Foul Play

Barlow Sisters #3

Jordan Ford

ISBN: 1979596522
ISBN-13: 978-1979596527

For HS

You're my heart and soul...the only one who can fill the space inside of me.

xx

#1

CHLOE

A Knight in the Darkness

The old church hall echoes with the sound of clanging utensils as hungry lost souls devour the one decent meal they'll get today.

I ladle a healthy portion of Bolognese sauce over the man's pasta and give him a kind smile.

"There you go, sir. Enjoy."

It's like he's not sure how to thank me, so he just takes the bowl and shuffles to one of the long rectangular tables in the middle of the room. His smelly odor lingers behind him and I wrinkle my nose, my heart squeezing with sympathy as I cast my eyes over the raggedy diners. I wonder how long it's been since some of them bathed, had a haircut, wore something brand new.

There's so much hurt and desolation in this room, yet beneath it all I can sense an underlying strength. They're close to the edge, but they haven't given up yet. They're fighting in their own way, and that's why I come here. It's a privilege to be around these people.

I was stoked that baseball practice was cut short this afternoon. I jumped at the chance to help Rahn set up for tonight's dinner service at the Catholic church. To be honest, I wasn't overly keen on sticking around to watch Holden and Maddie kissing, and Max has been so secretive lately, I didn't feel like spending the afternoon being lied to. So, I quickly texted Rahn, and thankfully she hadn't left yet. I ran to her place and we drove to the northwest side of town.

St. Michael's has been running this free dinner service for a couple of years now. Apparently one of the church's long-standing members left a huge chunk of money in his will, allocated specifically for setting up a food program for the homeless and any families who are seriously on the poverty line.

They set up the church hall every afternoon around four thirty, and the doors open an hour later. Every time I've come, the place has filled with the same forty or so hungry, helpless people looking for a small ray of sun in their day.

I love being a part of it.

Rahn's family knows the priest really well, and that's why she comes down once or twice a week to help. She's gotten to know a lot of these people, and she's now circulating the room handing out bread rolls and chatting with them. Talk about a ray of sunshine. She's the most effervescent person I've ever met. I bet she could convince anyone to do anything.

I love her.

And I'm so grateful to have formed such a quick friendship with her. I have a few friends back in Columbus that I've kept in touch with, but it can sometimes be a few days in between chats and it's nice to have Rahn to fill that gap. After my fallout with Mads, she was totally there for me. She hugged me when I cried and tried to bolster my spirits—a true friend.

I can see us spending a lot of time together over the next year or so, especially since my sisters will be leaving for college in a few months. I thought I wasn't going to be able to live without them, but since coming to Armitage, all three of us have kind of drifted apart. But that's okay. I have Rahn now.

Passing out another serving of Bolognese, I smile at the deadpan woman and her young son, my heart bleeding as the little boy sniffs and takes the bowl. His hands are so tiny, dirt caked under his fingernails. His shaggy hair is oily and his big brown eyes are too large for his face. He's adorable.

"I hope you like your meal." I grin at him and reach for an extra bread roll. "Why don't you keep this one for later?"

My wink makes a small smile twitch on his lips before he follows his mother to a nearby table. I remember them from a couple of weeks ago. They stopped by the food pantry to collect some breakfast and lunch food. Church people donate to it weekly— loaves of bread and boxes of cereal are handed out to those families struggling to scrape by.

I can't even imagine how difficult it must be.

I wish I had more time available to help Father Dan, but I can only come with Rahn when baseball practice finishes early or if she's willing to wait around and drive us over after things have already started. Due to family commitments, Rahn can only come a few times a week, but I tag along whenever I can.

I'm glad we got here on time tonight. Due to illnesses circulating, a lot of the volunteers aren't around, and Father Dan is seriously understaffed.

"We have to go." Rahn appears beside me.

I glance at her.

She winces and kind of bobs on her toes. "Sorry, but Mom's just called and told me I have to grab the boys. Some work emergency and she's held up. Dad's in LA this week, so it's up to me. Our neighbor is watching them but she has to go out. I need to get home or she'll be late."

"Oh, okay." I nod, kind of disappointed. I'm not ready to leave, and if we go, Father Dan will be down two more volunteers.

Glancing along the line of people who still need serving, and thinking ahead to the massive cleanup, I look back at Rahn and murmur, "You go. I'll be fine."

"What?"

"I'm not ready to leave. There's still so much to do. We can't leave it all for Father Dan." I point to the stout black man who has done nothing but good for this community.

"I know we're short-staffed tonight, and I feel really bad, but I've got to go." She flaps her hand between us.

I look at my watch, aware of the line backing up by the table.

"One second, sir." I hold my finger up to the man waiting for his meal. His quiet agitation is starting to show.

9

I can't bail.

"You go. Seriously, I'll be fine."

"I can't leave you here. I might not be able to get back to pick you up."

"I'll catch the bus home."

"From this part of town? No way!"

Biting my lip, I give her a determined look. "I'm not leaving these people in the lurch. I'll order an Uber. I don't care how much it costs."

She cringes, flicking her braid over her shoulder, obviously not happy with me. "But I have to go. My brothers need me."

"And these people need *me*." I rub her arm. "Don't worry, I'll be fine."

"I just want you to be safe getting home."

"I will be." I grin. "Seriously, go take care of your family. I'll text you as soon as I walk in my front door."

Rahn chews her lips, bobbing on her toes again.

"Just go." I giggle. "You don't want to be late."

My friend whines in her throat, so I turn her around and push her toward the exit.

She spins back to double-check. "You sure?"

"Yes, of course I'm sure." I smile, letting her know that I'm seriously not worried.

And I'm not.

I'm completely safe inside this building and when I leave, I'll order an Uber. It won't even be that late. I'll be home by like eight thirty.

Turning back to the pot of meat sauce, I grab the ladle again and ignore Rahn's indecision. I can see her bobbing out of the corner of my eye. She checks her watch and winces.

"See you tomorrow, sweets." I grin at her.

She groans. "Okay, fine. But text me when you get home."

"Promise." I wink at her and then serve the hungry man.

He mumbles a thank you and heads to a table near the back.

Smiling at the next person, I dish out some more food and keep doing that until my pot is empty.

Stepping back with a satisfied smile, I survey the room and pick up the last two breadbaskets. Father Dan is chatting with a single mother. Her kids are perched on his knee and one of them is giggling.

I grin and move past them, weaving around the tables to hand out the last of the bread rolls. It feels so good to be blessing people this way. It fills my heart in ways I can't explain. Helping others is what I want to spend my life doing, and I'm so grateful to Rahn for introducing me to Father Dan and giving me a chance to really give back.

After the food is gone, people slowly trickle out. A few of them will head to the abandoned warehouse three blocks from here, one or two will hang out in the nearby alleyways, and the biggest chunk will head home to their derelict houses which are coming apart at the seams.

I wish there was more we could do for these people, but when I mentioned it to Dad, he reminded me that the town could give some of these people a million dollars and they'd be back on the breadline within the year.

I argued that we should be giving them the money and then teaching them how to use it, but he just brushed me off. I guess he's been a cop on the streets for too long. That job really knows how to tarnish a person's hope.

Well, I refuse to give in to that line of thinking. There's hope for everyone, no matter who they are or where they come from.

Heading into the kitchen, I help Nancy with the last of the cleanup. The poor woman is standing by the sink, rinsing dishes and then loading them into the dish sanitizer. Her nose is red from over-wiping it. The cold she's been denying is getting the better of her and she looks miserable.

"Go home," I murmur, rubbing her back and forcing her away from the rest of the dirty dishes. "I'll finish up here."

"No, I really should stay."

"No." I grin. "You really should go home. I'm healthy and I have nothing else planned tonight.

Please, go get better."

She gives me a grateful smile and takes the towel I'm holding out to her. As soon as she starts drying her hands, I get busy finishing up. Before I know it, the kitchen is sparkling. I guess I have a little of my mother in me.

I snort and shake my head, grabbing my phone and jacket off the counter before walking back into the main hall.

The place is empty except for Father Dan, who is sitting beside a frail-looking man. They both have their heads bowed in prayer and I don't want to disturb them. Slipping out the front, I try to close the door as quietly as I can.

I ease onto the footpath and quickly text Rahn.

All done for the night. Ordering an Uber now. Will text again when I get home xxx

I press Send but the reception isn't good enough, so I walk a little way down the street until I can get a decent signal. Hovering under the streetlight, I finally get the message to go through and then open my Uber app. I haven't used it in Armitage yet, but hopefully it works just the same as it did in Columbus. And hopefully a driver won't take too long to get here.

"Well, hello." A crude voice I don't recognize

approaches from my right.

I flinch and step away, turning back toward the church. Instinct is telling me to freaking run, and I'm about to break into a sprint when someone steps into my path.

"Hey, sweet thing." A short man with crooked teeth gives me a half smile that's devoid of life. The streetlight casts a shadow across the right side of his gaunt face, making him look like some kind of ghoulish monster.

I jolt to a stop and spin, only to find the first guy closing in on me from behind.

"What's a pretty girl like you doing out here all alone?"

With a thick swallow, I inch away from him. He's tall and lean, his skin as dark as Father Dan's. He's holding a paper-wrapped bottle in his left hand, and the way his boots are scuffing on the ground tells me he's drunk.

I scoot back, only to bump into his friend, who chuckles in my ear while wrapping his arms around my waist.

"Let me go." My words spurt out in a trembling whisper.

My heart is hammering so hard I can barely think straight.

"Who you calling?" The man in front snatches my phone and smirks at the screen before tossing it aside. It smacks onto the ground and I wince. There goes my lifeline.

"You don't need an Uber, baby."

"Yeah, sweetness." The guy holding me gently skims his teeth across my earlobe. "We can take you for a ride."

His hot chuckle sears my skin and fear makes me buck away from him.

I open my mouth to scream, but he clamps his hand across my face, muffling my cries for help. His arms form a tight vise around me, and he starts pulling me farther away from the church.

No!

My mind is screaming at him to stop, but I can't seem to make a sound.

They're going to rape me.

I'd rather die than have these disgusting men touch me like that.

I'm horrified.

Terrified.

This can't happen!

I struggle and start to kick, repulsion making me panic.

"Calm down, cutie." The man lifts me off my feet while his friend laughs and takes a swig from his bottle.

Shit! Shit!

My entire body is trembling now, nausea

sweeping through me. I don't know what to do. I've got to get away.

I grunt and struggle some more, catching the guy's shin.

"Aw, fuck!" He loosens his grip for a second and my feet smack onto the ground.

I wriggle out of his arms and try to make a break for it, but his friend's instantly in my way, pushing me back into a dark alley. I hit the ground with a cry.

Pain rockets down my leg and my hands feel bruised from the impact.

I stay on the ground, inching away from my attacker as he towers over me.

"Please," I whimper. "Please don't do this."

Snatching me under the arm, he hauls me back onto my feet, reminding me just how small I am compared to him.

His breath reeks as he gets in my face and sprays my cheek with spittle. "Shut up and stop fighting. It'll only make it worse."

With a hard shove, he pushes me back against his friend, whose flirting tone has been replaced with a chilling whisper. "I'm going first."

I close my eyes, fear pulsing through me in such loud waves that I can't hear anything but my pounding heartbeat.

Tears burn behind my lids as sobs shake my belly.

I release my first cry when I'm thrown to the

ground. I scramble to get up but he pushes me down, straddling my hips and pinning me to the rough concrete.

"Don't," I sob. "Please! Stop!"

I catch his leering grin in the moonlight. It's ugly and only gets more repulsive when he reaches for my waistband.

He's going to tear my clothes off.

Oh God, help me!

I can't breathe as fear holds me frozen on the ground. Images of what he's about to do blind and hinder, until a noise behind us changes everything.

A *thunk* and grunt makes my attacker spin. He turns in time to catch a thundering fist to the face. He topples off me and doesn't even have a chance to cry out before the guy is on him, driving another sound punch into his nose.

I scramble back against the wall, hugging my knees to my chest and trembling as my rescuer goes to town. His arm works like a piston as he fires another two punches at him.

I'm sure he would have kept going if the other guy hadn't made it back to his feet and was now charging with a loud cry, his bottle raised like a club.

My rescuer spins, blocking the blow like it's a lame attempt and firing a fist into the drunken man's stomach.

I flinch as he doubles over, his loud groan echoing

down the alley. The street fighter stands tall, raising his knee and finishing the drunk off.

The man slumps against the wall with a pitiful moan before staggering over to his friend.

"Let's go," he slurs, wrenching his friend's jacket before giving up, jumping over him and limping away from the scene.

The guy who was going to rape me first whimpers and groggily stands, swaying on his feet as he looks down at me. Blood is streaming from his crooked nose, coating his teeth and lips.

A weeping gasp pops out of my mouth and I curl in on myself, covering my head until someone growls, "Get the fuck out of here. And if you ever show your faces around here again, you're dead!"

Sloppy footsteps scuttle away, but I stay in my little trembling ball until a gentle hand rests on my shoulder.

"It's okay. They're gone. You're safe now." The voice is deep and husky with emotion.

Cautiously lifting my head, I peek over my arm and lose my breath as, even in the dim light, I recognize the guy who just saved me.

Brushing a tender hand over the top of my head, his brown gaze coaxes me out of hiding and I'm soon facing the last person I expected to...

Vincent Mancini.

#2

VINCENT

A New Sensation

Chloe's trembling like she can't control her body.

Shit, I could have killed those guys.

When I was walking out of Pedro's, I got this weird sense that something was off. I heard a little scuffling around the corner and was tempted to mind my own business, but I couldn't shake the foreboding in my gut. So I turned back and walked around the side of the store to see two shadows and some poor girl struggling in their grasp.

I hate the fuckers who live in this damn place.

I gritted my teeth, knowing the consequences of brawling, but I couldn't leave some innocent chick in the hands of two sleazebags. Enzo probably knows them and will pound my ass for getting in the way, but I couldn't just turn my back on that shit.

With a heavy sigh, I walked over, wondering if I could try talking some sense into them first, maybe bribe them with the money I'd just taken from Pedro.

But then I caught a glimpse of the girl.

I don't know what made me recognize her voice, but the second she sobbed, "Don't. Please! Stop!" I knew it was Chloe and something inside of me popped.

Screw talking, I wanted blood.

I sprinted up with my fists at the ready. My punches were fueled with pure fury, and it felt damn good to feel their flesh fold beneath my knuckles.

Running my thumb over the reddened skin, I try to smile at Chloe, hoping to make her feel better.

She's still scared, probably thinking that I just sent those guys packing so I could have a turn with her.

The thought guts me and I shoot to my feet. Taking a step back, I want to give her space and let her know I'd never disrespect her that way.

I've been watching her since the moment she walked into my Biology class two months ago. She was like a vision, appearing through that doorway with her long blonde hair and sweet smile. I knew I'd never have a shot with her, so I didn't bother attempting to talk to her or even dream that one day I might. She's way too good for me. Just this afternoon, I found out that she was convinced I didn't steal that baseball gear. She knew it was a setup, and helped her sister, Maddie, prove it.

No one ever does shit like that for me.

Having Chief Barlow and Principal Sheehan show up on my doorstep last night to invite me back to school was freaking triumphant.

Enzo was damn pissed. He doesn't want me going to school. He wants me joining the family business with my cousin, Diego. But I refuse to become one of his thugs. I do what I have to do to stay alive, but as soon as I've graduated and can figure a way out of this place, I will.

I want to be a good person.

Just like Chloe.

Gazing down at her, my heart expands like it's taking a full breath. Maybe I was supposed to save her tonight. I owe her for proving my innocence.

Shit, even if I didn't, I still would have done what I did.

Chloe's like a delicate pink tulip—perfect petals

and pure sweetness.

My stomach convulses as my mind snares me with an image of what would have happened if I hadn't turned back and checked out that noise. Man, I'm so glad I listened to my gut.

Reaching out my hand, I swallow in an effort to find my voice. "It's okay. I'm not going to hurt you."

She hesitates for a moment, her wide blue eyes assessing me before she cautiously reaches for my hand. I wrap my fingers around her trembling digits and ease her off the ground. She's still a shaken mess and as soon as I let her hand go, she wraps her arms around herself and gazes down the alley with wide, fear-filled eyes.

"They're not going to come back," I assure her. "I'll never let them touch you again."

Her big blue eyes shoot to mine. They're glistening with the onset of tears and I can feel my heart disintegrating. She's still pale with shock. I wish there was something I could say to make it better.

"Come on, let's walk this way." I tentatively put my hand on her lower back.

She flinches, but I keep my hand in place, slowly guiding her back to the street. Her legs give out for a second and I catch her against me.

"It's okay," I whisper again.

Shaking breaths spurt from her nose like she's trying not to fall apart, and then she finally bobs her head and keeps walking.

I stay close and hear her inhale a full breath as we make it out to the lit sidewalk.

"My phone," she whispers in a voice so small I can barely hear it.

She's pointing at the ground behind me and I turn to check, spotting her pink phone cover immediately. I pick it up and wince when I notice the cracked screen.

"Does it still work?" Her voice is gradually getting its strength back.

I give her a closed-mouth smile and turn the device on. After a few seconds, it lights up and I can confidently assure her, "Yeah. Do you want me to call someone for you?"

She stares at me like she hasn't heard what I've said, but then she blinks like she's trying to force her brain to function.

Licking her bottom lip, she gazes out across the road and murmurs, "Uber."

My insides curdle with the idea of putting her into a strange car with some driver she doesn't even know.

Not that she knows me either, but…

"I can give you a ride home."

Her eyes flick to mine, surprise obvious on her pretty features.

Or maybe it's fear.

Shit.

I mean, I get it. I'm the scary guy at school, right? The one everyone avoids. I usually like it that way—it makes things easier. But in this moment, I wish I were as fucking normal as everybody else.

Scratching the back of my neck, I attempt a proper smile. It feels weird so I give up and tell it to her straight. "I can understand why you're not comfortable with that. I just hate the idea of you getting into a car with a complete stranger. If it's okay, I'll wait with you until it shows up, and then I'll follow it back to your place...to make sure you get there safely."

Her lips are slightly parted, but then they try to rise into a little smile. It doesn't really work, so she gives up and shocks the hell out of me. "I'll ride home with you. Thanks."

"Uh..." I let out a breathy snicker and then start nodding like some jackass. "Okay. Um...my car's this way."

I point down the street and she turns that direction, shuffling along with her arms still tightly wrapped around her waist.

It only takes a couple of minutes to walk to my car. It's a piece of shit that I got after my brother Nick was sent to jail. It's a rusty blue Camaro, and for the first time in my life, I wish I drove something classy like Holden Carter's Mustang. Chloe deserves to be driven in a freaking gold-lined carriage; I'm embarrassed that she has to sit in my crap-heap car.

The door creaks when I open it for her, and I wince when she gazes inside and no doubt wonders how the hell she'll fit in around all the trash.

"Let me just…" I lean in front of her and snatch up as many empty cans and chip bags as I can. Bundling them in my arm, I walk to the trunk and dump it all in there before closing Chloe's door for her.

Shit, she must think I'm such a freaking slob.

I walk around the car, trying to figure out what the hell I'm doing.

Just get in and drive her home. Make sure she's safe. That's all you've got to do, man.

Slamming my door shut, I fire up the engine and we rumble away from the curb. I don't know exactly where she lives, but I've got a good idea. I'll head to Main Street and she can direct me from there.

Chloe sniffs softly beside me. I turn to glance at her. Tears are running down her face. Her mouth bunches and she swallows like she's trying to hold in a sob.

Oh shit. What do I do?

"Uh…are you hurt?"

She shakes her head and whimpers before buckling forward and mumbling, "I'm fine."

She is so *not* fine. I should have killed those shitheads. Dammit, I had it in me.

Thoughts of Nick whistle through my brain, taunting me. I have the right blood running through my veins. But fuck, I don't want to be like him!

I grip the wheel while Chloe cries beside me. Her slow tears feel like talon scratches on my heart.

Tissue. I need a tissue.

I scan the spaces around me, desperately hoping for something I can give her while trying to keep my eyes on the road.

"Can you drive the long way home, please?"

"W-what?" I glance at her.

"I don't want to walk in the door crying. They'll want to know and I can't…" She presses the back of her hand against her mouth.

Her fingers are still quivering.

"They'll tell me off for not going home with Rahn when she begged me to. And then I'll get a lecture about safety and your neighborhood. They'll say I can never come back here. They'll stop me from helping at the church." She slashes at her tears. "I don't want to be scared off. I love working there."

Her sweetness squeezes my tattered heart into a ball of putty.

Most people would vow to never set foot in the northwest side again, but she's crying because she's worried they won't let her come back.

She's sweet…and crazy.

I lick the edge of my mouth and check the road

before glancing at her again. "So, you're, uh...not going to tell your dad about this?"

She shakes her head. "I know what they did was wrong and if they had..." She swallows. "If they'd succeeded, then yeah, I'd tell him, but..." She goes still for a second and her eyes slowly track across to me. "You saved me."

My lips twitch with a fleeting smile.

I should really say that she needs to tell the police about those guys. I could lecture her on the fact that they might try to hurt someone else. It's her responsibility to speak up. But her eyes... they're so full of gratitude right now.

I don't want to kill that look, so I keep my mouth shut.

I'll call the cops on my way home and give them an anonymous tip. I didn't know those guys, but I can give a good description over the phone. Hopefully they'll get picked up, and then after Chloe's had a few days to process how she's feeling, she'll find the courage to give an official statement.

I grip the wheel as another thought spikes through me.

I could forget about calling the cops and just ask Diego if he'd help me find them. We could make sure they'll never even want to look at another chick again.

"Take the next left." Chloe's soft voice distracts

me.

I turn down the correct road and feel my palms start to sweat. I'm such an alien on this side of town. Checking my speed, I make sure I'm cruising as legally as I can be. I don't want some cop pulling me over. The second they spot me with Chloe's blotchy face in the passenger seat, they'll jump to all the wrong conclusions.

Swallowing the boulder in my throat, I quietly follow her directions. She takes us the long way around school, weaving down quiet suburban streets until her tears have dried up completely.

"Can you pull over here?" Chloe points to the corner of a street.

I turn into it, shaking my head. "No, I need to make sure you get home safely."

"I will."

"Yeah, because I'm driving you to your door." My voice peters off as a strong nausea sweeps through me.

Shit, if her dad's home and he sees my car...

"Just drop me a couple doors down, then." She touches my arm and I silently vow to never wash my shirt again. "I don't want my dad making assumptions. He's really strict on guys and who we date."

Associating me with the word "date" sends an overpowering longing through me. Hopefully it doesn't show as I reluctantly pull the car up to the curb and let the engine idle.

"Which house is it?"

"Just up there." She points three houses down and I see the yellow Camry in the driveway. There's another car parked on the street outside their house.

"Whose car is that?"

"I don't know," Chloe murmurs, gazing at it before reaching for the light between us. Turning to face me, she swipes her hands over her cheeks and asks me, "How bad do I look?"

I can't tell her what I really want to say—that she's beautiful and could never look bad even if she tried—so I lick the corner of my mouth and murmur, "You're still a little pale."

"Are my eyes red and puffy?" She runs a finger under her lashes. "Does it look like I've been crying?"

Without thinking, I brush my thumb across her smooth cheek and smile at her. "You'll get away with it."

She pulls in a shaky breath, her expression softening when she smiles at me. "I wish I could walk you in my door and give you all the praise you deserve. I just can't imagine my dad buying it."

I grit my teeth and glance out of the windshield. "Yeah, probably best that you don't mention a Mancini drove you home."

She cringes, looking embarrassed by the truth.

I wave my hand through the air. "Doesn't matter."

"You know, a rose by any other name would smell as sweet."

"What?"

She smiles, flashing her straight white teeth at me. "It's Shakespeare."

"*Romeo and Juliet*, right?" I whisper, worried I might have it wrong.

She sits back with a surprised laugh. "You know Shakespeare?"

"I go to school too, you know."

"Sorry, I just…never pegged you for a guy who'd remember lines from a Shakespeare play."

I snicker, working my jaw to the side to try to hide my embarrassment. What kind of guy remembers Shakespeare, anyway? I'm such an idiot. Tapping my finger on the wheel, I will my brain to think of something intelligent to say, but I've got nothing.

"I think Shakespeare is beautiful, even if I don't always know what he's saying."

A smile tugs at my lips. "Yeah, me too. A rose by any other name… What does that even mean?"

"Oh, well I do know that one." She tips her head, causing her long hair to splash over her shoulder. I curl my fingers into a fist, resisting the urge to reach forward and run my hands through it. "It means your name doesn't matter. Who you are inside is what counts. You could have any name, Vincent, and it won't change the fact that you were a hero tonight. Others would have walked away, but you didn't, and I'll never forget that."

Leaning across the seat, she pecks my cheek and I suddenly can't move.

My lungs forget how to inflate and I'm speechless as she gives me one last smile and whispers, "Thank you."

She gets out of the car and I'm transfixed as she walks to her house. I keep the headlights on her until she turns into her driveway, and then I take a big risk and cruise past her place to make sure she's safely inside.

I spot her entering the kitchen and quickly accelerate away before anyone looks out the front windows.

My heart is still beating out of time as I race back to my part of town. It's a weird sensation. It's not fear. It's not anger.

It's something else.

Something foreign.

It's a feeling that I never want to forget.

#3

CHLOE

Can't Form the Words

I just kissed Vincent Mancini on the cheek.

Because he saved me.

The scariest guy at school beat the crap out of those assholes...to save me.

My confusion is still kind of potent as I creep through the kitchen door and shut it softly behind me.

Leaning my head against the wood, I relive the scene, fear pulsing through me as I imagine what could have been.

Thank God for Vincent—the one guy at school everyone tells me to avoid. Yet, in spite of my trembling limbs, I felt safe beside him. That's why I let him drive me home. I trusted him to get me here safely. To not harm me the way those other creeps wanted to.

"Chloe, is that you, hon?"

I flinch at the sound of Mom's voice and suck in a sharp breath.

Oh man, I hope my face looks okay. Lightly dabbing my cheeks, I try to think about warmth and sunshine, pasting on my best smile as I walk through the kitchen and out into the dining room.

"We're in here, sweets," Dad calls.

I can see his big foot resting on the carpet and have to take a second to gather myself. I should tell him about what happened tonight. He'll want to know so he can track those guys down and make sure they never touch anyone ever again.

If Vincent hadn't been there, tonight would have ended very differently. I close my eyes and shudder, wishing I were more like Maddie and Max. They would have fought like wild cats—claws, teeth, fists, whatever they could manage.

I could barely release a scream. It was pitiful.

My fingers start shaking again as I wipe my mouth. Creating a fist, I hide my trembles behind my back and inch a little closer to the living room.

I gave Vincent very valid reasons for keeping my mouth shut. But were they selfish? Should I be reliving my nightmare so justice can be served?

It's the right thing to do, but...

"What's taking you so long, kid?"

A familiar voice that I haven't heard in a long time distracts me and I can't help a surprised laugh when Uncle Conrad appears in the living room archway.

He spreads his arms wide, a happy grin on his face.

I smile and walk into his embrace. He wraps me in a bear hug, lifting me off my feet. Planting me back down, he stands back to assess me.

"Geez, you girls just keep getting more beautiful."

I snicker and shake my head.

"I know, that was lame, right? Way to sound like an old fart, Conrad."

I laugh at his self-deprecation.

"You're later than I thought you'd be." Mom checks her watch and looks up at me from the sofa.

"Oh, yeah, I..." My voice disappears as my heart starts thrumming again.

"You okay?" Mom smiles.

I bob my head. Do I do it now? Do I destroy

everyone's evening and create more drama than I think I can handle?

I don't want Uncle Conrad to know.

I don't want...

"Chloe's been helping out at a church on the other side of town, serving meals to the homeless," Dad explains to his younger brother. "It's a really great outreach. I love that Chloe's involved with it." Dad's smile is filled with pride as he grins up at me.

"Thanks, Dad," I murmur.

"My little girl with the heart of gold." He winks and I just can't do it.

I can't break that smile.

Not tonight.

"Sorry I'm late. It was busy tonight, we were understaffed, and things kind of went over time."

"Have you eaten?" Mom stands, ready to prepare me a late dinner.

"Actually, Mom, I'm good." I stop her before she leaves the room. "I just really want to go to bed."

My eyes start watering before I can stop them.

"Sweetie?" Mom's pale eyebrows dip into a frown as she runs her hand down my arm. "What's the matter?"

"Oh, I..." Shoving my hand into my pocket, I wrap my fingers around my phone and decide to sell a lie.

It's not like me.

I'm usually pretty honest, but I just can't seem to

form the sentence: *I was nearly raped tonight.*

"I broke my phone." I pull it out of my pocket and show her the cracked screen. "I'm sorry."

"Oh, sweetie," Mom chides, taking it out of my hand to inspect the screen. "It's just a cracked screen. That won't be too much to fix." She grins at me, her blue eyes dancing. "You look like you're ready to pass out. It's just a phone. I'm not mad."

"I just know how expensive they are. And you guys bought it for me for my birthday and made me promise to take really good care of it."

"Replacing the screen is easy," Uncle Conrad pipes up. "Don't sweat it, kid. I can sort that out for you tomorrow."

"Really?" I turn and beam him a grateful smile.

"Of course. That's what I'm here for."

Dad rolls his eyes while Mom lets out a soft huff.

It's no secret that she's not a huge fan of Dad's little brother. Heck, Dad's barely a fan, but we girls love him. Particularly Max. She'll be stoked that he's here.

I walk over to where he's taken a seat and peck his cheek. "It's nice to have you here."

He winks and I take the chance to slip away.

"Good night."

"Sleep well." Mom rubs my arm and passes my phone back to me.

As soon as I walk out of the room, the pocket of

36

air I've been storing in my lungs pops and my shoulders sag with relief.

I quickly text Rahn and hope it's the last lie I need to sell tonight.

Home safe. See you tomorrow xx

It's not exactly a lie. I am home safe...thanks to Vincent.

Her reply makes my phone vibrate.

Glad you made it! Sleep well xx

I can't imagine that happening. I shudder and close my eyes.

I probably didn't do the right thing tonight.

When Maddie was assaulted at school, she told Dad everything the second she walked in the door. Admittedly, she was beat up and bleeding.

Shit, that was only a week ago.

I can't come out with my incident yet. Mom will flip out and then start arguing that moving to Armitage was a huge mistake.

There have been moments when I one hundred percent agreed with her. But I don't know if I want to go back now. Even after what happened tonight.

Armitage is changing us.

Maddie's fallen in love with a jock.

Max is… well, I don't know what she's up to.

The point is, if we up and left now, Columbus wouldn't be the same. You can't go back and expect life to carry on as usual. Being in Columbus won't solve all our problems.

"Hey, you're back." Maddie catches me in the hallway.

She's drying off her hair and looking happier than I've seen her in a long time.

What's the bet she made out with Holden after school. They probably drove up to Cherry Top Hill or something.

I force a smile that she doesn't buy.

"You all right? You look kind of pale."

Do I? I blink and glance to the floor.

"Are you okay?"

"Yeah." My shoulder hitches and I swipe a finger across my mouth.

"What's wrong?"

"Nothing." I shake my head. "I'm just really tired."

"How was the soup kitchen? Tough night?"

"It was busy." I cross my arms, my heart starting to race as my mind tortures me.

I glance up in time to see Maddie's blue-green eyes narrow. She's about to ask for more.

My heart lurches, threatening to cut off my air supply.

I was nearly raped.

38

The idea taunts me and it takes everything in me not to buckle to the floor and sob out the truth.

"Seriously, I'm fine," I manage. "I'm just tired and I want to go to bed."

I drill her with a look that hopefully screams, *Don't push me on this!*

She takes a step back, slowly nodding while not believing me. "Sleep well, sis."

My lips quiver into a smile as I quickly brush past her and into my room.

I close the door on her. "You too."

Stumbling to my bed, I make it there before crashing onto it and fisting the covers.

They wouldn't understand.

Maddie would want to know why I didn't scream and fight my way out of it. Dad would want me to describe every detail. Mom would hear Vincent's name and immediately assume the worst.

They won't hear the truth.

Their shock and horror, their preconceived ideas, would mask what I'm saying.

I know I need to make it right and somehow let the police know about these men.

But I can't face it tonight.

All I can do is scrub my skin in a hot shower, throw away these tainted clothes, and curl into a ball, safe and warm under my covers.

#4

VINCENT

Just Like Them

It's nearly nine by the time I get home.

Enzo will be pissed, but what else is frickin' new?

My car rumbles and sputters to a stop outside the house I'm supposed to call home.

I'll never be able to. None of my immediate family even lives here. This whole block is Mancini central, but they're all second cousins and distant relatives I couldn't give a shit about.

The only Mancini I *do* care about is now in jail for murdering Todd McCrae. Bile surges in my belly the way it always does when I think about it. Nick said he didn't do it, but then all the evidence came out. It was impossible for him to deny it, so he shut the hell up and took the punishment.

So now I have to live in this stinking house with Uncle Enzo and his shithead son, Diego. I hate them both, but there's not much I can do about it right now.

If it wasn't for Selena, I probably would have split after Nick left, but Enzo's girlfriend convinced me to at least stick around and finish high school.

"Don't let the Mancini name ruin you, Vinnie. You could be different from all these guys. You *are* different. You stick with it, and one day your time will come. You'll get away." Her eyes glistened as she spoke, but she didn't shed any tears.

She's learned not to cry.

After trying to escape a couple of times, she's accepted her place in this "family."

The poor woman's only ten years older than me and I'm still hoping to set her free when I leave.

I don't know how we'll do it.

But for now, I just have to stick it out and at least get my high school diploma.

Mom would want that.

I sniff, trying not to think about the fact that Mom hasn't been around since I was eleven. She overdosed and we got shipped here to live with Uncle Enzo. My life has always been shit, but it's been ten times worse since moving to Armitage, and a million times worse since Nick got sent away.

He used to cover for me all the time, do the jobs I never wanted to. But now I'm stuck running his errands too.

Patting my jacket pocket, I shoulder the door open and trudge up the front steps. Thank God Pedro likes me. He owns the store near the church and Enzo makes him pay a monthly protection fee. Every person on that block pays something and unfortunately, it's my job to collect.

Rather than going in with a baseball bat and hitting the shit out of anything that moves—that's Diego's way—I've tried to build a rapport with these people. Most of them slip me the money without too much fuss. It's in everybody's best interest, I guess.

I just wish it didn't make me feel so scummy.

I'm taking money off these good, hardworking people. Money this family hasn't earned and we sure as shit don't deserve.

Anger fires through me and I shove the front door open, dropping Pedro's payment in Enzo's lap without a word.

"Hey!" the gruff man calls me back.

Everything about him is dark and threatening—from his black eyes to his towering persona. He's nearly fifty, but still just as scary as he's always been. The guy is stronger than me, tougher than me, and I've learned not to mess with him.

"You're late!"

"I got held up." I shrug.

"Doing what?"

"Nothin'."

Enzo's dark eyebrows dip into a sharp V. He snaps his fingers and beckons me over to his chair.

Holding back my sigh, I spin and clomp across the wooden floor. My boot steps are loud and reluctant.

Snatching my hand, Enzo digs his thumb into my bruised knuckles.

I wince but don't make a sound.

"Who've you been fighting?"

"Some jerks," I mutter and dish out an easy lie. "They wanted to take your money."

"Did you kill 'em?"

I scowl and Enzo just sniggers at me. He's always hassling me about killing people, comparing me to my loser brother. The guy used to be my hero, until he turned out to be just like everybody else in this damn family.

"Tell Diego what they look like. We'll track them down and teach them a lesson."

My gut twists with unease. "I taught 'em a lesson."

He scoffs, like my lessons are more like being whipped with a soggy tissue than bashed over the head with a baseball bat—Diego style.

"They won't be trouble," I softly argue.

Enzo shoots out of his chair, getting up in my face. He loves that he's a few inches taller than me. He loves that he's broader in the chest and can make me feel like a snot-nosed preschooler who is about to piss his pants.

It always takes so much to look him in the eye and not back down.

"I want those pieces of shit brought to their knees. Diego will get the boys together and deal with it. No one steals from a Mancini. You got that?"

"I got it," I grit out, hating this whole Mancini, mafia bullshit. He acts like the freaking Godfather and I just have to play along with it. "That's why I broke their noses."

I hold up my fist so my red knuckles are hovering just in his line of sight.

Easing back, he checks my hand again and I round off the conversation with a little nugget of truth, "I told them if they ever showed their faces on Fort Street again, I'd kill them."

His lips twitch before slowly rising into an impressed smile. "Finally learning something, huh?"

I clench my jaw and look away from him. "I'm going to bed. I've got school tomorrow."

He snatches my face and forces me back before I can step away. "Don't think me letting you finish school gets you off the hook. As soon as that final bell rings tomorrow, I want you cruising the street looking for these assholes. We don't give empty threats in this family. Take Diego with you."

Shit!

I force a nod and wrestle out of Enzo's grasp.

Trudging to my room, I bypass the den where Selena's watching TV. Diego seems to be out tonight, which is a huge relief. Creeping into my room, I shrug out of my jacket and throw it on the bed.

I still haven't called the cops yet. I thought I'd get a read on Enzo first, see if anything about the fight had gotten back to him. He could have dropped me a couple of names that I could pass on to the police. But he obviously doesn't know them, and as much as I'd love to serve up Mancini justice on this one, I won't be responsible.

I need to call the cops tonight.

It's times like this when I wish I owned a cell phone. I could just pull it from my pocket, hide in the closet and have a whispered conversation. But I hate phones. Phones link me to people, and I don't like it when Enzo can reach me at the drop of a hat.

It's been a constant battle between us, but every time he gives me a new phone, I lose it down the toilet, in a stream, or it "accidentally" gets smashed. I get a beating every time, but it's still not enough to stop me.

He gave up at the end of last year, and it's about the only fight I've ever won in this fucking house.

Slipping into the bathroom, I lock the door and flick on the shower. I get the spray pumping before turning on the radio. Finding my usual station, I turn up the volume, then climb onto the toilet seat and out the window.

I hit the ground and duck into the shadows, sneaking around the house and racing down to the payphone at the end of the street. It's one of the only ones left in Armitage, and the town council better not take it away. I've used it on more than one occasion. Shoving a few coins into the box, I call the Armitage Police Department. I've learned not to bother with 9-1-1; it's easier to call direct and leave an anonymous tip.

"Armitage Police Department, you're speaking with Mike."

Lowering my voice, I try to make it as gruff and scratchy as possible while I describe the two men who tried to hurt Chloe. The officer tries to get some personal details, but I deflect those questions, telling him it's not worth the risk.

He's not satisfied with this, and I'm running out of time.

With a sharp huff, I bark, "Just look for them before they're found by a Mancini and taken care of with another kind of justice!"

And with that, I hang up and run back home.

My boots scuff on the cracked concrete as I creep around the side of the house. As soon as I reach the bathroom, I jump up and grab the window ledge, pulling myself back inside.

"Hurry the fuck up, man!" Diego's home and pounding on the door.

I scramble out of my clothes and dive under the spray to wet my hair before turning off the shower. "I'm coming!" I holler, wrapping a towel around my waist.

Diego keeps pounding anyway. He's going to freaking break down the door if I don't hurry up.

Shit, I miss Nick.

It kills me that the guy who used to look out for me became just like them.

I don't want to be like that.

I don't want this toxic family to rub off on me too.

#5

CHLOE

My Almost Worst Nightmare

To say I didn't sleep well is an understatement. Every time I drifted off, my body would jolt awake with the feeling of tight arms around my waist and drunken threats against my skin.

48

At two o'clock, I gave up, flicked on my light, and tried to read.

The romance novels I'm into are always such a good distraction. I don't care what genre they're in; as long as they can take me to another world, I'm happy.

The reading worked...sort of.

I don't know what time I fell asleep, but I woke up with my thumb squeezed between the pages of *Eleanor & Park*. I've read the book before, but it's one of my favorites.

Trying to get ready for school was hard work, but thankfully Max and Uncle Rad left to do some breakfast and baseball thing, and Dad had already left for work. That just left Mom and Maddie to deal with, and they were so busy chatting about Mom's latest job application that they didn't even notice me.

Glancing down at my hands, I hold them out, relieved they've finally stopped trembling.

"What are you doing?" Maddie snickers as she pulls into the parking lot.

I quickly pull my sleeves over my hands. "Just checking my nails are clean."

"You should paint them again." Maddie switches off the engine and unbuckles. "You love that."

I wrinkle my nose. "Not during baseball season."

"True." Maddie laughs, her face lighting like the sun when she glances out the windshield and notices

Holden waiting for her.

He's got this loved-up smile on his face, and I'm once again caught between that emotion of being happy for them and gutted for me.

Holden's gorgeous, and underneath that arrogant jock persona is a really good guy. I wish he wanted me, but he loves Mads...and I seriously am happy for them.

I just wish that happiness didn't burn so bad.

Shutting the door behind me, I lean against the car and watch her jump into his arms. He laughs and spins her around before placing her back on her feet and kissing her thoroughly.

A little too thoroughly considering we're outside school.

I guess they're in that new, giddy, *I've never been happier* stage of their relationship.

I wonder what that feels like.

I mean, I know what that feels like, considering I've spent most of my teenage life crushing on guys. My problem is that I always crush on the wrong ones. If I look back over my high school—even my middle school—years, I've always been attracted to the coolest guys in school.

It makes sense, right? They're usually good-looking, sporty, smooth. Everybody likes them, so why shouldn't I?

Because they never like me back.

I don't know what's wrong with me. I obviously don't have the looks and personality to capture them. When Holden asked me to the homecoming dance, I finally thought I'd broken the cycle, but nope.

Here I am all over again…liking the wrong guy.

Except I can't like the guy anymore, because he's with my sister.

Clenching my teeth, I walk away from them and into the school. After my experience from last night, I should probably give up on guys altogether. But I have a romantic heart and there's this part of me that just knows I'm supposed to be in love one day. And maybe, if all the planets align correctly, someone will be in love with me too.

The right someone.

I wish I knew who he was.

Reaching my locker, I wrestle with my stubborn lock until it finally relents. Flicking the door open, I reach in to take out my books for the morning and am stilled by a white piece of paper sitting askew, like someone fed it through the air vents at the top.

Curiosity flickers inside of me as I reach for the note.

Glancing over my shoulder, I try to see who might have left it, but no one's paying any attention to me.

I'm guessing you didn't sleep well. I know today will be hard.

But nothing's going to touch you, okay?
You're safe. I'll make sure of it.
Thanks for letting me drive you home.

V

My heart does this weird double-kick, my nose tingling with tears as I read the note again. With a little sniff, I glance down the corridor, searching for signs of Vincent. But I can't see him anywhere.

I'll have to thank him in Biology. But that will look weird, right? Going up and talking to him.

People will want to know why.

Gossip will start. Rumors will spread.

I don't want that. And he doesn't need it either.

Even though I'd love to announce to everyone at this school that Vincent Mancini saved me last night, I don't think he'd want me to.

I don't even know why I feel that way.

I just have this sense that Vincent wants to keep his rescue mission on the down-low, the same way I don't want to utter my almost worst nightmare to anybody.

"Hey, sunshine!" Rahn jumps up to my locker and I let out a little yelp. "Oh, sorry." She winces, her brown eyes wide with surprise.

I let out a shaky laugh and tuck the note inside my

pocket. "I didn't hear you coming, you little stealth ninja." My joke feels weird and forced, but she laughs anyway.

"So you got home okay. Thank God!" She looks to the ceiling, her gestures always so dramatic. "I was seriously freaking out that I'd totally let you down by leaving early. I had visions of you being kidnapped on the way home or something."

I force out a laugh that probably sounds borderline maniacal, but if Rahn knew the truth, she'd never forgive herself. Clearing my throat, I get busy organizing my books for the morning.

"Don't worry about it. I told you to go."

"I know, but still…not exactly a best friend move."

I grin, glad she considers me a best friend already. We've only been hanging out a couple of months, but it does feel like we were born to be besties.

"I should totally pay for your Uber. How much was it?"

I stop her before she can reach for her wallet. "Don't be silly. It was my choice to stay."

"Are you sure?"

"Yes." I give her an adamant look, praying she won't press me.

Thankfully she tips her head and beams me a smile. "You're a sweetheart, you know that? Such a good heart."

"So I'm told."

"Only because it's true." She grips my arm and plants a kiss on my cheek. "See you in Bio, bright eyes."

Her long ponytail dances as she waltzes off to her locker. I watch her go, warmed by her sunny disposition. I'm so glad I have her at the moment.

Closing my locker, I head to homeroom, slipping the note out of my pocket and reading it again.

Rahn's not the only person I'm grateful for right now.

A soft smile tugs at my lips as I soak in Vincent's words. The fear that's been pulsing through me all night eases just a little…

You're safe. I'll make sure of it.

#6

VINCENT

Locker Notes

Chloe's reading my note.

And she's smiling.

The coarse rope that's been binding my heart ever since sliding the note into her locker starts to unravel.

I rub my cheek, remembering the soft brush of her lips against my skin.

No one ever dares to get close enough to kiss

me…to let me in.

I usually like it that way. My scowling glare and on-the-edge temper provides protection on both sides. People can't afford to get close to me and my insane family, which is why I push them all away. And keeping them at arm's length stops me from forming any kind of bond that will inevitably get broken.

But this morning as I was getting ready for school…thinking about the kind of night Chloe must have had, I couldn't *not* do something.

It's only a note.

It can't do any harm, but the fact that she's reading it while she's walking to class fills me with something I don't even recognize.

I like this feeling, and I want it to stick around, even though I know it won't.

Good things don't happen to people like me.

Pure things like Chloe shouldn't even come near me.

But at least she knows she's safe. I just wanted to offer a little comfort. And I think I did, which makes me feel like a million bucks.

I'm actually in a good mood when I slip into homeroom. As usual, I take my seat in the back of the room and warn people off with a stony-faced glare. That shit really unnerves people.

I keep my scowl in place, only softening it slightly when Chloe's eyes brush across mine in Biology class.

She keeps glancing at me, and as much as I love those blue-green eyes, it makes me twitchy.

Twitchy with longing.

Twitchy with the truth that this yearning can never be satisfied.

By lunchtime my good mood has disappeared and been replaced with that standard charcoal cloud that seems to swirl in my chest on a regular basis.

I skip lunch the way I always do. I hate being in the cafeteria. Pulling a squished piece of bread from the bottom of my bag, I tear a mouthful off and slowly chew the plain, boring meal while shuffling through the hallways.

This is standard operating procedure for me.

Sometimes I head downstairs and loiter near the music room so I can hear Velocity rehearse. Other times, I roam the halls. And occasionally, I'll head to the library. Today I go for hall roaming, and by the time I've finished my piece of bread, I'm at my locker.

The bell's not due to ring for another fifteen minutes, but I decide to get prepped for afternoon classes anyway.

Reaching for the lock, I feel that uneasy vibe shudder through me. Ever since Luke Frost planted that mitt and those drugs in my locker, I've been nervous of what I'll find. It's only been a couple of days since returning to school, but I'm still cautious. Being set up sucks. I should find Luke and beat the shit out of him, but I guess I understand why he picked me as his scapegoat. Thanks to my family's reputation, I'm the perfect fall guy.

Pushing the lock up and then down, I give it a little rattle and it pops open. It took me weeks to come up with that technique. My locker got a fair share of abuse in those early days, until I could figure out the damn lock.

No wonder people avoid me. There are still dent marks in the metal from my boots.

Licking the edge of my mouth, I pull the door back and freeze when I spot a white sheet of paper folded in half.

My heart starts pounding as I slowly reach for it, and with my breath on hold, I open it up and read...

You're right...I didn't sleep well. I hope the nightmares don't last too long.

I still haven't found the courage to tell anybody, which makes me feel kind of bad. Like I'm a coward. But I just can't seem to form the words.

I wish I had your strength. To just step up and beat those guys the way you did... You don't even know me and you ran into a fight to save me from something hideous.

You're an honorable warrior.

I wish more people knew that, but somehow I sense you

don't want them to.

Thanks again for what you did. It's a privilege to know the truth.

C

I scan the note again, rereading her words until they're memorized.

I'm not even aware of the shuffling in the corridor around me until the bell rings and I'm brought back to earth.

An honorable warrior.

Holy shit. That's a title right there.

It's not really one I deserve, and I should tell Chloe that.

Snatching a pen from the bottom of my bag, I quickly rip a sheet of paper from the back of my English notebook and write her back.

I'm no warrior. And you are no coward.

I was just in the right place at the right time.

You have no idea how good it felt to pound those guys. What they were trying to do to you made me sick to my core.

No girl deserves that.

Especially a girl with a heart like

yours.

You deserve only respect, because you are one of the nicest human beings I've ever seen. Watching you at school...the way you are with people, I

"Mancini, move it! The bell rang five minutes ago!" Principal Sheehan barks at me.

"Yeah, yeah, I'm going," I mutter under my breath, grabbing my stuff and haphazardly folding the note in half.

I race down the corridor, passing Chloe's locker on my way. I shouldn't put my note in yet. I haven't even proofread it. It's not finished. But before I can stop myself, I slide the paper through the vent and run to class.

It's not until I'm walking in late on Mr. Moreno's lesson that I suddenly regret what I did. My mind is scrambling for what I put in that note. Was my tone right? What the hell did I say? How the fuck did I end it?

Shit! I think I've just totally screwed this up.

Slumping into my seat, I grip my pen, nearly snapping it in half as I can do nothing but sweat it out and hope like hell the note spontaneously combusts before Chloe finds it and thinks I'm some kind of creepy stalker.

#7

CHLOE

No One Else Knows

I can't stop smiling.

Vincent's notes are so sweet. They reveal a side of him I never even knew existed. Talking about me deserving respect. Wow.

As I stand on the baseball field, pitching to my sister, I can't stop reeling at the idea that Vincent Mancini is not the guy I thought he was. He puts on this angry persona to push people away. I'm not sure why exactly, but underneath it all is a sweetheart.

A sweetheart I want to get to know.

Maddie catches my pitch and stands tall to lob the ball back to me. It thumps into my mitt and I set up to send a slider her way.

I'm not the world's best pitcher. I mean, I'm not bad, but I just don't see myself doing this after high school. Heck, I might not even bother with it next year. Once my sisters leave for college, I'm not sure I'll have it in me to drag my butt onto this field without them.

I wonder how Dad will feel about that. He probably won't care as long as Max is playing college ball. Poor Max. I mean, she seems to love baseball, but sometimes I worry that Dad puts too much pressure on her. She's definitely been off since we moved to Armitage.

I glance at the batting cage as soon as Maddie's caught my pitch. Max is swinging at Holden's pitches, making him work hard to strike her out. My lips twitch at the frustration on his face. I share a look with Maddie, who's now walking toward me. She chuckles, like it's fun to watch her boyfriend have to sweat it out in order to best her sister.

Swinging her arm over my shoulder, we lean against each other on the mound and take a quick break.

"You seem brighter today."

I roll my eyes. "I told you, I was just tired last night."

"I'm glad that's all it was." Maddie kisses my cheek and then heads across to Holden.

She's got a bounce in her step like she's never had before. I guess being in love brings out the happy in people.

I wipe my forehead with the back of my arm and fight a grin.

I do feel brighter this afternoon, and I'm pretty sure it's because of Vincent.

By the time we walk in the door, I've already started formulating my next note. As soon as dinner's over, I'm going to escape to my room and figure out exactly what I want to say. For some reason, Vincent finished his note mid-sentence, which makes me think that he was rushing to scribble something down before the bell went off and he ran out of time. I bet he put that note in my locker on impulse. Like he did it before he lost his nerve.

I giggle, finding the idea of me making someone nervous completely absurd.

As I wait my turn for the bathroom, I pull out a

sheet of paper and decide to start writing something now.

These notes are enlightening. I kind of like seeing this side of you. It's like a privilege no one else gets. I don't know if that's the right way to look at it or not, but thank you for being so kind to me.

"Bathroom's free!" Max shouts.

I hide my note away and run to the shower.

We've never been allowed long showers in our house—three girls, one bathroom, I'm sure you can imagine—so I rush through my cleanup and am soon standing in front of the mirror combing my hair.

"Hey, you're home early." Mom sounds surprised.

I go still as my parents meet up in the hallway outside the bathroom. I can tell it's Dad because I'm sure I heard them kiss.

"You look tired." Mom's voice is soft, and I seriously should not be straining to listen in on their conversation.

Dad grunts. "I feel like I'm always tired."

"Did you have a good day though?"

"Yeah, as good as I can. I spent most of the morning trying to help the guys narrow down an anonymous call that came in last night. Apparently some girl was attacked near Fort Street."

"Oh no," Mom whispers while my heart catapults into my throat.

"I've got a feeling someone stepped in before they could violate the girl. The tip gave very clear descriptions of what went down and the men's physical descriptions. Hayley picked one of them up this afternoon. His nose was broken and he had some pretty nasty bruises on his face. He's of course denying everything. Says some young guy tried to beat the crap out of him and steal his wallet. Said it was a Mancini."

"Do you believe him?"

"My gut's telling me not to, but I'd really like to find this guy who called in the tip...and the girl who was attacked."

My heart is seriously lodged in my throat right now. It's a struggle to breathe as I lean my ear against the wood to catch the rest of the conversation.

"Do you think the person who called in the tip rescued this girl somehow?"

"Maybe," Dad murmurs. "But why hide that? He's a hero."

"He might be worried that he'll get in trouble for beating the guys up."

"Yeah, I guess so. That poor girl though. Must have been a nightmare for her."

"Thank God she was saved. You said Fort Street,

right?"

"Yeah." Dad sighs.

"The church Chloe volunteers at is on Fort Street. Do you think we should still let her go? If there are guys like that lurking in the neighborhood, she's vulnerable. So is her friend."

"She'll hate us if we don't let her keep helping."

"I know, but after what happened to Maddie at the school... I just can't stand the idea of my babies being in danger."

"They're big girls now." Dad's voice rumbles with emotion. "But I think you're right. Chloe needs to stay on this side of town until we lock down this second suspect."

I frown but stay quiet, not wanting to alert my parents to the fact that I've been eavesdropping. I wait until they move out of the hallway before easing the door open and sneaking to my room.

I'm kind of annoyed that they've made the decision without even talking to me about it, but I understand. If I put myself in their shoes, I wouldn't want my daughter going off to that part of town either. Man, if I admit the truth, they won't even let me leave the house.

Plunking onto my bed, I gaze at the pen on my nightstand and my mind immediately jumps to Vincent.

Anonymous tip.

Wow. He really is a hero.

Snatching the pen, I grab the note and try to finish it before the dinner call.

Just so you know, Dad said that one of the guys who attacked me last night was picked up this morning. Apparently someone called in an anonymous tip last night.

Smart move. You're braver than me.

I'm glad you're letting the police handle it. I'm glad you trust them to do the right thing.

I don't know your full story so I'm only guessing here, but it must be hard to trust the law in your part of town. I hate preconceived ideas, but unfortunately they exist, and that must make you feel quite vulnerable sometimes.

Just so you know, you never have to worry about me. I'm big on believing that there's goodness in all of us, but people have their different reasons for not letting it show.

Thank you for showing me your goodness. It's a beautiful thing.

I stop and tap my pen on the paper for a second, deciding just how far to go. Part of me wants to open up to him, so he can see a part of me too...a part that no one else knows.

Pursing my lips, I grip the pen in my hand and

then grin.

I like chocolate raisins.

Random, I know, but Maddie's lactose intolerant, Max doesn't have a sweet tooth, and my parents are all about healthy living. So, when no one's watching, I go for it. I can finish an entire box of Raisinets all by myself. I always feel sick afterward, but it's so worth it.

Now you know something about me that no one else does.

I kind of like that.

Hope to read from you again soon.

C

#8

VINCENT

Secret Letters

Your notes are enlightening too. I always figured you were kind, but you seem to have an extra batch of empathy that most people lack. I like the way you look past appearances and make your own guesses. There's always a backstory, right?

So, you're a Raisinets girl, huh?

Give me a Butterfinger any day of the week. I'm also pretty good with M&Ms. No sharing required, if you know what I mean.

You do, don't you?

I feel like I could write you anything, and you'd know what I meant.

V

You're sweet. I love that you're a candy freak like me. Can I call you Butterfinger boy? Or maybe the M&M man :)

There's nothing like sugar to really comfort the soul though, right?

Oh man, that's so bad! Talk about unhealthy living, but seriously...sugar is good for the soul. I truly believe that ;)

I'm also a fan of romantic movies and novels. They're good for the soul too. Anything where love wins... you can't beat it. Love is the strongest weapon on this planet. That's what I want to spend my life proving to people.

C

You amaze me.

I wish you were right, but unfortunately hate is like a nuclear bomb. I live with it every day. It's this disease that eats and devours anything good around it. I wish I could look at the world the way you do.

I wish love was stronger than all the bullshit.

V

It is.

Love will ultimately win. People deserve happy endings. They deserve to be understood and cared for. I know that's often not the case, which is why there are people like you...and me. You go in with your fists at the ready to physically defend. My style's different—I hug, I listen and try to encourage with my words. But they're both forms of love, and if enough people could do that, this world will be a better place.

Am I sounding cheesy right now?

I'm not delusional. I know the world will never be at peace, but I'm going to do my part to spread the love and create peace where I'm able.

That's why I want to get into humanitarian work. There's a world of people out there who need to be shown a little love and kindness. There's a whole world in Armitage that needs the same. I'll focus on that for now ;)

C

Folding Chloe's note in half, I press it against my chest before slipping it into my pocket. This girl is amazing. Her attitude toward life. Her outlook. I've never met anyone like her.

We've been passing notes for just over a week now and with each new letter, I fall a little harder. It's dangerous and I should stop. Someone like Chloe shouldn't be with me. She's too innocent and hopeful to truly understand the darkness in this world. She wants to save it with hugs and words, but she's dreaming.

Problem is she's making me dream too.

She's making me imagine what life outside of Mancini-land could look like. For the first time ever, I'm really thinking ahead, finding the courage to imagine rather than just tell myself I have to get out.

She's helping me see what "get out" looks like.

It's inspiring.

No doubt dangerous, and possibly a waste of time, but...

I don't want to stop.

If anything, I want to get closer.

Which is why when Chloe turns the corner and starts walking my way, I step into her path before thought can stop me.

She glances up and kind of jolts when she sees I want to talk to her. We haven't spoken two words since the night I dropped her at home. It's all been through secret letters. But I want to hear her voice again.

Tipping my head to the left, I spin and start walking away, hoping she's understood and will follow me.

I don't stop walking until I've made it down the flight of stairs and am tucked into a private alcove near the music room. Hardly anyone ventures down here during lunchtime...except for Velocity, and they're always too busy playing to notice me.

Holding my breath, I lean against the wall and hope.

My fingers curl into a fist, my heart rate accelerating as excitement and fear battle for top position.

She's not going to come.

She won't follow. Why would she?

"There you are."

Her soft voice makes me jerk and bolt away from the wall, nerves scouring my insides.

She's right there. Close enough to touch.

Her blue eyes sparkle with a smile. "Are you okay?"

"Yeah," I rasp, then clear my throat. "Uh, thank you for your notes."

She tips her head, her nose wrinkling. "You don't believe me, do you? You don't believe in happy endings."

"I wish I could," I murmur, drinking in her beauty while I can.

She's going to say no. She's going to prove me right.

Pulling her sleeves down over her hands, she leans her weight to one side and smiles at me again. She's waiting for me to explain why I brought her down here.

My throat goes dry. I've never asked a girl out before. Not like this, anyway. I usually hook up with chicks at clubs or parties. It's spontaneous, spur-of-the-moment stuff that has no lasting effect. I'm usually supposed to be working for Enzo, so the girls are a nice reprieve.

And Chloe's nothing like them.

"Did you want to talk to me about something?" she finally asks.

"Um..." I swallow, then lick the corner of my mouth. "Yeah, I... Do you want to go out sometime?"

Her lips part, like this question was the last one she was expecting.

"Just to hang out and talk. You know, so I don't have to wait hours for your reply."

"Oh, I..." She bites the tip of her tongue between her lips, crucifying my hope and reminding me that my worldview is more realistic than hers. Girls like her don't date assholes like me.

She looks to the ground. "I'm not sure. I—"

"That's okay. You don't have to."

"No, it's just—"

"See ya later."

I push past her and walk away before she can come up with some lame excuse.

She should just tell me she doesn't want to, but that's not her style.

She's too nice.

Too sweet.

She'd never just come out with the ugly truth like that.

Shoving my hands in my pockets, I storm up the stairs, my mood blackening as I stalk down the corridor.

"Fuck this," I mutter, veering for the exit.

I'll get detention tomorrow but I don't give a shit. Right now, I just want to drive up to Cherry Top Hill and stare at the view for a while. No one else will be there at this time of day, and it's a quiet space where I can vent a few screams and punch the air for a while.

It's a hell of a lot better than sitting in some classroom trying to learn when I know deep down that it's a big fat waste of time.

I'm not getting out of this shitty life.

I shouldn't let Chloe's notes affect me so bad.

I shouldn't have let myself dream.

#9

CHLOE

Best Friends with Classified Information

I step into the dark alcove with a frown. Leaning against the wall where I found Vincent, I wonder how else I could have played it.

Part of me wanted to chase after him, but that

angry, rejected look on his face told me he probably wouldn't have listened anyway.

Truth is, I'd love to go out with him. I'd love to have a back and forth conversation. I'd like to watch the way his lips move when he forms an answer, stare at his chiseled jawline while the muscles clench and unclench.

There's something so strong about his face. I've been spying it any chance I can get and between that and his letters, I'm scoring myself a great big crush.

But he's Vincent Mancini.

I mean, I don't care, but everyone else sure will.

They won't see past his family name and angry scowls to the sweet guy underneath. I could try and tell them, but they won't hear me.

How am I supposed to get out of the house to even go on a date with him? Mom and Dad are still being super cautious, even though Dad's apprehended the second attacker. He can't charge him with attempted rape because I still haven't stepped up. I was prepared to, but I heard Dad say that the guy had illegal drugs on him and they'll charge him with that instead. So I don't have to admit the truth anymore.

It's still a cowardly way out, but I'm worried about his reaction.

Rahn's already sad that I can't go to St. Michael's with her anymore. If I can just give it a couple more weeks, Mom and Dad will cool down and I can go again.

Rahn.

I stand up straight.

Maybe she can help me.

Turning out of the alcove, I'm about to walk down the corridor when the music room door opens. I recognize Max's laughter before I see her. Ducking back into the alcove, I hide away and play spy.

She's walking out the door with Cairo. He has a loved-up look on his face. His hand is on her lower back and he smiles before bending down to kiss her. She leans into it, threading her hands around his neck and deepening the kiss.

Oh really!

Well, this is interesting.

So Maddie gets Holden and Max has Cairo.

I wonder if Maddie knows about this. I sure didn't.

Max leans her forehead against Cairo's cheek. Oh my gosh, she's one hundred percent smitten! She whispers goodbye, pecks his lips one more time, then walks up the stairs without him.

I see, they're going secret with the whole dating thing. Cairo watches her walk away, looking kind of dismal about it. I bet he wants to hold Max's hand and claim her in front of everyone, but she won't let him do it.

But why?

I snicker and shake my head. Because of Dad. She's afraid if she tells someone the truth, she'll lose Cairo. It's not like Dad's going to open his arms and welcome some longhaired rock star into Max's life.

Pursing my lips, I consider what my sister is doing. You know, her reasoning is kind of valid. And if she can do it, maybe I can too.

Determination fires through me. I wait for Cairo to leave and then subtly follow him up the stairs. As soon as I'm back in the hallway, I run to Rahn's locker.

She's there, busily chatting with someone who's only half listening.

"Hey." I bounce up to her, already giddy with my plan.

Although I'm kind of nervous too.

But Rahn's a romantic like me; surely she'll understand.

"Can we talk?"

"Sure." Rahn checks her watch. "We've got like five minutes before the bell goes."

"I've got a free period now. Do you?"

She looks thoughtful and then gives me a wicked grin. "I can have a free period now."

"I don't want you to get in trouble." I wince.

"It's just PE." She sticks out her tongue. "I'll tell Coach Keenan that I've got major cramps. As soon as you mention anything to do with the female anatomy, he goes pale and excuses you from anything. As long as I'm there before the end of the period, it'll be okay." She giggles and threads her arm through mine. "So, hey, why weren't you in the cafeteria at lunch?"

"That's what I need to talk to you about."

Her black eyebrows wiggle. "Oooo, intrigue. I love it!"

"Oh yeah, I'm pretty sure you're going to adore this, once you get over your shock."

"O-kay."

Pulling her toward the library, I figure we can pretend we're working on an assignment together.

I pick a table in a quiet corner at the back and lean my arms against the wood. Rahn leans in too, her brown eyes dancing with excitement.

"You've got to swear that you will not say anything to anyone."

"Okay."

"No, I'm serious. This is super top secret."

"Got it." Rahn gives me a serious look. "I promise. I won't utter a word to anyone."

"Okay." Pulling in a breath, I go to start talking, then stop and squeeze her arm. "Oh yeah, and you need to be quite open-minded on this one."

Her eyes narrow. "Chloe Barlow, what are you into?"

I cringe and softly whisper, "Vincent Mancini."

Her lips drop with a gasp. Slapping my hand over

her mouth, I glance over my shoulder to make sure no one's watching.

"Shhh," I whisper. "It's a long story."

"Then you better start talking," she mumbles beneath my hand.

I release her and, with a jittery smile, launch into the week I've just had. I'm really careful how I word the near attack at the church. As expected, Rahn feels awful, but I distract her with all the positives that have come out of it.

She's eventually won over by the romance of it all. I even show her one of Vincent's letters and she totally swoons.

"I can't believe this. What a sweetheart."

"I know, right?"

"So why does he always look like a scary asshole?"

"It's a front." I shrug, folding the letter and tucking it back into my bag. "I don't know exactly why he does it, but I want to find out those details. I want to find out everything about him." I look to the ceiling and can't help a dreamy smile.

It's really sinking in that Vincent Mancini asked me out, and unlike Holden Carter, I feel like he really means it.

"Aren't you a little scared? I mean, what if he's just putting on a front to get you somewhere quiet and alone?"

"I honestly don't think he is. And before you remind me of my Holden Carter experience, I just want to say how different this is. When it comes to romance, I've always been the chaser. I've flirted and put myself in their line of vision, done everything I can to make them want me. But with Vincent, I haven't even tried. I've just been myself. I swear these notes feel like pieces of his heart. I trust him."

Rahn bites her lip, still looking cautious.

"He saved me. I don't think he has any dark ulterior motives."

"I just want you to be safe. His family is—"

"I don't think he's going to let me anywhere near his family."

"Okay." Rahn bobs her head. "Okay, so... all right. I'll help you, but you've got to promise that you'll go somewhere public and safe."

"Public?" I cringe. "I wouldn't be asking you to keep this a secret if I was happy to go public."

"No, I mean, a busy area, like..." She sits up and snaps her fingers. "There's a fair near Brazenwood. It runs over Spring Break. That would be the perfect place to go on a date."

"But won't there be Armitage people there?"

"Maybe." Rahn shrugs. "But it's a fair. There'll be plenty of places to hide and if anyone spots you, you can just say you bumped into Vincent and were having a little chat."

I give her a skeptical frown. "Like that'll fly."

"Hey, it's the best solution I've got, and I won't agree unless you promise that you're going to hang out somewhere open and public."

I roll my eyes with a sigh. "Okay, fine. I promise. I'll find him and ask him to take me to the fair."

"Good." Rahn nods. "Then I will officially cover for you, saying that we're off doing something girly—like a movie and milkshakes afterward."

"We'll have to get our stories straight."

"We will." She grins.

"Are you sure you don't mind doing this for me?"

Taking my hand, she gives it a squeeze. "You're my soul sister. Of course I don't mind."

"Thank you." I lean across and kiss her cheek. "You're the best."

"Yeah, well, I expect a very detailed rundown of events the next day...and you can buy me lunch while you're telling me about it."

"Deal."

She winks and giggles before grabbing her stuff and hauling ass to the gym before the bell rings.

Grabbing a pen and sheet of paper out of my bag, I quickly compose a letter to Vincent. I hope he gets it before the end of the day. I can't wait to wipe that sad, rebuffed look off his face.

#10

VINCENT

Smile

I pull my car into school, already dreading homeroom and the fact that I'll get bawled out by my teacher and issued an after-school detention. It's happened plenty of times before. I'm not due for another lecture from Principal Sheehan yet, but if I skip out again, it'll come.

Sometimes I want to tell them the real reasons

why I skip out on school, but that'll just open a whole big-ass can of worms that I'm not prepared to deal with.

No, I just have to keep my head down and get this next year and a half over with.

My grades are currently good enough to get me a diploma next year. Even though I can't see how I'll use it, I'll have it. And Selena says that counts for something.

Yet another hopeful female.

My mind skips to Chloe.

Closing my eyes, I lean my head back in the seat, feeling like such a frickin' idiot for even trying to ask her out. I should never have tried to step things up a notch. The letters were enough, and now I've totally screwed it up.

Shit!

Shouldering my door open, I slam it shut and get a couple of looks from those parked nearby. I give them all my best death glare and they shy away, scuttling toward the school.

I must look like one mean bastard.

Of course Chloe wouldn't want to be seen with me.

With a sharp huff, I hitch my bag and trudge into school. The bell will be going soon, so the hallways are kind of full, but they part like the freaking Red Sea when I walk in.

I hide my eye roll and stalk past the nervous student body until I spot Chloe standing in the corner staring at me. She's the only set of eyes brave enough to do it. Her lips curve into a smile, so I deepen my scowl, trying to put her off.

Rather than the hurt sadness I expect, she gives me a *don't you look at me like that* kind of frown, and I'm startled by it.

My head jolts back, my scowl changing from mean to confused when she tips her head the exact same way I did yesterday.

I hesitate, not sure if I should follow her. I'm not up for a second rejection, even if she does word it sweetly and has the best excuses in the world. I don't want to hear it.

I plant my feet, set on turning toward my locker, until she spins and catches my eye. Her eyebrows wrinkle with a silent plea and it tugs me toward her before I can stop myself.

Thumping down the stairs, I turn the corner and find her in the same alcove as yesterday.

"Hi," she whispers with a smile.

I lift my chin at her, then glance away. It's a protection technique, but I feel like a douchebag greeting her that way.

"I'm guessing you didn't get my note yesterday."

I clench my jaw, desperate to know what it says, but also not. It'll just be a sweet excuse.

"I put it in your locker before last period. I was hoping you'd get it before you went home."

"I left school early," I mutter.

"Oh." Her eyes are assessing my expression. I can feel them on me, delving, searching for some way to understand me.

I sniff and swipe a finger under my nose before turning for the stairs. "I'll go check it now."

"Wait." She grabs my arm before I can walk away. Her long fingers curl around my bicep and I gaze down at them, wishing I could brush my thumb over each of her knuckles. "I'll just tell you."

I hold my breath, preparing myself for the sweetly worded rejection.

"You didn't give me a chance to explain yesterday. The reason I said I wasn't sure is because I didn't know how I could make it work. My dad's really strict about guys, and my mom's a little paranoid after Maddie got beat up. They've even said I can't help at St. Michael's anymore, which totally sucks."

I glance at her sad expression but can't think of anything to say to make her feel better.

"The truth is, I want to go out with you, even if it means sneaking around behind my parents' backs." She winces. "I know that sounds bad, but I just don't think they'll understand. Which sucks, and I'm sorry. I'm sorry they've already made up their minds about you. I wish I could help them understand, but I'm worried if I even mention that I like you, they'll freak out."

She likes me?

I can't breathe.

"I'm sorry. I hope you're not offended."

"I'm not," I croak. "I'm used to it."

Her smile is filled with empathy as she squeezes my arm.

I cover her hand with mine and her smile grows a little wider.

"Anyway, I was just trying to figure out how I can make this work and so I told my friend. Rahn knows everything now, and she's going to cover for me."

"So, you...you *want* to go out with me?"

"Of course I do." She giggles like I'm being silly for ever doubting it. "You just took me by surprise yesterday. I didn't think you'd want to..." She shakes her head, looking embarrassed. "I don't know. I guess I'm still trying to work you out."

I snicker, wishing I had something intelligent to say, but I'm kind of reeling here. Chloe likes me. She *wants* to go out with me.

"So, unless you have a plan already, I'd love it if you could take me to the fair in Brazenwood. Apparently it runs over Spring Break, and since that starts after school tomorrow, I figured maybe we could check it out."

"The fair," I murmur.

"Yeah, have you ever been to one?" Chloe runs her finger down her face, capturing a stray hair that's stuck to her lip gloss.

My lips twitch with a smile. "Yeah, I've been to one."

"It's a pretty good first date location, don't you think?"

First date. Holy shit. Those words sound so sweet coming from her. It makes me realize that I've never really been on a first date. I hook up at parties and clubs. I go where Enzo tells me to. I don't do romantic dates.

But taking Chloe to the fair...

"Yeah, it's perfect." I grin.

"Wow." She giggles. "You have a great smile. You should show it off sometime. It'd shock the hell out of people."

I snicker and raise my eyebrows at her teasing wink.

The bell rings, breaking up our awesome little moment.

"So, do you have a phone I can text you on? We can set up a time."

I cringe and run a hand through my hair. "I don't do phones."

"Really?" Her face buckles with confusion. "Why not?"

"I don't like people being able to get in touch

with me."

"Okay." She nods, obviously finding it weird but nice enough not to say it. "So…"

"So, meet me at that park two blocks from school. You know the one with the blue slide?"

"I do. What time? What day?"

"Uh…Monday. Six o'clock."

"I'll be there." Her glossy lips pull into a smile that melts my insides.

She's so freaking beautiful.

I can't say anything as she brushes past me and makes her way to class. Leaning my head back against the wall, I gaze up at the ceiling in awe.

I'm going on a date with Chloe Barlow.

The smile on my face feels wide and foreign, but I just can't stop it.

I'm going on a date with Chloe Barlow!

#11

CHLOE

Figuring It Out

I check my appearance in the full-length mirror Dad hung on the back of my door.

Turning to my side, I study my profile and hope I look okay.

I've kept it simple with a black skater skirt and a white off-the-shoulder top that tucks into it. The sleeves finish at my elbow. I've paired the ensemble with my white Converse and my gold hoop earrings. I might take my short leather jacket too, in case it gets cold.

Trying it on, I assess whether I've killed the outfit with too much black. Maybe I should go for my denim jacket instead.

I switch it out and then decide that maybe I should go for the pink hoodie I always wear.

Crap, just make a decision, Chloe!

I can't believe how nervous I am. I've been so excited about tonight...until I started getting ready to leave. Rahn texted me, asking for photos of my outfit choice, and that's what set off the storm of butterflies. They've been fluttering in my belly all afternoon.

Grabbing my phone, I snap a quick selfie and ask for Rahn's opinion.

She responds within seconds.

Love it! Sweet but hot. Casual but classy. You've hit the balance perfectly xxx

I bite my lip and check my appearance once more before reaching for my lip gloss. I'm not a huge makeup wearer, but I love having shiny lips.

I'm just dabbing a little extra gloss on when Max knocks on my door. "Can I come in?"

"Sure," I squeak, ordering my nerves to calm

down already!

"Wow, you look pretty." Max points at my outfit. "I thought you were just kickin' it with Rahn tonight."

"I am." I screw the lip gloss stick into the tube. "But that doesn't mean I can't look nice when I'm doing it."

"True." Max raises her eyebrows before crossing her arms to study me.

"Do you need something?" I keep my eyes as wide and innocent as possible.

"Uh...yeah, I was going to ask if I could borrow your leather jacket."

"Sure." I grab it off my bed and hold it out to her. "Where are you going?"

Max's mouth curves up on the left side. "Where are you going?"

I pause and we eye each other for a second, like we're waiting for the other to break.

"I'm going out with Rahn," I repeat.

My sister snickers. "Do you want me to drop you at her place?"

"Um...no, I can... I'll walk."

"Okay, liar, liar." Max starts putting my jacket on.

"Like you can talk." I laugh and cross my arms. Not that I really have time to do this right now, but I am not the only liar in this room.

"What's that supposed to mean?" She frowns.

"Two words." I hold up my fingers. "Cairo Hale."

Max's eyes bulge and she looks over her shoulder before shutting the door and whispering. "How did you hear about that? Did Maddie tell you about Saturday night?"

"No." My eyebrows dip. "What happened on Saturday? I thought you were at Zane's house playing PS4."

"That's what I wanted everyone to think."

"Where were you really?"

She gives me a sheepish grin. "Holden and Mads took me to this club in Cullington."

"So you could meet up with Cairo. I knew there was something going on between you guys. I saw you kissing outside the music room last week. Why didn't you tell me?"

She blanches and shoves her hands into her pockets. "The music room? What were you doing down there?"

I deflect her question by repeating mine. "Why didn't you tell me?"

She gives me a pained frown. "Because I didn't want you to feel like the only single girl in the family. You went on about how grateful you were that I didn't have a boyfriend."

It's impossible not to smile. That was kind of sweet and thoughtful.

I have to fight the urge to tell her about Vincent.

But I don't think she's ready. Sneaking around with

Cairo is SO different than sneaking off with Vincent Mancini.

"So, is he your boyfriend?"

She nods, her grin growing into a thousand-watt smile.

I giggle. Wow! Max has a boyfriend. I honestly thought it might never happen for her in high school.

I jump across the room and wrap my arms around her shoulders. "You are too cute. So happy for you, sis."

"Thanks." She squeezes me, then steps back. "Sorry I didn't tell you."

"No worries." I brush my hand through the air, not wanting her to feel bad. Right now I kind of need to keep my own secrets, so I'm glad I don't owe her any. Glancing at my watch, I move to the door but stop when Max asks me the weirdest question.

"Hey, sis, you're not doing anything illegal tonight, are you?"

"What?" I spin around with a surprised laugh. "No! Of course not."

"Then why won't you tell me where you're going? Why lie?"

Resting my hand on the frame, I glance at my nails, which I painted pink this afternoon, before looking at my sister. "It's just one of those situations where Mom and Dad will never get it, and the less people who know, the better."

Max nods like she totally understands what I mean. "Got it. I won't ask again."

"I'll tell you eventually. I'm just figuring it out right now."

"Totally get it." Max raises her eyebrows. "Just be safe, okay?"

"I will be," I assure her, believing it with every fiber of my being.

I'll be with Vincent. There's no safer place than that.

#12

VINCENT

A First First-Date

I hover by the slide, pacing from the ladder to the circle of sand the children land in.

I can't believe how freaking nervous I am.

This feels like my first date...ever.

I guess it kind of is.

Smoothing a hand through my hair, I glance over my shoulder and stop short when I see a vision walking toward me.

Her blonde hair cascades over her shoulders like a golden waterfall. The breeze catches a few strands, making them dance as she waves and smiles at me.

I step forward, meeting her on the edge of the grass. I wish I had something smooth to say, but all I can do is gaze at her, from the top of her head to those white sneakers on her feet.

"You look really pretty," I manage.

"Thank you." She tweaks her jacket sleeve and tucks a lock of hair behind her ear.

Maybe I'm not the only nervous one.

That thought relieves me in a weird way, and I pull in a full breath before pointing to my car. "Shall we go?"

"Yes, please." She tucks her hand through the crook of my arm and then starts talking like I'm her best buddy, telling me about her morning and how she slept late because Sunday night she went out with her Uncle Conrad and they did back-to-back movies.

"We got home at like one and I'm so not great with late nights. I'm a big sleeper. There's nothing better than snuggling up in bed and drifting into dreamland. I love falling asleep while reading. That's the best."

She's talking faster than usual and it makes my heart squeeze with affection.

We reach my car and I open the door for her, feeling like a gentleman for the first time in my life.

"Thank you." She slips in and I wait for her to notice.

It doesn't take long.

I watch her face light with a smile as she picks up the box of Raisinets I bought on my way here.

As I get into the car, she gives them a shake and starts laughing. "You are so sweet. Do you want some?"

"Are you sure you want to share?" I fire up the engine while she giggles some more.

That's seriously a sound I will never get sick of.

"I'll break my own rules. You know, just this once." She winks and I hold out my hand for a few.

We head out of town, munching happily. Chloe talks most of the way. She's pretty damn easy to listen to.

As we reach the town limits and I turn toward Brazenwood, she finally takes a breath and says, "Man, I've spent this whole time talking and haven't asked you one question. I'm sorry. I guess I'm nervous, not because of you...just because of...you." She snickers and shakes her head. "That doesn't even make sense."

"I get it." I smile at her and look back to the road. "I'm nervous too. I just want this night to be perfect."

"Me too. But what a huge expectation. No

wonder we're nervous. You know what, we need to just switch off and talk like we're writing to each other. We don't need to have all this first-date pressure. Let's just hang out like we've been doing for the last week or so."

I nod. "Good idea."

"Okay, so questions I have yet to ask you."

"Uh-oh."

Chloe laughs. "No, they're easy ones, I promise."

"Okay. Shoot."

"And you have to say the first thing that pops into your head."

"Am I allowed to ask you the same stuff afterward?"

"Totally!" Her eyes are so bright and beautiful. "Okay, so first one is...favorite color."

"Orange," I say, then wrinkle my forehead. Was that seriously the first color that popped into my head?

"I like orange too. It's such a happy color."

"I like orange juice." I shrug.

She giggles and fires another one at me. By the time we reach Brazenwood, I know her favorite authors are Simone Elkeles, Rainbow Rowell, and Abbi Glines...whoever the hell they are.

She couldn't pick just one book—that was impossible—so she just rattled off author names and we decided the first three that came to mind must be the winners. She's a sucker for romantic movies, loves any genre as long as there's a love story involved. Her favorite sandwich is chicken salad, and she'll basically eat any dessert, unless it's rice pudding.

I answer every one of the questions she throws at me, because they're all light and easy. Most of them can be answered in one or two words, although she takes more like twenty to thirty for her answers. I don't mind. I could head east all the way to North Carolina listening to her talk. We haven't even reached the fair yet and I already feel like I've had the best date I'm ever going to have in my life.

The Ferris wheel lights appear down at the end of the country road and Chloe gasps. "Aw, it's going to look amazing when the sun goes down."

Twilight kicks in around eight, so we've still got an hour to go before it's fully dark. It's kind of nice that we're going to get the best of both worlds this evening.

I pay the parking attendant a couple of bucks, then find a spot in the back corner of the parking lot. The fair's already in full swing. Chloe gives me a nervous smile as I help her out of the car.

"Wow, it's busy."

"Yeah, it gets pretty crowded. You still want to go?"

She hesitates, then bobs her head. "Yeah."

With my breath on hold, I take her hand as we

walk for the entrance.

She doesn't let go or shy away from my touch.

Chloe's holding my hand!

Shit, I feel like a fifth grader with a crush, but there it is. My insides are frickin' sparkling right now and there's nothing I can do about it.

We line up behind a bunch of families and couples. Some are clumped together—groups of friends out for a fun night. Chloe squeezes my hand and smiles up at me. We don't say anything as we wait, just stand there grinning at each other.

"Would you lovebirds stop staring at each other and move it along?" The person behind me taps my shoulder and I instinctively tense.

"Sorry about that. First date." Chloe winks at the man and he laughs—all tension diffused in a microsecond.

I hate that I'm so wired for combat. If she hadn't been there, I would have turned around and glared the guy down. My hands would have been clenched into fists, my entire body ready to pounce if he came at me.

Dammit. Why do I have to be that way?

Chloe's gentle tug pulls me forward and before I know it, she's chatting with the guy behind us, asking about his family and talking to the little girl. I'm kind of in awe of her ability to interact with anyone.

"Have a fun first date!" the little girl shouts at us

as we walk away from the entry booth.

The people around us chuckle and I find it in me to turn back and wink at the little girl. "Thank you."

Her toothy grin makes me warm on the inside. So this is what it's like to be normal.

"What do you want to do first?" Chloe bounces on her toes beside me. "I bet you're kickass at those shooting games."

I frown. "Why do you think that?"

"Because you noticed me, so you must have a really good eye." She tips her head back, laughing at her own joke, and I can't help but join her.

I don't laugh much, so it feels kind of weird, but also really good.

I steer her toward the shooting games and have some fun competing with her. This fair is going to suck me dry, but I don't want to deny Chloe anything. And so the day turns to night while I shell out my cash, buying her games, rides, and eventually a huge stick of cotton candy.

Licking the pink sugar off my fingers, I grin down at her. "You having fun?"

"I'm eating cotton candy at a fair!"

"I'll take that as a yes."

She nods. "And I know you're having fun too."

"And how do you know that?" I nudge her with my hip.

"Because you're smiling."

"Yeah, feels kind of weird," I admit.

"Looks kind of beautiful."

I stop and gaze down at her. Her blue eyes, her sweet words, they bowl me right over. Turning to face her, I skim my finger across her cheekbone and over her ear. I want to kiss her so badly right now.

Running my fingers gently through her hair, I'm just thinking about leaning in when a voice makes me jerk back.

"Vinnie. Hey, cuz. What are you doing here, man?"

Shit!

I turn my back on Chloe, hoping to block her from view as I face off with my cousins. "'Sup, Diego." I raise my eyebrows at Rex and Carlo too. "Why you here?"

"Was in the neighborhood." He looks back at his cousins before peering over my shoulder. "Who's the chick?"

His dark eyes drill into her and I want to punch him in the face.

But I know better.

Stepping to the side, I block his view again and go for a casual shrug. "I don't know."

"You come together?" His dark gaze drifts to me.

I hold it and sell the lie as best I can. "Of course not."

I'm trying to sound disgusted by the idea, even

though I feel the exact opposite.

Shit! I've probably just killed the date. I don't want Chloe thinking I'm ashamed to be seen with her or something.

But Diego can't know.

I have to protect her, so I glance over my shoulder and mumble, "Later."

Her expression flickers with confusion, but I have to walk away.

It's a scummy thing to do.

All I can hope is that she'll let me explain when I find her again.

#13

CHLOE

Things Are Not Always As They Seem

"Well, if you're not going to play with her, I will." Diego's dark eyes drink me in like I'm some kind of ice cream he's never tasted before.

Vincent whips around, fear washing over his

expression before shooting daggers at the guys. "Leave her alone. Let's go."

"Aw, come on. Where's your sense of fun, man?"

Diego goes to move into my space, but Vincent grabs his jacket and yanks him back. "Don't be a dick. Let's just go."

Moving like lightning, Diego grabs Vincent's collar and pulls him forward. "You want to mess with me?"

"No," Vincent seethes between gritted teeth.

"If I want to talk to the girl, I'll talk to the fucking girl!"

A muscle in Vincent's jaw works as he stares the guy down. The other two have moved in as well, and I get the distinct impression that it'll be three on one if this turns into a fight.

I can't let that happen, but I'm not quite sure what to do. I don't want to leave Vincent, but I don't want him getting hurt trying to protect me either.

"I'm gonna go find my family," I murmur and rush away before anyone else can say anything.

My heart is hammering as I scurry around the corner. I'm half expecting Diego and those other two guys to chase me down, but as I duck into the shadows behind the main tent and look behind me, the space is empty.

I'm alone.

Without Vincent.

Wringing my hands, I stand there wondering what

the hell I'm supposed to do. I check my watch and decide to wait ten minutes for him to come find me. There's no point walking around the fair looking for him if he's now stuck with those people. Diego called Vincent "cuz." I wonder if they're related or something.

My heart aches for him.

I could tell the second that guy uttered the word "Vinnie" that he was an unwelcome guest to our party. The way Vincent turned and blocked me with his body. I wasn't offended or surprised when he denied me being someone important.

Yet again, Vincent the Protector was in action.

Chewing my lip, I glance at my watch again.

It's been fifteen minutes and still Vincent hasn't found me.

He must be caught up with those jerks. Nibbling my thumbnail, I tentatively step out from hiding and work my way around the tent. I'm scanning for both Vincent and those assholes who broke up our date. I don't see anyone I know, so I decide to head to Vincent's car. It's in the very back corner of the parking lot. If those guys are still lurking around when he walks to his car, I can hide behind another vehicle and wait it out. There's no way Vincent will leave without me. I refuse to believe he would.

Glancing over my shoulder, I scan the fair as I walk out of it. Nerves are attacking me from all sides.

Walking through this dark parking lot alone is kind of terrifying, especially after what happened to me on Fort Street.

The darkness is no longer a protective cloak. Shadows are no longer innocent shapes, and walking alone isn't as easy as it used to be.

My breath hitches as I pick up my pace, sprinting for Vincent's car and screaming when I round the back corner and find him waiting for me.

"It's me. It's me." He holds up his hands. "I'm not going to hurt you."

I sag against the car, breaths puffing out of me as I recover from my panicked run.

"I am so sorry." Vincent's voice quakes. "I couldn't let them think we were connected. And then when you took off, I had to stick with them for a while so they wouldn't get suspicious. When I finally managed to drop them, I didn't know what to do, or where to start looking for you. I'm sorry. I just couldn't have you around *him*."

"Are you talking about that Diego guy?"

He nods, his jaw clenching tight.

"He was kind of scary."

"I never want him to touch you, ever. I don't even want him looking at you," Vincent spits.

I reach out for him, brushing my hand down his arm in an attempt to calm him. "Who is he?"

"My cousin. I live with his dad. I...I hate it." He

leans forward, resting his elbows on the roof of the car.

Shuffling a little closer, I study his moonlit face. His expression is so tormented, my heart can't help but ache for him. "Thank you for protecting me tonight."

My soft words make him flinch and he turns to gaze down at me. "I thought you'd hate me for killing the date."

I smile and shake my head. "You can't kill this date. It's not even over yet."

Brushing his thumb across my cheek, he gives me a pained smile. "I better take you home."

It hurts a little, but I don't say anything. I'm only disappointed because I'm not ready for this night to be over. I can sense he wants to get me out of here though. The feeling's only amplified when he asks me to duck down until we're out of the parking lot.

I do it, but as soon as we're in the clear, I sit up and ask him to tell me his story.

"What story?" He frowns, gripping the wheel until his knuckles are white. The muscles in his forearms flex tight and I study the shape of them. His arms are strong. Everything about him seems strong, like he could take on an army if he had to. Maybe he already has. Maybe his house is a constant battlefield.

I lean back against the headrest, my throat thick with emotion. "Your story, Vincent. Everyone has one, and I'm guessing yours is a lot sadder than most. Why do you live with family you hate? Where are your parents?"

His nostrils flare while he clenches his jaw and does everything he can to not look at me.

After a few minutes of silence, I finally concede. "Sorry, it's not really any of my business."

"My dad left when I was four. I don't really remember him, and I've never seen him since he walked out the door. Mom had depression and she got addicted to who knows what. My brother basically raised me. She overdosed when I was eleven and we got shipped to Armitage. Uncle Enzo's the only relative who was willing to take us. It's been shit, especially since Nick was sent away. He used to look out for me, but..." Vincent's chin bunches for a second until his expression returns to a hard look that no doubt keeps him safe.

"Was Nick the guy accused of murder?" I ask quietly.

"Yep. Accused, convicted, sentenced to life in prison."

"How old is he?"

"Twenty-two."

"Wow. That's so young," I whisper, my eyes smarting as I think about what life in prison really means for him. "Do you think he'll get out on parole?"

"Eventually." Vincent shrugs. "Maybe. I don't

know. It'll be years away though."

"Do you ever go and see him?"

Vincent pulls in a breath and holds it for a second. "I've been a couple of times. It's hard to look at him, you know? He used to be my hero and then he just...became one of them. It happened so fast, I didn't even see it coming."

"I heard he said he was innocent."

Vincent scoffs. "All the evidence was there."

I shrug. "Evidence can tell a lie if it's planted correctly. You should know that."

He gives me a sidelong glance but doesn't say anything.

"Have you ever asked him his side of the story?"

"I don't want to know."

"Why not?"

Vincent rubs a hand over his mouth. His fingers are shaking slightly, tension radiating from him like he's a nuclear weapon primed to explode.

I bite my lips together, but don't take back the question. Sucking a breath in through my nose, I turn to look out the window until Vincent's soft, broken voice makes me turn back.

"Because what if he did it? What if he can't look me in the eye and tell me he's innocent? My brother can't be a killer. I don't want him to be."

"But you don't mind him being falsely accused and convicted?"

"The evidence was there, Chloe!"

"And you don't believe it! If you're too scared to talk to him in case he admits to being guilty, then there must be a part of you that believes he's innocent. You just said your brother can't be a killer."

Vincent huffs and shakes his head. "Just stop, okay? Since his conviction he hasn't said shit about being set up. He hasn't appealed. Nothing."

"Maybe he figures it's pointless. Maybe he's given up."

"Or maybe he's guilty!"

Vincent's thundering angst shuts me up. Gazing down at my hands, I let silence fall between us. I don't want to aggravate Vincent, even if I do think he should talk to his brother. Why would Nick claim he was innocent and then shut up about it? It just feels a little off. I don't know the guy, but if he used to be Vincent's hero, then there must have been something good about him, something worth looking up to. Right? Maybe the murder was an accident...or not Nick's fault at all.

Everything is not always as it seems. Vincent is living proof of that, and I hate the idea that his hero is now stuck behind bars, especially if he's not guilty.

Man, I wonder if he is.

I can't decide which is worse—him actually being a killer or him serving time for a crime he didn't commit.

Vincent wants him to be innocent. He needs to know that the person he always looked up to hasn't let him down.

Crap, I'm probably dreaming.

Nick is probably guilty.

But what if he's not?

If he's anything like his little brother, how could he possibly be capable of pulling the trigger on an innocent man?

I want to find out.

I'm *going* to find out. I don't know how, but I'll figure out a way.

Vincent saved my life. Maybe this is a chance for me to give a little something back.

#14

VINCENT

Whatever Keeps Her Safe

Shit. I just yelled at Chloe.

I am a date killer.

Of course I was going to fuck it up.

I'm Vincent Mancini. I don't know how to do

anything else.

This silence is suffocating. But I don't know how to break it.

Grinding my teeth together, I focus on the road. I keep my eyes ahead, determined to get Chloe home safely.

Is she ever going to talk to me after this?

Probably not.

Clearing her throat, Chloe leans toward my radio. I don't even know if the thing works. I wince as she flicks the knob, expecting it to fall off, but it doesn't and the car fills with a song I don't even know. It's haunting and beautiful, the guy's voice hitting me right in the heart.

"'Ashes,'" Chloe murmurs. "I love this song. It's so sad but beautiful."

I glance at her, my heart filling to overflowing as I take a mental snapshot.

"Vincent," she whispers.

"Yeah." I can barely rasp the word.

"I know you probably think this date has been ruined or something, but you should know that I've had a really good night. Until Diego, everything was perfect. And after Diego, everything has been raw and tense, but I'm still sitting in your car. And you're driving me home while we listen to beautiful music. I don't care who your family is, or what they have or haven't done. None of that changes the fact that *you* are a good human being, and I'd go out with you anytime."

My throat is so thick I can't even swallow. Talking's off the menu.

All I can do is look at her.

She smiles at me and then turns back to face the front, closing her eyes and softly singing along with the song.

There'll never be another like Chloe Barlow.

But I don't see how I'm ever going to keep her. She deserves so much better than me.

That familiar sadness that's been living in my chest ever since Mom died spreads through my body, settling like a heavy blanket over my soul.

I didn't kiss Chloe goodbye. What's the point of torturing myself?

She pecked my cheek like she did last time and slipped from the car. I kept my lights on to guide her home and then drove past her house.

I wonder what it's like in there.

I bet it's a home, with parents who say "I love you." Home-cooked meals. Conversation around the dinner table. Teasing banter. Stories about the day. I bet they hug each other when they're sad. There'd be no fists in their house.

Pulling up to my crappy home, I gaze at the peeling clapboard exterior and fight the urge to take my car and drive until I run out of gas. But what would be the point? I'd just get shipped right back here. Even if I am seventeen, and old enough to leave home, what would I leave with? It's not like I'm rolling in cash. It's not like I can get a decent job when I don't even have my high school diploma.

I have to stick it out.

Slamming my door shut, I thump up the stairs and walk in to find Selena on Enzo's knee. Diego is sitting on the other couch, staring at the TV like a zombie.

As soon as I shut the door behind me, his head snaps in my direction and he's off the couch like lightning.

"How was your date?"

I glare at him, my stomach clenching tight. "What date?"

"The blonde. I knew you were lying. Did she dump your ass for ditching her?"

I point at him. "Shut up."

"Boys, boys." Enzo scowls at me. "What's the problem?"

"I told you, Pop, Vinnie was out with a girl and he lied about it."

"What girl?"

"He's talking shit." I point at my cousin and know right away that I'm in for it.

"You calling me a liar?" He gets in my face, puffing out his chest like an angry gorilla.

Dammit!

I'm about to get pounded, and I'm never allowed to hit back or Enzo jumps in to support his son. The first and last time I brought my fists to the table, they broke two of my ribs. Nick was in jail by then so I had no backup, and they went to fucking town on me.

I glance at Selena, who closes her eyes, dread washing over her expression.

Diego fists my collar, breathing his beer stench all over me. "You calling me a fuckin' liar?"

I don't say anything as he shoves me back. My hip crashes against the table, the empty beer cans rattling and falling to the floor.

"Who was she?"

"No one," I mutter.

Diego's fist plows into my side. I grunt and do my best to hide the pain.

"Who was she?"

I suck in a breath. "You can hit me all night, Diego, but I'm telling you, she wasn't my date. I don't know her!"

"You seemed hell-bent on defending her."

"Only because she didn't deserve your dirty hands trying to grope her."

Diego's nostrils flare and he lashes out again. I block the punch, only to score myself a thunder fist to the stomach.

I hiss and bend forward just as Diego's knee comes rocketing toward my face. The taste of blood explodes in my mouth and I hit the floor.

Curling into a ball is my safest bet. I just need to ride it out until Diego's had his fill or Enzo gets bored of the show.

He shouts at me the whole time, demanding Chloe's name, but I keep my mouth shut. Covering my head, Diego gets in a solid kick before stepping back. I make the mistake of unfurling and score myself a fast one to the face.

"Her name!" he screams in my ear.

"That's enough, Diego!" Enzo shouts. "He would have told us by now. Leave him!"

My cousin stands back, puffing from exertion.

Pain radiates through my body as I stagger to my feet. Enzo looks across the room at me. "If I find out you're lying, it'll be much worse than this."

"She was nothing. A stranger." I wipe my lip with the back of my hand but it doesn't stop the blood dripping off my chin.

"Go and clean him up." Enzo pats Selena's butt and forces her off his knee.

She does as she's told and I'm soon sitting in the bathroom being patched up by my uncle's young girlfriend. Her hands are trembling as she dabs my wounds.

"Nick would never have allowed this," she whispers.

"Nick's not here," I grumble.

Shit, I'm hurting all over.

But at least I kept Chloe out of it.

I can go to bed with a clear conscience. And if I know what's good for me, I should probably stay there for as long as I can.

#15

CHLOE

Can't Stop

It's been three days since my date with Vincent.

I haven't heard from him or seen him since, and I miss him.

It makes me miss school, which I know sounds weird. It's Spring Break! I should be living it up, but I can't get him out of my head.

I want to find one of his notes in my locker. I want

to feel connected to him.

"You're thinking about him again, aren't you?" Rahn's lying on her bed, her feet swinging in the air as she thumbs through a magazine and hums along to "Crush" by David Archuleta.

She invited me over as soon as I got up this morning and I jumped at the chance. Maddie's helping Holden at Cresthill Home for the Elderly, and Max is sneaking out to hang with Cairo. Uncle Conrad is covering for her. They left with their mitts and a baseball bat, but I know he'll be dropping her at Cairo's place before going off to do something else. It's nice of him to help Max out this way, but part of me wonders if she should just tell the truth.

I swallow at my hypocritical thinking and go back to coloring Rahn's book that she got for her birthday. It's one of those really detailed coloring books and Rahn tires quickly, so I'm taking over to finish off the page.

"Purple?" I hold up a dark shade of my favorite color.

"Nice." She grins. "Now answer my question."

My lips twitch and I finally give in. "Of course I'm thinking about him."

"It did sound like a nice date...until his cousin showed up."

I figured I'd tell Rahn everything. I want her to understand how protective and sweet Vincent is. She seems to be coming around to the idea.

Outlining the flower petal, I start to shade in the middle and finally admit, "I'm worried about him."

"Why?" Rahn's braids splay over Zac Efron's glossy headshot as she looks up at me.

"Sounds like he hates where he lives. He misses his brother. His family doesn't care about him. I just wish I could rescue him from that horrible situation. I wish his brother wasn't in jail for murder."

Rahn gives me a sad smile. "I know we want to save the world, but unfortunately sometimes we can't."

I blink, hating her answer.

"I want to see him. Make sure he's okay."

"Yeah, well, you can see him when school goes back."

"That's still three and a half days away!"

"You must be the only teenager on this planet complaining about not being at school right now. This is our last break before the summer."

I slump back in her desk chair, tapping the end of her pencil against my bottom lip. "I wonder if I should go see him."

"What?" Rahn sits up. "You're just going to show up at his front door?"

I sit forward. "Do you know where he lives?"

"No! And thank God, by that look on your face. Seriously, Chloe, don't be insane. After what happened to you, I can't believe you even thought for a second about going back to the northwest. Stay put. Right here where you're safe."

I wrinkle my nose at her and go back to coloring.

It's not like I'm planning on waltzing in there after dark. I was thinking about an afternoon excursion. I glance at my watch and note the time. If I left in the next half hour or so, I could be there and back before dinner.

I just want to see him. Maybe if I wander around town and ask a few questions, I can track him down.

Keeping the thought to myself, I color until the field of flowers is complete.

"There you go." I plop the book on her bed. "You've only got the sky and birds to go."

"Ooooo, it's pretty!" She grins at me. "Thank you. I figure I need to finish at least one page."

I snicker. "I'm surprised your mom thought this would be the ultimate gift for you."

"Me too." She sits up with a frown. "Seriously. Sometimes I feel like my parents don't know me at all."

"I'm pretty sure every teenager in the world feels that way."

We laugh together and I stand up, reaching for my hoodie.

"You have to go already?"

"Yep." I bob my head. "I promised Mom I'd clean

my room this afternoon. Apparently Max and I are making her hair turn gray." I roll my eyes. "She needs a job, so bad."

"I'll cross my fingers for you guys."

"Well, she has another interview tomorrow. It's a second one, so things are looking good."

"What's the job?"

I shrug. "Something to do with management and marketing. It's for that store on Main Street. You know, the one that sells everything from cheese sticks to garden hoses."

"Oh, you mean the one no one ever wants to go into because the store is so overcrowded that you can barely move?"

"That's the one." I zip up my sweatshirt and flick the hood back. "If Mom has her way, the place will be revolutionized."

"I bet she'll turn it into the most popular store in town."

"Well, she's capable." I grin and lean down to peck the top of Rahn's head.

"Thanks for hanging with me."

"Always a pleasure, never a chore." I wink.

"Hey, you want to come fundraising with me tomorrow? I'm doing chocolate sales on Main Street."

"Sounds good. Text me. If I'm free, I'll be there."

"Coolio. See ya later, Blondie."

"Take care, Pigtails." I wave and walk for the front door.

I feel kind of bad that I just lied to Rahn, but there's no way I'm wasting my afternoon at home cleaning my room.

Turning for my place, I walk down the street and veer left once I'm away from Rahn's house. I then pick up my pace and run to the bus stop at the end of her street. I only have to wait two minutes and I'm soon sitting on a bus bound for Fort Street. My stomach is a mass of jitters, but I'm comforted by the daylight.

Admittedly, it's pretty bleak daylight. Dark clouds are hovering overhead, threatening to open up at any moment. I look out the window and ignore the small voice in my head, reminding me this is a really bad idea.

You don't even have an umbrella.

You have no idea where Vincent lives.

Are you seriously just going to walk up to random people and ask around?

The thought is unnerving, especially in that part of town. What if I bump into those rapists again?

No, they're behind bars now, and surely there will be some good, helpful soul that will want to point me in the right direction. I could start near St. Michael's. Maybe I'll bump into someone I've met through the free meal service.

Although, will mentioning the name Mancini do

me any favors?

Crap, this is a bad idea!

But I want to see Vincent, so whether it's stupid or not, I'm going to spend my afternoon looking for the guy I can't stop thinking about.

#16

VINCENT

A Greenhouse in the Rain

I've been stuck in my room for nearly three days and I can't handle it anymore. Enzo usually leaves me alone to recover after a beating. He'll be on my case by the weekend, asking me to run errands, collect money, and play messenger boy.

Only eighteen more months of this shit.

That's what I keep telling myself, but I'm a big fat

liar. I don't see how I'll get out anytime soon. Not unless I steal money from Enzo, and that will never fly.

He'll either kill me for my betrayal or make sure I get charged with a crime and given the heaviest punishment possible. It won't be hard; the judge already has it in for me, although he did only saddle me with community service after that shoplifting incident. I should have known better than to steal something from Main Street. If I'd gone for any of the stores in my area, I could have mentioned the name Mancini and gotten away with it.

I don't know what the hell I was thinking. It was just after Nick got sent away, and I guess I was acting out or some shit.

The community service wasn't too bad. Picking up garbage and cleaning local areas. There was something kind of satisfying about making this town look better.

Lifting up my hood, I walk out the front door and head right. I have no particular destination. I just want to walk for a while.

It's going to start raining soon, but I'm not turning back. I need air, space, freedom.

My body is still kind of sore and stiff. I roll my shoulders and shove my hands into my pockets. I haven't looked in the mirror this morning. When I checked last night, my bruises had a red-purple hue to them. They'll be yellow by the weekend and gone by the time school goes back. At least I don't have to miss any classes. Last time Diego lost it with me I was off school for a week.

My mouth's healed up quick, with only a little swelling left on my lower lip. It doesn't hurt anymore, which is good. And I didn't lose any teeth, which is even better. Thankfully Diego's never left permanent damage. Well, damage that people can see, anyway.

I hunch my shoulders and keep trudging forward.

The wind's picked up a little. The cold swirl against my skin tells me that winter's not quite ready to let go. It'll battle it out with spring until we get consistently warmer weather. Bring it on.

Checking both ways, I cross the street and wander onward. I pass an old guy with a broken shopping cart. He's muttering to himself while scratching his unkempt beard. I don't bother acknowledging him. He probably doesn't even know I'm here anyway. Another block later, I reach St. Michael's and gaze up at the tower, the cross on top of it. It's so grand and out of place here. I bet when it was built, it fit perfectly. I bet people came in droves every Sunday. That was before the town turned to shit and the most popular time became the free meal every night.

I glance down the street, shuddering at the reminder of what nearly happened to Chloe the last time she was here.

The rain starts to fall in light droplets.

I hunch over a little more and figure I should probably turn for home, but the thought only stirs a moaning complaint within me. I don't want to go back.

With a heavy sigh, I walk forward, aware the rain is only getting heavier. I guess I could take shelter in Pedro's for a while, but...

I jerk to a stop, squinting through the rain as I spot a pink hoodie dashing around the corner.

My heart lurches into my throat the second I recognize her.

Chloe?

What the hell is she doing here?

Fear flashes inside me, a hot, intense wave that makes me surge forward into a run.

She looks up to see me coming and an instant smile transforms her wet face. She's so damn pretty it's hard not to be affected by it.

"What are you doing here?" I bark.

Her smile falters, her sweet expression disappearing behind a look of horror. "What happened to you?"

She reaches out for me but I veer back, worried someone might see us together.

The rain is starting to pelt down now. I can't drag her into Pedro's—he might talk.

"You have to get home." I look down the street,

trying to remember where the nearest bus stop is.

"No way! I'm not leaving until you tell me what happened."

"Chloe, you shouldn't be here." I gaze down at her, desperate for her to get it.

It's not safe.

My family's not safe.

I can't handle it if she gets hurt.

Her eyes start to glisten and she looks across the street, licking the water off her lip before saying, "I know this part of town and I don't go very well together, but you and I do. So I'm risking it anyway, because I want to see you." She blinks and looks back up at me, her voice quaking with emotion. "What happened to you? Who hurt you?"

Damn. She looks ready to cry. Like somehow my bruises are hurting her too.

She sniffs, her face a mask of anguish.

"Come on." I capture her hand before I can think better of it and head toward the nearest alley.

She stiffens as we enter it, but I tug her through as fast as I can and keep running until I spot the empty, overrun yard. Ducking through the hole in the fence, I help Chloe through and then we run to the old, abandoned greenhouse.

I haven't been in here for a couple of years. I'd sometimes hide out after a belting from Enzo. Nick would always find me in here.

Shouldering the stiff door open, I usher Chloe inside.

Rain pings off the glass above us and I glance up to watch the tears trickle down the sloping roof. Chloe lets go of my hand and moves past me, surveying the center table of smashed pots and rotting wood.

This place has always been abandoned. Grass and weeds are growing up through the floorboards, and there's a smashed window down the end. A little graffiti decorates the back corner. I run my gaze across it before staring at Chloe.

She's reached the far side where a bunch of musty sheets are piled in the middle. Old, but still dry.

Turning to face me, she wipes the droplets off her cheek and stares me down. "What happened to you?"

I flick my hoodie back and reveal it all. I've got the feeling she's not going to leave without the story, but I keep it brief. "Diego was in a bad mood."

Her expression crumples with a mixture of disgust and sympathy.

I'm not used to people feeling sorry for me, and I'm not sure I like it.

Leaning against the edge of the table, I shove my hands in my pockets. "It's no big deal. I'm okay."

"It's not okay," she retorts, approaching me with swift steps.

She's right beside me now, her big blues gazing up at me like I'm important.

"You got beat," she whispers. "And I'm not cool with that."

Her fingers tremble as she gently runs them over my face. My instinct is to shy away, but I hold myself steady, transfixed by the feel of her smooth fingers.

It's too hard to talk, so I just look at her, wishing I could read her mind. Her gaze caresses me, her lips curving into a fleeting smile before she rises to her tiptoes and brushes her lips across the bruise on my cheek.

My heart starts hammering so hard I'm sure she can feel it through my chest. She's pressed against me, leaning across to kiss my other cheek and then my chin.

Pulling back, she hovers near my swollen lips. Her breath whispers against my mouth and there's only one thing I can do.

Cupping the back of her head, I decimate whatever space is keeping us apart.

Her lips are soft and supple, pressing against mine like they were made to be there. They're wet and cold from the rain, but a quick fire is building inside of me.

I kiss her top lip, then move to the bottom, intoxicated beyond anything I've felt before. She's so soft and sweet.

Resting my free hand on her hip, I pull her a little closer.

My body's taking point on this one and before I can even think about what's happening, I'm skimming my tongue against hers.

Electric bolts fire through me, sparking a ravenous hunger I've never felt before. Tipping my head, I deepen the kiss and forget about everything but what Chloe Barlow is doing to me right now.

#17

CHLOE

Sweet, Naïve and Stubborn

Vincent's tongue is warm and commanding. I like the way it feels against mine. Our slow dance is in sync and natural. I've never found a rhythm so easily with a guy before, and it just reinforces the fact that I was supposed to come and find Vincent today.

Poor, beat-up Vincent.

I pull back with a gasp. "I'm not hurting you, am I? Is your mouth okay?"

He doesn't even wait a beat before he's whispering against my skin. "Your kisses could never hurt me."

I smile and lick his tongue, heat spreading through me as we deepen the kiss again. I love how strong his body is, the way his sure fingers grip my hip and pull me a little closer.

Our wet clothes stick together.

I'm pressed right against him, my arms around his neck, my heart beating in time with his.

The rain above is the perfect soundtrack, and my romantic heart is full to overflowing right now.

Eventually Vincent pulls back for air, resting his forehead against mine for a moment.

His breaths are shaky and he still can't seem to find his voice.

"I knew I'd like kissing you," I whisper and lean back so he can see my smile.

"You thought about it before, huh?"

"Maybe."

His eyes sparkle with a smile. "Is that why you came today? So you could kiss me?"

"That was just an added bonus."

His hands run down my arms as I step back.

Threading my fingers between his, I look him in the eye and admit, "I've been worried about you. And I had every reason to be." My forehead bunches; I can feel my eyebrows wrinkling together. "He should not be treating you like that. You need to tell my dad."

He's shaking his head before I've even finished talking. "I know you think that works, but..."

"He'll listen to you."

A scowl flashes across his face. "It's too risky."

"Involving the police is too risky? The police are there to serve and protect. That's their job."

"It's not that simple, Chloe." Gently tugging me closer, he wraps his arms around my waist. "Justice doesn't always win. The police can't always get the bad guy. They can try, but then if Uncle Enzo or Diego don't get convicted or get a really small sentence for assault, my life's not worth it. They'll kill me if I betray them."

Those words are like a knife to the heart.

"You can't...you can't live like that." Tears scorch my insides, rising up my throat and building on my lashes. "It's not fair."

He swipes his thumb beneath my eyes and softly whispers, "It's okay. I'm going to be okay. I'll be free one day."

"How? When?"

"I don't know. The only step in front of me right

now is my high school diploma. Once that's done, then I'll think about what's next."

"That's over a year away!"

"I can do it. I know how to survive. I just have to do it their way until I can get out. Sure, it was easier when Nick was around. He'd step in. I wasn't outnumbered." He dips his head, his swallow thick and audible. "I miss him."

As if my heart wasn't breaking before.

Resting my hand lightly on his beat-up face, I press my forehead against his. "We need to get him out of jail. We need to prove he's not guilty so he can be acquitted and you can have your bodyguard back."

He gives me a pained smile. "It's not that simple."

"I know that." My soft voice grows strong with conviction. "It'll be really hard. And we might fail. But we have to try. We need to get your brother out."

His shoulders slump as he leans away from me and looks up at the rain. "I don't know how."

"I think we need to start by asking him what really happened. Obviously everyone who could help him gave up for some reason."

"Or he's guilty," Vincent mutters.

I lightly thump his shoulder and wriggle out of his grasp. "Would you stop saying that?" I swallow, hating his doubt. It only fuels my own. I want to be convinced that Nick is innocent, and negative talk won't help us. Licking my lower lip, I stare Vincent in the eye, hoping I sound stronger than I feel. "If your brother is anything like you, he's not guilty. And it's not fair that he's stuck in some prison while the person who set him up is walking free somewhere. I can't just ignore that. I won't."

An emotion I can't decipher flickers over Vincent's face.

"You need to go see him and find out the truth. Once we've got that, we can work backward, dig up the right evidence and hand it to the right people."

"Your dad," Vincent mutters.

I cross my arms. "I know you don't like him, but—"

"I think it's more a case of him not liking me."

"He doesn't even know you." I spread my arms wide. "Besides, he was the one that stopped you from getting expelled."

"I bet he'd hate the thought of his daughter hanging out with me. I bet he'd expel my ass if he knew that."

I have to concede with a huff. Turning my back on Vincent, I stare out at the rain trickling down the dirty glass panes.

An involuntary shiver runs down my spine, the cold, bleak air nipping at me.

Vincent moves behind me, his slow footsteps closing the distance between us. His hands touch my shoulders and very slowly glide down my arms until I'm completely enveloped.

Resting his chin on my shoulder, he whispers, "I haven't seen Nick in a while. I should probably go visit him. Maybe when I'm there, I could ask. I've never outright asked for the truth before. Maybe it's time."

Turning my head, I press my smile against his cheek. "I want to come with you."

He tenses. "No. You are way too beautiful and sweet to be walking into a prison."

I roll my eyes. "Don't put me on some pedestal. I might be sweet—naïve, even—but I'm also very stubborn and when I believe in something, I won't back down." I turn in his arms so I can look him in the eye. "I believe in you, Vincent, and I'm helping you whether you want me to or not."

He tightens his hold around my waist and I'm waiting for his gruff refusal.

But it never comes.

Leaning forward, I rest my chin on his shoulder and can't help a small, triumphant smile.

Looks like I'm visiting my first prison tomorrow.

#18

VINCENT

Mouth Shut

I made Chloe wait in the car. She's kind of annoyed with me, but there's no way I want her walking into some prison. We "discussed" it for most of the two-hour trip, but finally, about five minutes from the parking lot, she conceded on the one condition that I'd tell her every single detail when I got back to the car.

I promised her I would.

And I will.

Because telling Chloe stuff makes me feel better.

She believes in me.

She believes in Nick.

That's the only reason I'm here.

The prison door buzzes, allowing me entry into the visitation room. I follow the prison guard's instructions and take a seat on the chipped wooden stool in front of the Plexiglas cubicle.

Gazing at the black phone, I wait for my brother to join me.

About two minutes later, I see him shuffling in. He's surprised to see me, probably because the last time I came, I was so mute he told me I didn't have to come again.

"It's a long way, you know? And you've got school. You take care of you. I'm fine."

I went along with it because it seemed easier somehow, but now as I watch him thump into the seat in front of me, a wave of brotherly love storms through me so fast I'm nearly taken out.

I grit my teeth as we stare at each other. His brown eyes assess me, a hard look washing over his face as he takes in my bruises.

I reach for the phone.

"Hey, big bro." My voice is kind of croaky, so I clear my throat and grip the receiver. "How you been?"

"Is that Diego's work?" He points at me.

"I'm fine, man. It's Spring Break, so I'm not missing any school."

He lightly thumps the counter in front of him and lets out a soft string of curses.

I wait it out. It never takes him long to rein it in.

"I wasn't going to come, but..." I drop my gaze, wondering how much to say.

Do I mention Chloe?

Do I tell him that she's motivated me to be here?

"I told you, you don't have to, Vin. I hate you seeing me like this. I wish I'd never let you down."

I glance up, looking him right in the eye. "Did you?"

He frowns at me, his dark eyebrows wrinkling.

"Did you let me down? Did you kill that guy?"

His jaw works to the side.

"I need to know."

"I don't want you to get caught up in this, bro." His eyes flash with warning. "Just let me do my time. It's better for everyone."

"That's bullshit, man! Tell me the truth. Did you kill that guy?"

The phone goes slack in his hand and I'm worried he's about to hang up on me. He lightly taps the receiver against his chin before closing his eyes and slowly lifting it back up.

"No." He says the word so softly I nearly miss it.

"No?"

He shakes his head, his nostrils flaring when our eyes connect.

Relief spikes through me, followed by a healthy dose of anger. "Why have you never appealed?"

"My lawyer told me it was pointless. The evidence is too compelling."

"Your lawyer's a dick. I never liked that guy," I mutter darkly, remembering the public defender with his potbelly, cheesy smile and pointy-toed shoes.

Nick tips his head in agreement, then sighs. "Look, he's probably right, and I can't afford a new one. The best I can hope for is early parole."

The best he could hope for?

"But you shouldn't be in here, man. You're innocent. You—"

"It doesn't matter. They don't care about that shit."

An irate snort puffs out my nose. "Who did it?"

"I don't know, and I don't want you finding out." His brown eyes, so like mine, flash with warning.

"Why? We have to. You shouldn't be in here."

"I can't, man." His expression turns dark and stormy. "You need to leave this alone."

"No." I tap my finger against the Plexiglas. "You need to tell me what happened."

"It won't do any good. I'm not getting out of

here."

"Tell me everything that happened from the time that guy was killed to when you got arrested." My voice is full-on shaking, but my glare obviously has more power because Nick's shoulders deflate.

Pressing the phone against his mouth, he softly whispers, "You sat through the entire trial. You know the details."

"Tell me the parts that are true."

Fear swamps his expression before he pulls it back into line, clenching his jaw and gritting out, "I don't want you getting mixed up in this. I was saving for your college fund, working for certain people that Enzo didn't know about."

He was what?

I blink, trying to ignore the emotion surging through me.

My brother was doing extra work to put me through college?

Clearing my throat, I shuffle in my seat and sniff. "So, you think it was them?"

"It doesn't matter what I think. It doesn't matter that I got a text telling me to pick up that car and take it to the chop shop in Brazenwood. When I got there, Todd McCrae was already dead inside of it."

I swallow. "They said you shot him trying to jack his car. The gun had your fingerprints all over it."

"Because it was my gun! That didn't mean I pulled

the trigger on anyone. My boss made all of us carry in case we needed protection."

"But the ballistics matched."

"Because someone else used it. That night I went to collect the car, I didn't know where the hell my gun was. I didn't exactly want to fess up to my boss that I'd lost it, so I went to the pickup unarmed. I never thought..." His voice trails off and he shakes his head. "Look, it's done, man. There's no fighting these people."

"Who sent you that text?"

Nick obviously doesn't want to tell me who he was working for. He must suspect them of setting him up.

Shit!

I huff and try again. "Why was that text never presented as evidence in court? Why didn't anyone ask you about it?"

"Because it doesn't exist anymore." Nick's voice is dark with defeat. "And my lawyer advised me against admitting that I usually carried an unregistered weapon. I was dead in the water before the trial even started," he mutters. "Someone wanted Todd McCrae dead. I can't figure out why, but they were smart enough to put the murder on me. And I'll take it."

"What?" I snap.

"You don't know who you're dealing with. I'm keeping my mouth shut for you. So you do the same for me, you hear me? Do *not* get involved." His steady gaze is telling me to obey him. "You wanted to know if I'm innocent, well I am. Now, just focus on being a teenager. Graduate for me, man. Please. Stay out of trouble."

Before I can reply, he hangs up and stands from his chair.

The guard jumps to attention, cuffing my brother's hands and ignoring my cries for Nick to come back.

I stand and watch him disappear behind the thick door. My head is pounding as I slowly return the phone to its cradle.

He's staying silent for me?

What the hell is he talking about?

Feeling kind of numb, I turn and head back to the parking lot. I don't know what the hell I'm supposed to tell Chloe. My brain can barely compute what just happened. My brother's innocent. He was set up, but he's happy to do the time?

That's bullshit!

Something's got him scared.

It should scare me too, but I can't think past the righteous anger burning my numbness to dust.

Someone set up my brother...and scared him enough to take the fall.

I'm not okay with that.

I am so not fucking okay with that!

#19

CHLOE

Looking in the Wrong Direction

I jump when Vincent wrenches open the driver's door and slams it shut behind him. He grips the wheel, breathing like a bull ready to charge.

"Are...are you okay?"

He shakes his head. It's a stiff, minimal head movement. His knuckles are white, his jaw muscles going to town as he smashes his teeth together.

"He's innocent, isn't he?"

"Yeah," Vincent growls, firing up the engine and speeding out of the parking lot with a squeal of tires.

We tear away from the prison like we're trying to outrun a tidal wave.

Vincent swerves around the next corner and I'm thrown into the passenger door.

I can't help a small gasp and he immediately slows down.

His expression crumples with a pained apology as he starts to pull the car to the side of the road. It's a lonely country lane—the only route into the prison. There's barely space to pull over.

"There's a rest stop just past the intersection. Do you remember?"

He nods and accelerates forward, but much slower this time.

We putter down the road and through the intersection before pulling into a quiet spot that looks over a small gorge.

The car hiccups to a stop and then we're drenched in this stony silence that I'm trying to work out how to break. I'm worried if I ask too many questions, it will shatter like glass.

But Nick's innocent! I mean, I know it's just his

word, but Vincent believes him, which means I do too.

Licking my bottom lip, I unlatch my seat belt and turn to face him.

"I'm sorry," I whisper, reaching for his hand and tracing a slow pattern with my thumb. "It's not fair."

My touch seems to calm him, so I keep holding his hand even though he's not talking.

"Does he know who did it?"

Vincent shakes his head. "He doesn't want me finding out either."

"Why not?"

"He seemed scared." Vincent's dark eyebrows dip together. "Said he was staying silent for me. I don't understand that."

"Maybe someone's threatening him. Or you. Maybe he's had some kind of warning that if he appeals, bad things could happen."

Vincent's eyes flick to mine. "He told me to stay away from it. He's probably right."

"Yeah, probably." I tip my head. "But I don't think we should."

"Of course you don't," he scoffs, wrenching his hand out of mine and tipping his head to the roof.

I gaze at his tormented profile, my heart breaking and opening up at the same time. "Do you really want to let this lie? That's not who you are. You'll put up with injustice against yourself, but you'd never take it for someone you care about. You're a warrior. You put your life on the line to protect others."

"I'm not a warrior."

"Yes, you are." My voice is strong and adamant.

"I can't fix this, Chloe!"

"Yes, we can!"

"We?" He scowls at me. "And how am I supposed to protect you through all of this? If Nick doesn't want me getting hurt, I sure as shit don't want you to!"

I smile, his words warming me even though they're being yelled.

Reaching for his face, I comb my fingers through his short black hair. "I know this seems huge and scary and dangerous."

"Because it is." He works his jaw to the side.

"I know, but we can be careful. We can look into things without people even knowing. All we need is a starting point and then slowly we can uncover some evidence. We just need enough to set Nick free. Once we have it, I can take it straight to my dad. Then he can protect us." Vincent opens his mouth to argue, but I speak over him. "My dad might not understand that I'm crushing on you big-time, but he hates injustice as much as I do. He'll help us."

Vincent's eyes flick to mine, and very slowly his puffing breaths ease. Finally, the edges of his lips curl at the corners. "We can't go to him without something decent."

"Well, what do we have?"

Vincent taps the wheel with his finger. "Nick was doing some work on the side, trying to earn some money so he could send me to college." He lets out a pained sigh, his jaw clenching as he tries to rein in whatever emotion he's fighting. "He never told me about it, but I think he was working for some guy in Brazenwood."

"Why do you think that?"

"Because he just told me he was supposed to pick up a car and deliver it to a chop shop there."

"So he *was* stealing cars?"

Vincent nods, then cringes and scrapes a hand through his hair.

"Do you know their names?"

"No, he wouldn't say. If it's the Mendez brothers, they're complete assholes. Maybe that's why he's scared. Maybe they've threatened to come after me or something." He frowns and shakes his head. "But they wouldn't take on a Mancini. They're not completely insane."

"So, if it's not them, who could it be?"

Squeezing his eyes shut, Vincent cups the back of his head. "I don't know."

Curling my fingers around his neck, I give it a little massage, hoping to relax him. "Are there any other crime syndicates in that area?"

He swallows and slowly opens his eyes. "Not that I know of. Enzo doesn't like us going into Brazenwood. He knows better than to start some kind of war with the Mendez brothers."

"Okay." I bulge my eyes, finding this conversation kind of heavy. "So, what happened that night? Nick went to pick up a car and..."

Vincent keeps rubbing his forehead, his face puckering. "He said he got a text to go collect and deliver this car, but when he got there McCrae was already dead inside. The cops showed up. Saw the body. Saw Nick standing there and arrested him on the spot. Assumed it was a carjacking."

"But what proof did they have? They can't convict him for standing beside a dead body."

"They found a gun with his fingerprints all over it. Ballistics matched the bullet to the gun."

"And where was the gun?"

"On the floor of the car he was supposed to be stealing."

My lips part. Damn, that evidence is really compelling. It takes me a moment to find my voice as I will myself to not waver on my conviction. Nick told his little brother he was innocent. We have to believe him.

"Okay, so someone could have easily stolen his gun, used it and then planted it in McCrae's car, right?"

Vincent nods.

"It sounds to me like he was set up by his boss."

"Yeah, but we don't know who the hell that is. Nick refused to say, and he looked scared when I pressed him on it."

"Well someone else must know. What about his lawyer?"

Vincent scoffs. "That idiot won't help. No one's going to talk to us."

I purse my lips, staring out the car window while I think about my dad and what he goes through when investigating something. There are always reports and those little notebooks they write in. That's all evidence and permissible in court.

"There have to be notebooks from the night Nick was arrested. Records. Statements. Maybe I can ask Dad to look into it for me."

Vincent gives me an incredulous look. "And when he asks why you want to know that stuff? What are you going to tell him then? That you're helping a Mancini?"

"Stop saying your last name like it's a curse word," I scold him. I hate the way he does that. It just fuels his own belief that his bloodline makes him automatically bad.

He huffs and clenches his jaw again. The way he's going, his teeth will be buried back inside gums soon.

"Okay, fine, you don't want to involve my dad. Do you remember who the arresting officer was? The detective who investigated this case? Maybe we can talk to them."

Vincent worries his lip, still staring out the window like he doesn't want to look at me.

"I just want to help," I whisper. "Please let me."

Glancing my way, a soft smile curves the edge of his mouth as he reaches for my hand and starts playing with my fingers.

"There wasn't a detective, just the chief of police."

"The chief of police?" My nose wrinkles. "That's weird. They don't usually conduct investigations."

Vincent shrugs. "He was the guy who arrested Nick that night, so he took the case."

"Okay." I shake my head, still finding it a bit strange.

"He retired early, after Nick was convicted. Got seriously ill and left town."

"Do you remember his name?"

"Scott Tannon. I don't even know if he's still alive."

"Well, there's only one way to find out." I smile, pulling out my phone and getting to work.

As weird as it might sound, this whole thing is kind of thrilling. If we can talk to this guy, find out some answers, dig out the real truth, it's going to open up a whole big book of secrets.

A book that might set Nick Mancini free.

#20

VINCENT

A Losing Battle

Chloe found a bunch of people named Scott Tannon on her phone. It's going to take us some time to work through them. She doesn't seem perturbed by this. If anything, she's excited, which kind of worries me.

Nick was jittery when I visited him, like he wanted me to leave this alone. Like maybe he wished he hadn't said so much.

But he's my brother. Now that I know he's innocent, I can't turn my back on him.

Leaning against the blue slide, I cross my arms and wait. It's moments like this where I wish I did carry a phone so at least Chloe could get in touch with me.

When I dropped her back on Friday, we agreed to meet up again today. Ten o'clock at the blue slide. Chloe said she'd work through the night to condense it down to a few decent leads.

I wish I could have helped her, but the second I walked in the door, Enzo had me running errands, collecting fees, delivering things in paper bags. I don't want to know their contents. Although I probably should, because if I ever get busted, it'll be on my head.

I didn't get home until 3:00 a.m. I'm kind of tired this morning, but I wouldn't stand up Chloe for anything.

She's working really hard to sneak out with me. Yesterday Rahn covered for her again, but she feels bad about using her friend. Rahn was happy to go along with it, but Chloe was worried that she sounded disappointed on the phone. I don't know what excuse she's using today.

It kind of sucks that she has to find any at all, but I can't change my name right now, so she has to lie.

Shoving my hands in my pockets, I push off the slide and walk to the edge of the park when a mother with two young kids appears. She gives me a cautious look and I force a smile, hoping I look harmless enough.

She doesn't buy it, so I sigh and move away from the area, not wanting to ruin her kids' playtime.

I'm not sure which way to walk. I don't want to miss Chloe if she takes a different route. We're both trying really hard not to be spotted by someone who knows her parents. They'll no doubt put her on full lockdown for sneaking around with me.

I need Chloe to help me on this one. I need her strength.

Glancing over my shoulder, relief washes through me when Chloe appears around the corner. The second she sees me, her face lights with a grin. I tip my head toward the park and walk away from her, getting into my car and driving down the street.

Hopefully she'll pick up my signals and meet me around the first corner.

It's an anxious two minutes as I tap my finger on the wheel and worry that she thinks I've abandoned her.

The passenger door creaks open and I release the breath I've been holding.

"That was incredibly double-oh-seven of you." She grins before planting a kiss on my lips.

Threading my fingers around the nape of her neck, I get lost for a moment before she pulls back.

Her blue eyes twinkle as she stares at me. I drink her in.

Shit, I wish we were meeting under better circumstances. I wish I were picking her up so I could take her out for the day. What do normal couples do on the weekends? Go shopping? Catch a movie?

"So..." Chloe plunks back in her seat and pulls a sheet of paper from her pocket. "It took hours but I did manage to narrow it down to three men named Scott Tannon who have all been police officers. One of them works for the police department in Bakersfield, another has retired to LA, and this one lives just outside of Cullington. There's no contact information listed, but I called a bunch of places this morning looking for his information and a sweet, clueless librarian totally believed that I was a courier trying to track down Scott Tannon because a book order had accidentally been delivered to us." She gives me a triumphant smile while my eyebrows pop high. "So I figured we've got all day...why don't we just show up at this address and see if he's the guy we're looking for?"

"What if it's not him?"

"What if it is?" Chloe slips the note back in her pocket and gives me a hopeful smile.

It's impossible to counter her sunshine, and my

lips twitch with a grin as I pull away from the curb and we rumble out of Armitage.

"Can't believe you lied to a sweet librarian," I tease her.

She giggles. "I did feel a little bad, but everyone else I tried was adamant that they didn't give out personal information. I nearly fell off my bed when this sweet woman started rattling off his address."

"She could get fired for that kind of thing."

Chloe frowns and gently swats my arm. "Don't make me feel worse! Crap, it was probably her first day on the job or something."

She groans and covers her face with her hands.

I laugh and rub her thigh. "Don't worry about it. It's for a good cause."

"That's true." She sneaks a look at me and I'm taken by how a girl can be so adorable, intelligent, kind, and stubborn. There are so many angles to her, so many points of beauty and brilliance.

I want to discover every single one of them.

Chloe leans forward, fiddling with the radio until some song she likes is playing. She quietly sings along, "I've got to be me..." and I'm yet again affected by her presence.

She's like a warm spring breeze that curls around your senses, filling you with the hope of summer and good times to come.

The farther we go, the more I relax; by the time

we drive through Cullington, I've nearly forgotten why we're here. Until I reach the T-junction on the other side of town and am directed left, then left again down a quiet country road.

We end up making three more turns before we hit gravel and slowly wind our way down a long, narrow driveway.

"You sure this is it?" I murmur.

"According to Maps it is." She taps her phone to light up the screen. "Although my reception is getting sketchy. I'm down to one bar."

As soon as we pop through the trees, a small cabin appears and two dogs start barking. And not that happy, yappy kind. It's more the *I'm going to rip your throat out* variety.

Chloe tenses beside me when I stop the car and a German shepherd goes ballistic against the glass.

I reach for her hand and give it a squeeze. "I'm not going to let him touch you."

A shadow catches my eye and I glance out the window to find another beast on my side. His throaty growl and sharp fangs keep me put until a weathered-looking guy in brown slacks and a checkered shirt appears on the porch.

He's holding a shotgun like it's no big deal. His pale brown eyes assess us as he slowly walks to the car. With a sharp whistle and a click of his fingers, he calls his dogs off. They obey immediately, scampering onto the porch but standing ready to fight if he calls on them.

"Can I help you?" He leans against the roof of my car, the muzzle of his gun tapping the glass.

My window groans as I wind it down. I give up about halfway and murmur through the gap, "Hey, Mr. Tannon."

I look him in the eye and he flinches with recognition before going very still.

"Thought I recognized this damn car. What are you doing here?"

"I just want to talk."

"Who sent you?"

"No one. I'm just looking for answers."

His face hardens and he shakes his head. "I can't help you, son."

"Please." My voice cracks.

Chloe leans around me. "Just one conversation, Mr. Tannon, and then we'll leave you alone. We promise."

His eyes narrow, his long nose twitching. "I know him, but I don't know you."

"I'm Chloe, Vincent's girlfriend."

My heart does this weird hiccup. I've never had a girlfriend before, and I definitely didn't think I'd be lucky enough to get Chloe as one, but there she is, announcing it to this guy like it's common knowledge.

I'm rendered speechless, gazing at the side of her face like this is some kind of dream that's going to disappear the second I open my eyes for real.

"We know we might not be able to change anything, but sometimes understanding can bring a little peace, you know?"

"Understanding this won't help you, and it certainly won't give you peace."

"We just want to know a little about the investigation. That's all. Please. Please help us."

With a deep huff, he steps back from the car and starts walking for his house.

Chloe and I glance at each other, wondering what it all means, until he turns on the porch and barks, "Are you coming or not?"

We scramble out of the car and inch past his dogs.

"Ratchet, sit!" the man barks when his dog starts growling at me.

I swallow and duck through the screen door before it shuts on my butt.

The house is dim and sparsely furnished. The guy obviously lives alone.

"I would offer you something to drink, but I've only got water."

"That's okay." Chloe smiles at him while taking my hand and sidling up against me.

I rub my thumb over hers and wait for an invitation to sit down.

It doesn't come until he's plunked into a cane chair by the window and leaned his gun against the wall. "Well, are you going to sit down?"

We drop in unison onto the couch opposite him. I bring Chloe's hand onto my lap and thread our fingers together.

"So, how'd you find me?"

Chloe and I share a nervous look and I'm just formulating a lie to protect her when she goes and spurts out the truth.

The ex-police chief blinks a couple of times, his mouth opening in surprise before he lets out a snickering laugh. "Well, I guess after that kind of effort, I should at least let you ask me a question or two."

"Thank you." Chloe smiles in relief, then pulls out her notebook and flips it over. "You arrested Nick that night, didn't you?"

He nods but doesn't say anything.

"Could you, uh, tell us about that?" she prompts him.

"What do you already know?"

I adjust my jeans and clear my throat. "Only what Nick's told me. He got a text, telling him to pick up a car at a warehouse in Armitage. He was supposed to drop it off in Brazenwood, but when he showed up, there was a dead body in the driver's seat."

"Todd McCrae," the man mutters.

"Exactly." I nod. "So, you took Nick in. What was he like?"

The man rubs a calloused hand over his mouth. His long, bony fingers are split and dirty. He obviously works this small piece of land and does everything he can to stay out of society's way. "He tried to run. I had to chase him down and wrestle him into those cuffs. He was angry, cursing up a storm, shouting that he was innocent."

I frown. Why did Nick run if he was innocent?

"I had to fight him into my car."

"What were you doing at the scene? Had someone called it in, or did you just get lucky cruising by?" Chloe asks.

Scrubbing a hand over his face, the man shuffles in his chair. "We had a suspicion that the car thefts in the area were linked, and that night I got an anonymous tip that another car would get jacked near the warehouse on Vine Street. We were so eager to get these jerks that I didn't think twice about where the tip came from. I just followed it, decided to cruise the streets in the area before I headed home. I pulled into the lot and Nick was standing by the car, the door wide open."

Chloe scribbles down some notes. "Did he have the gun in his hand?"

The man's face puckers with regret. His headshake is minimal, his voice dropping to a quiet rasp. "He was trying to deny his guilt, but he was standing over the body. He ran!"

"Where was the gun, Mr. Tannon?" Chloe repeats her question.

"We found it in the floor of McCrae's car."

"It could have so easily been planted there."

"I know that now," he grits out. "The whole case was a mess. Nick claimed he got some text about the car but when I tried to look into it, I was stonewalled. My gut kept telling me this kid was innocent, and I wanted to fight for him. But every time I got close to the truth, I was pushed back."

"By who?" I snap.

Mr. Tannon goes really still, his eyes darting to the floor as he rubs his mouth again.

"Please, sir. Won't you help us?" Chloe's voice is soft, coaxing him to look up.

"I can't tell you what you want to hear." He sighs and looks back to the floor.

"We're only asking for the truth."

"I don't have it for you. I've only got theories. Dangerous ones that are gonna get you in trouble."

I sit forward, my frown deep and obvious. "What are you saying?"

"This is bigger than you think it is. I tried for justice for your brother and I got shot down. Sometimes, you have to turn your back and get out of town."

"You gave up on him?" I shoot to my feet.

The man holds up his hands to calm me, clicking his fingers at Ratchet who's growling from the doorway.

"It was a battle I couldn't win, and I had to think about the safety of my family."

"What family?" Chloe whispers.

An aching sadness washes over his expression before he mutters, "They're safer without me."

"Mr. Tannon—"

"I'm warning you kids." He cuts Chloe off, pointing at her with a look of desperation. "You stay out of this. I wouldn't let any of my officers go near it. I faked cancer and split for the sake of my family and the people I care about. You don't know who you're dealing with."

"I'm not afraid," she argues calmly. "My father's the chief of police in Armitage, and he can—"

The guy lets out a scoffing laugh. "Tell him good luck with that. And if you love your old man, you won't be dredging up this case."

Anger spurts inside of me, and if it wasn't for those damn dogs, I'd be fisting this guy's collar and shaking the truth out of him.

"Why the hell did you invite us in if you aren't even gonna tell us anything?" I lift my hands in frustration.

He gives me a pained smile, his eyes filling with

tears. "I wanted to tell you I'm sorry. What they did to your brother was wrong, and I couldn't make it right."

The fury inside me is dampened by the tear trailing down his cheek.

"I know he's not where he should be, but at least he's alive. He's keeping his mouth shut, and he'll get out on parole for good behavior. That's gonna have to do."

"But that's not fair." I grit out the words.

"Life isn't, son."

My upper lips curls. "My uncle will bust your ass if he knows you locked up his nephew for no good reason."

"I didn't lock up anybody. I tried to dig deep. I wanted to keep the investigation open."

"Who stopped you?"

He looks away, shaking his head again. "Too many powerful players to take down. I knew it, Nick's lawyer knew it. We backed away to protect the people we love and I'm not telling you more, or the people you care about most won't make it. You understand me?"

My gut scrunches into a tight ball as I turn and catch Chloe's eye.

"Do yourselves a favor and turn your back on this thing." Lurching out of his chair, he takes my shoulders and gives them a soft squeeze before murmuring another quiet apology and guiding us to

172

his door.

Chloe and I walk to the car in numb silence.

Slamming my driver's door shut, I run my hand over the wheel and whisper, "Holy shit."

"I know." Chloe's cheeks are pale. "What the hell is going on?"

With a sniff, I shake my head and start the ignition. My arms are trembling for some reason and I have to hold the wheel with two hands.

"We should just drop it."

"Are you kidding me?" Chloe's voice pitches high.

"You heard what he said," I snap.

"Yeah, I did. He's covering up one great big injustice because he's scared."

"And for good reason!"

"Just because he's gone into hiding doesn't mean we have to."

"Chloe, don't do this to me," I whisper. "Don't put your life on the line for my family. We have to drop this."

"Vincent, no."

Slamming on the brakes, I pull the car to a skidding stop on the edge of the gravel road.

Her chest is heaving with surprise as I turn to face her.

Taking her face in my hands, I caress her jawline with my thumbs and hope to hell she can hear me. "I don't want you to get hurt. I can't handle that."

"I won't—"

"You don't know that!"

Her eyes start to glisten and I lower my voice, confessing the truth in a barely there whisper. "Good things never happen to me. But here you are, for reasons I can't even understand. And I don't want you to get hurt or tainted by your involvement with me. I need to keep you safe. I don't want to lose…" My voice disappears as emotion cuts off my air supply.

"It's okay." She skims her fingers down my cheek, her smile delicate and pure.

I suck in a ragged breath and lurch for her mouth. She tempers my kiss with a softness that calms me and we melt against each other.

My arms are still quivering. I wrap them around her, sliding my hand up her back and securing her against me.

It brings home exactly what I've got right now…and exactly what I don't want to lose. As much as I hate the fact that Nick's in jail, I won't take on this beast and risk Chloe getting hurt.

Sometimes you just have to let things lie, even if it leaves a bitter taste in your soul.

#21

CHLOE

A New Name

Vincent drops me back near the park. Because no one's around, he takes his time and thoroughly kisses me goodbye. It's hard not to feel gooey as I step out of the car and wave to him.

But as soon as he's gone, the day swamps me again.

Our conversation with Scott Tannon niggles,

eating my brain to the point where I know I won't be able to drop this.

I know it's big. It's scary.

But we can't just let this injustice fly.

I want to know who's gone to all this effort to set up Nick. It's not just some simple cover-up when you've managed to persuade the accused, the lawyer, and the police to keep their mouths shut.

What are they really hiding?

Why did they really kill Todd McCrae?

I stop on the sidewalk.

That's it.

That's the question we should have been asking. We've been going about this all wrong. Rather than working backward, we should be starting at the beginning.

With Todd McCrae.

Breaking into a jog, I run home, figuring a couple of hours on my laptop might unearth a whole bunch of answers.

I shove open the back door and make a beeline for my room, nearly jumping out of my skin when Dad says, "Hey, Chloe," from the living room.

"Oh!" I pat my heaving chest and let out a nervous titter.

Dad chuckles and glances up from the book he's reading. "Where've you been?"

"Um…" I puff and point over my shoulder. "Just

hanging out."

"With your sisters?"

I swallow and shake my head. "No...Rahn. You know, just more fundraising stuff."

Man, it feels weird lying to Dad this way, not to mention the fact that I'm using Rahn for cover *again*. I need to make sure she doesn't feel like I'm taking advantage of her. Crap, I'm a bad friend.

I catch myself worrying my lip and quickly stop before Dad notices. I'm surprised his eyes aren't narrowing with suspicion. Can't he hear my thundering heart? There's an earthquake ripping through my body at the moment.

"Where's Mom?" I glance around.

Dad's lips twitch with a triumphant grin. "She's signing her new contract."

"She got the job?" A smile jumps onto my face. "That's great! Man, she is going to revolutionize that place."

"Oh yeah." Dad laughs.

"You must be relieved." I tip my head and wink at him.

"I think we all will be."

We share a look that says it all before breaking into laughter. It's nice seeing him relax for a minute. He's usually so intense and focused, but he's got the house to himself and he's obviously enjoying some time out.

I wonder where Uncle Conrad is, but stop myself from asking because I really want to get down to my room and start Googling: *Todd McCrae, Armitage, CA.*

"Hey, well, I'm gonna go to my room."

"Okay, sweets. Enjoy the peace."

"Sure thing, Dad."

I suck in a breath as I spin away. The urge to turn back and let it all out is kind of strong. It'd be great to have Dad's support on this one, but I understand why Vincent doesn't want him involved. Besides, I don't want to be banned from seeing my new boyfriend, either.

I like to think that Dad's a little more open-minded than that, but when I put myself in his shoes, I get it. Vincent's family is trouble, and I wouldn't want my innocent kid near them either, even if she is falling for the diamond among the charcoal.

Clicking my door shut, I grab my laptop and plunk onto my bed.

The late afternoon turns to dusk without me even noticing.

By the time I'm called to the table for dinner, I've found out as much as I can about Todd McCrae— reporter for the Armitage Gazette.

I also have the name of someone who might be able to shed some more light on this mystery— Camila Montes.

Todd McCrae's girlfriend.

It's probably dumb, but I decide to visit Camila alone. I feel kind of bad for not involving Vincent, but he asked me to drop this and I don't want him to be annoyed, especially when this visit could lead to nothing.

Max gave me the keys to our car. Cairo's going to drop her home, so I'm a free agent for the afternoon. It's worked out well actually. Having avoided my family for the last half of Spring Break, I felt like I couldn't say no to their lunch invitation. Max was actually kind of insistent, so I went along, wondering the whole time how I was going to get away.

Thankfully Holden got a text and he had to split. Maddie went with him. I took it as a sign and quickly came up with an excuse to leave.

Checking Maps on my phone, I follow the directions and turn left onto the next street, then take the second right. Camila's little house is number 18. I slow the car and gaze at the white garage door. A palm tree is growing in the front yard, looking like a lonely soldier refusing to give up his post.

Nerves pummel me as I step onto the sidewalk. I don't know how this will go down. I just hope she's open to talking to me. It's probably the last thing she feels like doing on a Sunday afternoon, but I didn't want to call ahead because she might have hung up on me or told me not to come.

At least this way it's a surprise attack and I might have a better chance of getting through the door.

Pulling my sweater sleeves down, I hold my breath and walk down the concrete path to her front door. The doorbell makes a weird squawk when I push it, but thankfully no dogs are going crazy at me this time.

I nibble on my lower lip while I wait, hoping she's home. School starts up again tomorrow and my free time will disappear. I feel like this is my only chance to really get some information.

The door clicks and I flinch, pasting on a smile just as a short, heavyset woman opens the door. Her black hair is styled in a pixie cut that frames her round face.

"Hi." I smile.

She frowns. "Who are you?"

"My name's Chloe. I was wondering if I could have a few minutes of your time."

Her dark eyebrows dip even further together. "You're not about to sell me something, are you?"

"No." I grin at her, raising my hands to show her I'm not carrying anything.

"Then what do you want?"

"I just want to talk."

Her face puckers with a guarded scowl. "You're not a reporter, are you?"

"Me? No, I'm a student at Armitage High."

"Oh." She wraps her long knitted sweater tightly around herself. "Well, what do you want to talk about?"

I swallow, wondering how to broach this. "I'm looking for some answers to an unsolved mystery..." I sigh. "I'm trying to help my boyfriend, and I think you might be a good source of information."

Her wide mouth trembles as she sucks in a breath. With glistening eyes, she shakes her head and murmurs, "If this is about Todd, I don't have anything new to tell you."

She goes to close the door, but I shoot out my hand to stop her. "Please. I know talking about him must be really hard. I'm sorry for your loss."

With a soft huff, she stops pushing the door against me.

"It's just...something feels off to me. Nick Mancini being the killer doesn't make sense."

Camila's face takes on a hard, brittle edge. "Don't you dare try to prove him innocent. He killed the man I wanted to marry."

"I don't think he did."

Her olive skin pales.

"I know all the evidence is there, but something

doesn't add up, and you can't tell me that you're happy for an innocent man to be behind bars when Todd's actual killer is walking free."

Her nostrils flare, tears building on her lashes and spilling over.

"I'm sorry. I'm not trying to upset you. I just hate injustice so much. My boyfriend misses his brother terribly and it's not fair...the conditions he has to cope with." I shake my head. "He needs his brother. And sure, if I didn't care about him so much, I would be completely unaware and no doubt happy for Nick to serve his time. But I'm telling you, he didn't do it."

Her forehead wrinkles.

"So, if there's anything you can tell me that might shed some light on this situation, I'd—"

"Why are you doing this?" Her wide brown eyes spark. "You're a high school student. If the guy is innocent, it shouldn't be your job to prove it."

"Everyone who could have helped him has gone into hiding. They're all scared, and I want to figure out why."

She looks to the floor, quietly sniffing while she thinks. Her knuckles pale as she grips the door, but then, very slowly, she pulls it open for me and silently ushers me inside. I follow her into a small living area and take a seat on the brown couch when she points at it.

Grabbing a tissue from the box, she dabs her face

and crumples into the armchair adjacent to me. "I always thought it was weird that Nick Mancini went on about his innocence and then never appealed. I saw him at the station the night he was arrested. He was shouting that he was innocent. He looked so scared, like somehow he knew it wouldn't matter either way."

I gather my hair and pull it over my shoulder so I can play with the ends while I'm talking. "Leading up to that night, was Todd doing anything different, or did he say anything to you that seemed out of the blue or unusual?"

Pressing the tissue under her nose, Camila takes a second to compose herself. "The afternoon he was killed, Todd told me that he was onto something big. Something that would set us up for the future. He didn't say what it was, but he was really excited. Things had been tough for us and it felt like a way out of Armitage. We'd be able to get married and move to a nicer place, so I didn't bother asking for details. Todd liked to sit on stories and get them perfect before giving them to his editor. I was used to him being secretive about his work, so when he left for a meeting at eight o'clock that night, I didn't even think to question him." Another tear breaks free, trailing down her cheek unnoticed. "I didn't know it'd be the last time I'd see him."

"So you're pretty sure he was working on a story?

How would that set you up for the future?"

"I don't know." She frowns. "He was working for the *Gazette*, and maybe he thought this could get him front page and he'd start working his way up to editor-in-chief. He was very ambitious and determined to be out of this place as soon as we could. He was just clocking up some experience here and then hoping to head to LA or New York or somewhere big so he could get a real high-flying job."

"Do you know if he had any photos or notes that might be useful? Maybe he'd already started his story."

Camila swipes her cheek with the tissue. "The police already came and took all of that. It was evidence and I've never gotten it back."

"Who came? Was it Police Chief Tannon?"

She shakes her head. "No, it was the female detective in charge of the case. She was very kind and sympathetic."

It's hard to hide my confusion. What female detective?

"What...what was her name?"

"I can't remember it now." Her eyebrows flicker as she tries to dredge it up.

"Do you remember what she looked like?"

"Sure. She was short, Latina like me, but very beautiful, dressed impeccably. Long black hair in one of those low ponytails, perfect makeup. You know the kind. She even had a beauty spot on her upper lip." Camila touches the left side of her upper lip. "She looked like a model, but was obviously a well-trained detective. She wore glasses."

I manage a closed-mouth smile in spite of my trembling insides.

As far as I know, no one at the Armitage PD looks like that. And the only cop who was working the Mancini case was Tannon. He made that very clear when he spoke to us. He wouldn't let anyone else touch the case, because he knew something was off.

I don't know who that woman was.

But I need to find out.

#22

VINCENT

The Ultimatum Backfire

Yesterday was torture. I spent the whole day missing Chloe, worrying about Nick, and trying not to think about what Tannon said.

I'm a bad person for wanting to drop this. But that guy scared me. He warned us that looking into this will only lead to trouble, and I can't put Chloe in danger.

I need to see her.

Running up the front steps of Armitage High, I weave through Monday-morning hallway traffic and make sure I swing past Chloe's locker. She's standing there chatting with Rahn. Her smile looks kind of forced, like she's only half listening to her friend.

The second she spots me, her expression transforms, lightening around the edges until she's giving me a full-blown grin.

I glance around me, sure every student within range is being warmed by her rays. But no one seems to notice and I scratch the back of my neck, tipping my head toward the corridor before loping off.

Looking over my shoulder, I see Chloe kiss Rahn on the cheek and then hurry after me. Rahn looks a mixture of worried and annoyed as she watches her friend rush away.

Shit, I really hate the way people see me sometimes.

When I reach the bottom of the stairwell, I notice the music room door is open, so I head a little farther down the hall and click my fingers when Chloe pops into view.

She grins and runs toward me, leaping into my arms with a giggle. I capture her against me, lifting her off her feet and stepping into the alcove so I can kiss her in privacy. Pushing her back against the wall, I let my tongue do the talking, swiping it into her open mouth and feeling my agitation immediately dissipate.

She threads her fingers into my hair. I love how good that feels. It tells me that she's as into this kissing thing as I am.

Our lips dance, working in time until we both pull back to catch our breath.

Chloe grins. "Good morning to you too."

I snicker and rest my forehead against hers. "I know it's only been a day, but I missed you."

"I missed you too." She's still playing with the ends of my hair.

I kind of never want her to stop.

"I have something to tell you," she whispers.

"Yeah?" I lean back so I can smile down at her.

Her expression takes on a nervous edge and I'm immediately alert.

"I know you want to drop this thing, but I couldn't turn my back on it."

I squeeze my eyes shut. "Shit, Chloe, what did you do?"

"Just a little more research. I didn't look into the case, specifically. I started with Todd McCrae. I thought maybe he was murdered for a reason and Nick was just another cover-up, you know? Everyone thought it was a carjacking, but maybe there was more to it."

I groan and let her go.

"Just hear me out. I found Todd's girlfriend." She captures my wrist before I can turn away from her. "I went and saw her, and—"

"What?" I snap.

My heart has just taken off, fear for Chloe nearly blinding me.

Does she not get how dangerous this could be?

Why the hell is she playing with fire?

"She told me that Todd was onto something big. She didn't know what it was, but he was really excited. Said it was going to set them up for the future."

I go still, curiosity tugging at me in spite of my fear.

"And then she told me that the female detective in charge of the case came and took all his photos, notes, *everything*, saying it was evidence."

"What female detective?"

"Exactly." Chloe bulges her eyes. "Now, she couldn't remember her name, but the woman was a short Latina...really beautiful, apparently."

"Well, that narrows it down," I mutter.

"Yeah, I know, but...the thing is...I really think we should bring Dad in on this."

"Chloe, no." I hold up my palms to emphasize what I'm trying to say—*stop this!* "We have to drop this."

"But how? We can't just turn our backs."

"Yes, we can." I point to the ground, leaning close to her face and begging her to hear me. "Everyone we've spoken to has told us we can't win this one. I don't want you getting hurt. I don't want anyone getting hurt! Things are fine the way they are."

"No, they're not! You need Nick, and it's not fair that he's locked away for someone else's crime. Whoever shot Todd McCrae is still out there somewhere."

"Yeah, and that person probably won't hesitate to shoot you either! You want to bring your dad in on this? Scott Tannon *left* his family in order to keep them safe. If your dad starts nosing around, that puts you in jeopardy, and I'm not okay with that."

"Vincent, come on…"

"No!" I shout. "You leave this alone, Chloe. I mean it."

Her eyes glint with defiance as she crosses her arms and stares me down. "I can't do that."

My heart splinters, a thick shard digging into my gut as I pull the only card I have left. "Then this is over."

"What?" Her arms drop in time with her mouth.

"I obviously can't stop you, but I can't watch you do this either. I've told you how I feel. How I want to keep you safe. How I want to be with you. If you care about me at all, you'll leave things as they are."

"But I do care about you." Her lips tremble,

piecing my heart back together until she smashes straight through it again. "Which is why I need to find the truth and set Nick free."

My nostrils flare, my jaw working to the side as I look away from her.

"Vincent, come on."

"No!" I'm too angry to speak, too rejected to do anything but walk away.

She's choosing to put her life in danger instead of be with me.

"Vincent!"

I keep walking, thundering up the stairs and hoping it'll be enough to have her give up on this thing.

But she doesn't follow me and I'm soon walking to homeroom without my secret girlfriend.

Shit! I thought my speech would work.

Now what the fuck am I supposed to do?

#23

CHLOE

Deaf Relations

My eyes are sore and gritty. I squint against the cruel sunlight and pull my cap down a little farther.

Stupid baseball game. I don't even want to play today.

It's an away game too, so it just elongates the whole damn thing.

Most of the team were stoked to get out of class

early so we could make it to Cullington on time, but even that didn't make me feel better.

I haven't slept properly since Vincent basically broke up with me in the hallway. That was nearly three weeks ago, and I'm exhausted.

I can't believe he gave me an ultimatum—him or the truth.

Why did he have to do that?

He doesn't get it!

He wanted me to choose him, but I *am* choosing him. If you care about someone, you put their needs above your own.

I've written him a note every day since, trying to explain myself, but he hasn't replied to any of them. He won't speak to me. He makes a point of looking the other way when I try to catch his eye.

Talk about torture.

I know what he's doing. He's convinced he's keeping me safe by staying out of it. And maybe in some ways, he is. I haven't raised it with Dad yet—I kind of wanted Vincent's blessing before doing that— so I've just been quietly researching on the internet. I popped into the library to drag up some of Todd's old articles. I was looking for anything that might trigger some kind of clue, but so far I've come up empty.

I need to tell Dad what I know.

He's been doing shitty hours at work this week,

but I have to pin him down this weekend. Maybe if I solve this, Vincent will be open to being with me again.

Max stomps toward me, giving me a half-hearted high five before plunking down on the bench seat.

"Nice batting, sis." I nudge her with my elbow.

"Whatever," she grumbles, brushing a few stray hairs off her cheek.

"What's up with you?"

She dips her head forward, holding onto the bill of her cap so I can't see her face.

"Max?"

She groans. "Audition and big game are on the same day."

"What?"

Her shoulders slump with a sigh and she looks over at me, talking softly so no one can hear us. Holden's up to bat, so Maddie's thoroughly distracted.

"You got this, babe!" She claps.

I lean in a little closer to hear Max's grumbling. "I thought I could do both, but I've just found out this afternoon that the game and the audition are at the same time. Austin told me, and I was too scared to admit that it's going to clash with the game."

"So you haven't told the band yet?"

"No. How am I supposed to let them down that way? They specially let me in, which is a really big deal, and now I can't even make it because of stupid baseball!"

"Aw, Maxy, I'm sorry." I rub her shoulder. "What are you going to do?"

"I don't know! I can't let Dad down, but how the hell am I supposed to tell Cairo that I can't make it to the audition?"

"Well, which do you want more?"

My sister gives me a telling look.

"Then you've got to tell Dad."

Max scoffs. "Yeah, right."

"What are you so afraid of?"

"He won't get it. Dad's impossible to talk to."

"He's not that bad."

"Yes, he is." Max gives me an emphatic look. "He only hears what he wants to hear."

I shake my head, silently disagreeing with her. Sure, talking to Dad is hard work, but it's not impossible. He acts like a grizzly bear sometimes, but at the end of the day we're his daughters and he loves us. It's all about how you word things.

You know what, I'm going to prove Max wrong. I'll test Dad out tonight and see if I can't get him looking at things from my perspective. Maybe it'll give Max the courage to try it out herself.

Dad's in a good mood after finding out that we won the game. Uncle Conrad came along for the ride so he's given Dad a play-by-play rundown, talking Max up the way he's always done.

Maddie chips in with her own bits of information and dinner ends up being a jovial, chatty affair.

Except for Max and me.

We're pretty damn quiet...and no one even notices.

After dinner, Maddie excuses herself to go help Holden at Cresthill. Mom and Dad have really warmed to Holden, especially when they found out about his volunteer work.

"You doing anything with Rahn tonight? It is a Friday." Mom grins.

"Uh, no, she's got a family thing, so I'm just kicking around here tonight."

"We could go catch a movie." Max looks at me hopefully and I instantly know she's saying, *Be my cover for Cairo. Please, please!*

"Sure, I'll just help Dad with the dishes first. It's my turn."

"Cool. I'll go get ready." Max practically skips away from the table.

"You can go, sweets. I don't mind doing this."

"No way." I grin at my father. "You've been doing horrible hours. I'm not going to leave you alone with a pile of dishes on your first night off."

He winks at me and we clear the table together.

Dad starts rinsing and stacking the dishwasher while I clear off the table. Soon all that's left are the pots and wineglasses Mom likes us to wash by hand.

"Hey, Dad." I grab a dishtowel and spin it around my finger while the sink fills.

"Uh-huh?"

"You know that murder case from just over a year ago?"

"The McCrae one?"

"Yeah. Have you ever looked into that?"

"No." He glances over his shoulder with a confused frown. "Why would I do that?"

"I don't know." I shrug. "Don't you think it's weird that Nick Mancini swore he was innocent and then went quiet about it?"

"Uh...no. Guilty people do that all the time."

"But surely you get a feel for who's telling the truth and who isn't."

"Sometimes. And other times people fool you. There are a lot of conmen in this world."

"I know." I bob my head. "But from what I've heard, the case doesn't add up to me."

"From what you've heard?" Dad snickers. "Honey, we don't reopen old cases unless we have something solid to go on, and Nick Mancini's word is hardly solid. Not to mention the rumors you've no doubt heard." He puts the pot in the rack and gives me a quizzical frown. "What's got you asking this anyway? Vincent hasn't been threatening you or anything, has he? Forcing you to manipulate me somehow?"

"What?" My nose wrinkles. "No, of course not. Why would you think that?"

"Because you said someone told you that something was off. The only person that could truly benefit from Nick's release is his family."

"Well, Vincent has never asked me to come to you."

"Good. I hope he's never asked you anything."

"What?"

"Look, sweets, I know your style is to always give people the benefit of the doubt, but that can be dangerous. Some people are just born bad, and there's nothing anyone can do about it."

I plunk the pot on the counter, kind of annoyed. "How can you think that way? You're a cop. Aren't you supposed to have hope in humanity?"

"My job is to protect the good people by putting the bad guys away. That's my hope. That's why I work so damn hard, so that I can protect and keep innocent people out of harm's way. And the Mancini family makes it very difficult for me to do that."

"But not all of them, right? I mean, you've never had to arrest Vincent."

"I've had to investigate him."

"And it turned out he was innocent."

"That doesn't mean the rest of his family is. People are right to stay clear of them."

I snatch the small pot and furiously start drying it. "I still think people judge when they don't have all the facts, or they don't understand the backstory. Sometimes the best people can be dressed like wolves, and wolves can be dressed like lambs."

He gives me a confused look, then snickers. "That's true, but are you calling the Mancinis lambs now?"

"No." I let out an awkward chuckle. "But what if Nick was innocent and he got put away for a crime he didn't commit?"

Dad flashes me a sad smile. "Sometimes that happens, but I don't think that's the case with this one."

"But—"

"Chloe, you have to trust me on this. You're not out there dealing with that family. They're a bunch of merciless thugs who don't care about anything but money and power. You just don't see it because I don't tell you about it."

"I see Vincent at school." My heart is hammering so hard right now as I imagine admitting that I've actually made out with Vincent, and the fact that we're not speaking at the moment is breaking my heart.

I can't see that going over so well, especially when

Dad keeps talking.

"You don't hang out with him. You don't go home with him, thank God. The environment he's being raised in has to have a bad effect on the poor kid. That's probably why he's got such a foul temper, why he always chooses fists over a calm conversation."

I frown.

Dad rinses off the frying pan and lays it in the rack. "I'm not trying to sound harsh, but that boy should be given a wide berth. I don't want you trying to be nice to him or becoming his friend. And I'm allowed to say that, because I'm your dad and it's my job to keep my daughters safe. I know you want to save the world, Chloe, but not everyone can be saved. I wouldn't say that if I didn't care about you. Your sweet heart makes you vulnerable sometimes." Drying off his hands, he gently holds my face and makes me look up at him. "I love my girls more than anything. It's my privilege to provide for you, and guide you in the right direction. I want you to have the best life you possibly can."

Max steps into the kitchen and Dad lets me go, taking the dishtowel from me. "I'll finish up. You girls go enjoy your movie."

"Thanks, Dad." Max throws me my jacket, then grabs my hand and tugs me out of the kitchen before I can even put it on.

"I don't know what you were talking about in the

kitchen. I only heard the last part, but I was right, right? He didn't hear a word you said."

I harrumph as Max unlocks the car and starts laughing at me. "I told you!" she singsongs.

Buckling up, I cross my arms and lean back in the seat while Max gets the right music going before reversing out of the drive.

"Cairo's meeting us at the theater."

"Awesome," I mutter, so not in the mood to play third wheel. But what else am I supposed to do?

It's not like I can show up at Vincent's door.

Crap, I can't even call him!

Max starts singing to "Sugar, We're Going Down," oblivious to my internal angst.

I should just make my life easier and drop this whole thing.

But the thought of letting an innocent man stay behind bars makes my stomach curdle.

I have to figure out who these people are and expose them.

I just wish I didn't have to do it alone.

#24

VINCENT

Pointless Dreams

It's been three weeks since I told Chloe to drop this and be with me.

She hasn't.

The reason I know this is because every single note she's left me explains yet another reason why we can't turn our backs on my brother.

It makes me feel like shit.

He's my family and I'm putting her safety above his freedom.

But my stupid-ass plan didn't work, and after weeks of catching Chloe's heartbroken gaze on me, I can't take it anymore.

Screw this shit.

I need her.

I'm sick of sitting in the background of her life, following her wherever she goes to make sure she's safe. I'm like her freaking stalker right now.

I haven't slept in weeks.

I'm tired, grumpy and miserable.

This can't be my life anymore. It's shitty enough without this extra crap added on top. I need to convince Chloe that we should be together, no matter what.

If it means going to her father, then so be it.

The man might scare the shit out of me, but I care about Chloe more than my own fear.

He no doubt thinks I'm not worthy of her...and he's probably right.

But it's not like I choose to steal money from people or be Uncle Enzo's delivery boy.

I do it for my own survival. And I do it in the nicest, most peaceful way I can.

Does that make me a bad person?

I rub my forehead.

Shit! Probably!

She's too good for me.

But...

I don't want to live without her anymore. She makes me want to be a better person. She makes me *want* to be worthy of her.

When we're together, I am a good guy. I'm her warrior.

Gazing down at the note, I reread my instructions with a thick swallow before folding it in half. I check both ways and then slip it into her locker.

In order for the coast to be clear, I had to wait until the late bell had already rung. I'm going to get in trouble for missing the first ten minutes of class, but it'll be worth it.

Pumping my arms, I run down the hallway, my boots loud and intrusive in the quiet corridor.

I puff in to class and get told off by Miss Jenkins, but her sharp words bounce right off me. I might be getting my girl back. Nothing can touch me today.

I hover near the bus stop, pacing back and forth while I wait and hope, wait and hope.

I never got a reply from Chloe. Shit, did she even go back to her locker before baseball practice this afternoon? What if she didn't get the note?

Raking a hand through my hair, I hover in the shadows, hoping no one I know notices me. The bus stop is just around the corner from Pedro's. This is my block and I've tried hard to establish good relationships while collecting "protection pay," but there's still the odd person who hates or fears me.

I can't wait to get away from this trash heap.

Crossing my arms, I lean against the building, trying to keep the dark feelings at bay while I wait for my ray of sun.

Please come. Please find my note. Please agree to meet me.

Nervous energy pulses in my head and I'm pacing again before I can stop myself.

The bus pulls around the corner and I tense, holding my breath until its brakes squeak and the only person I want to see steps out the back door.

I sag with relief as she walks toward me with a sweet smile on her face.

Before she can say anything, I take her hand and lead her down a couple of back alleys until we're safely hidden in the greenhouse.

The second I close the door behind us, I spin and capture her face in my hands.

"I've missed you," I murmur, kissing her smile, her cheek, her neck.

She giggles and wraps her arms around my waist,

sliding her hand up my back and gluing us together.

I hold her like she's precious, because she is.

She smells like vanilla. I subtly sniff her hair as she rests her cheek on my shoulder.

We don't say anything. We just stand there, holding each other and making up for too many weeks of radio silence.

Finally her hands move and she pulls back to look up at me.

Her eyes sparkle with warmth. "I'm so glad you changed your mind. I've missed you, and I haven't been able to think straight these last three weeks."

"Me neither."

"So now we can solve this thing and just get on with being together?"

I tense, putting my hands on her shoulders and taking a step back. "You sure you don't want to just drop it?"

Her reprimanding look makes me sigh.

"I tried to raise it with my dad, but he says cases aren't reopened unless there's some solid proof, so we just need to find something. I've been doing some research on the internet, trying to find Latina detectives in the area, but I'm coming up short. You know, I think that lady who visited Camila wasn't even a cop. I—"

"Stop." I place my finger on her lips.

She goes still, her eyes studying my expression.

"I don't want to waste this time talking about the case. I asked you here so we could hang out for a while. Talk."

"But—"

"Chloe, we can't solve this, okay?" I swallow, nerves making it hard to speak. "I know you really want that, and yeah, if I can keep you safe, I want that too. But there are no guarantees." I lick the side of my mouth and gently take her hands in mine. "But there is one thing we *can* try to control. You and me. Us, together. And if you want, I'll come with you and I'll meet your parents. I'll say whatever I have to, wear whatever you want me to. I'll be the guy they need me to be so that you and I can be a couple, like Holden and Maddie are."

"Vincent." She's shaking her head. Not a great sign.

My tattered nerves rub together, creating an electricity that's hot and irritating. I pull in a breath to temper my anger. I never want to lose it with her. Never.

"Please, Chloe. I want to be able to take you out, hold your hand, kiss you goodbye at the end of a date. Let's tell your parents about us. Let's tell the whole freaking world."

Her lips pull into a sweet smile that gives me hope until she rests her hand on my cheek and whispers, "I want to do all those things too, but we have to clear your family name first. Don't you see?"

I pull away from her, turning my back and pacing to the glass before spinning around and letting my anguish really show. "And don't you see that I'm trying to be worthy of you, and I have nothing to do with any of this murdering bullshit! I'm so sick of my family name dictating who I am! I'm a good guy."

"And so is your brother!" Chloe throws up her arms. "If we can prove he's innocent, then all that stigma against you guys disappears."

"That's not true," I scoff. "I'm still Enzo's nephew, still have to do shitty things for the guy. I'm still a Mancini."

"If Nick is innocent and gets out, you don't have to live with Enzo anymore. You don't have to be a part of that."

"It's not that simple, Chloe." I sigh and scrub a hand down my face. "Can't you just tell your dad that you like me and want to be with me? Can't you just tell him that being with you makes me a better person?" My voice cracks. I turn my back on her, staring out the dirty glass and lamenting the fact that my dreams are never going to come to fruition.

Even if she does tell him, he probably still won't believe her.

I should just shut the hell up and let her go.

#25

CHLOE

Mine

I gaze at Vincent's back. His shoulders are so broad and tense, his stance so strong.

Yet he's breaking on the inside, and I'm partly to blame.

He just wants to be seen for who he really is, and no one will give him a chance. If he hadn't saved my life that night, I probably would have gone the rest of my life assuming that Vincent Mancini was a bad boy who should be avoided. I never would have known.

And he hides it. Most of the time he keeps his guard up because he knows no one will truly give him a chance if he suddenly starts acting like the guy he is.

But he wants to do it for me.

Because he thinks I make him a better person.

Pulling my sleeves down over my hands, I cross my arms around myself and slowly step toward him.

He stays where he is, keeping his eyes trained on the filthy glass.

Stepping over the broken floorboard, I stop behind him, resting my cheek against his broad back and looping my arms around his waist.

"I can tell my dad the truth. I'll tell him whatever you want me to. I don't know if he'll believe me or change his mind about you though. And I hate that, but it's true." My eyes glass with tears and I sniff, hoping my voice doesn't shake too much. "I guess that's why I haven't said anything. I don't want to do something that will stop us from being together. When you gave me that ultimatum, it broke my heart because you said if I care about you, I'd walk away from this. But I *do* care about you, which is why I want your brother to be free. I want *you* to be free. So if I care, I should be fighting for that. I should fight for you, because I think I lo—" I swallow the word before I can say it. I don't want to embarrass him, and it feels way too soon to declare my love for the guy.

The words just kind of popped out before I could stop them.

Do I love Vincent?

Yeah, I think I do.

He starts to turn, so I step back and keep my eyes on the ground.

I don't know what he's about to say to me, and I'm suddenly petrified that he's going to pat me on the shoulder and reject me in the nicest way possible.

Pulling in a shaky breath, I inch away. Maybe I can just wave him goodbye and bolt for the door.

But he reaches forward, gently capturing my chin and forcing my head up. His brown gaze is tender and sweet, his lips curling into a soft smile. "I think I lo...you too."

I let out a breathy laugh, made shaky by a mixture of relief and elation. There's a sprinkling of fear in there—the healthy kind that no doubt plagues everyone who's falling in love.

I've had crushes before, but never anything this intense. I've never told a guy I lo—ed him, that's for sure.

Closing the space between us, Vincent dips his head, capturing my mouth in a smooth, perfect motion that reminds me how in sync we are. Yes, it's fast. Yes, I never expected to feel this way about him,

but I'm going with it.
Because it feels good.
It feels right.
He feels like mine.

#26

VINCENT

Whispers and Kissing

Chloe's tongue in my mouth is a song. Her soft lips fill my heart; her warm body and kind words make me feel like a different person.

She thinks she loves me.

I could fly right now.

Cupping the back of her head, I cradle her against me while tasting her kisses from every angle. The exploration and study of her mouth is something I will never get sick of.

We're meant to be together.

And even though it'll be a fight, I'm willing to do it.

Hope is a powerful thing, and as I'm kissing Chloe, I'm filled with it. My mind jumps forward to next year, being a senior with Chloe by my side. Graduating and maybe even getting into a community college. I don't know where Chloe's going, but I'll travel to see her. I'll get away from this place and become the man she deserves.

Chloe pulls back for air, her giggle light and free as she rests her forehead against my lips. I kiss her soft skin before guiding her to the pile of musty sheets on the floor. Plumping them up, I take a seat and pull her down to sit on my lap. She fits perfectly, wrapping her arm around my shoulders and grinning down at me while the light fades outside.

"How long can you stay?" I whisper, unable to resist kissing her neck.

"Max is covering for me, but it is a school night, so I've probably got until ten at the latest."

"Ten," I murmur against her skin, wondering how long we can last in the greenhouse. I should probably take her out for dinner, feed her, treat her like a lady.

"Let's stay here until the last minute," she whispers, tipping her head to give me better access to her neck. "I don't want to leave you until I absolutely have to, and this greenhouse feels safe and secret somehow, you know?"

"What about food?" I kiss the spot beneath her ear.

"What's food?" She grins, turning her head to capture my mouth.

I spin her around so she's straddling me and so goes the rest of our night, whispered conversation interrupted with kisses. Kisses that heat me to boiling. I have to pull back a couple of times and ask her about something random and mundane. I unearth a box of Raisinets from my bag and we munch on those, then share my bottle of water. She knows what I'm doing every time I pull away from her and giggles at me before answering or popping a few more candies in her mouth.

We chat until things cool down and then inevitably start making out again.

If I didn't care so much about her, I'd let myself go, peeling her clothes off piece by piece until I could lay her down beneath me and have all of her. But I'm not taking Chloe's virginity. Not in this musty greenhouse. Not this soon. I don't even have protection on me.

Although, that's not really the point.

As much as I'd love to wriggle my fingers beneath her shirt and explore the shape of her body, take things to the next level, I'm not going to. I'm not turning this into something more until we're both ready. It's a big step. With Chloe, it would be an epic step, because getting intimate with her would be off the charts.

I've never loved a girl before.

And I'm not rushing into sex with Chloe. I want this thing between us to slow burn, because I want it to last. I want to keep loving her for as long as she'll let me. I want to know everything about her, starting from the inside and working my way out.

She burrows down in our makeshift sofa so she can rest her head in the crook of my neck. I smile, loving the feel of her, wishing we could fall asleep right here and wake up together in the morning.

I glance at my watch, wondering how much longer we have, and nearly jump out of my skin.

"Shit! It's ten o'clock."

Chloe jumps. "Really? Already? Crap."

"Your dad is going to kill me."

"No, he's going to kill *me*. We have a game tomorrow, and he hates any of us being too tired to play."

"Come on. Come on." I jump up, taking her hand and pulling her to her feet. "I'll drive you home."

"You'll need to drop me at the end of my street."

I frown at her.

She laughs and shakes her head. "You honestly

think walking me in the door past curfew is the best way to play this? I need to talk to my parents first, okay? Don't worry, they'll come around, but it's going to take a little time and tact. Please trust me."

I lean into her, planting my lips on her mouth instead of saying yes.

When I pull back she smiles, and even though the light is dim, I can make out the look in her eyes.

Oh yeah, she loves me.

A grin breaks across my face, wide and foreign, yet so damn satisfying.

I drive her home as fast as I can and drop her close to her house, lighting her way until she disappears up the driveway.

Shit, I hope she's not in too much trouble.

I wince, driving past her house to make sure she's inside before turning around and heading back to my place.

#27

CHLOE

The Safest Place in the World

The kitchen door squeaks when I open it. I wince and click it shut as quietly as I can. It's twenty past ten and most of my family will be tucked up in bed already. Especially the night before a game. Dad's kind of strict on that.

Holding my breath, I tiptoe through the kitchen and past the living room where Uncle Conrad is snoring. I stifle a giggle; he sounds like a foghorn. Creeping down the hallway, I nearly make it to my room when I'm brought up short by a snap from Mom and Dad's room.

"Chloe, is that you? Get in here."

I cringe and head down to the end of the hallway.

"Hey, sorry I'm late."

"Where have you been?" Mom asks, checking her watch and then sitting up and turning on the light. "Why didn't you text?"

"My battery died," I murmur, looking to the floor.

"Couldn't you just have used Rahn's phone?"

Shit! I didn't know what Max's cover was going to be. Rahn's a safe bet. I'm glad she went with that.

I glance up with a remorseful frown and punch out the closest truth I can manage. "Okay, fine. I forgot. I'm sorry. I lost track of time and then when I *did* notice, we just jumped in the car and raced here."

"I hope she wasn't speeding." Dad rubs a hand over his face while I roll my eyes. "You know, I don't want you hanging out with Rahn on school nights if she's going to be bringing you back this late. You have a game tomorrow."

I look to the floor, wondering how I'm ever going to admit what I was really up to...or how I truly feel about Vincent Mancini.

"You know we trust you, Chloe." Mom tips her head the way I do. "You're the one we never have to worry about."

"I know." I wince. "And I'm really sorry I missed curfew. It won't happen again. I appreciate your trust."

Guilt singes my insides as I look between their smiles.

I think of Vincent and the night we've just spent together. How badly I want to do that again. How badly I'd love for them to know who he really is.

I can't tell them I was with him tonight—that won't do him any favors—but maybe I can tell them something.

Nerves attack me from all sides as I inch into the room and perch on the end of the bed. It's hard to know which side to pick—both parents could erupt at this revelation—but I'm compelled to do it anyway.

"Actually, there's something I have to tell you guys. I should have told you weeks ago, but I was worried you'd freak out."

Dad groans and covers his face. "Please tell me you haven't fallen in love with some loser and he's got you pregnant."

"Dad!"

"Reece!"

Mom and I complain in unison. She slaps his arm

while I worry my lip.

"I'm not in love with a loser," I clarify. "And I'm not pregnant. I'm still a..." I frown at Dad, too embarrassed to say the word *virgin* in front of him.

He gives me an apologetic smile, which I'm about to wipe clean off his face.

I look down and start tracing the swirling pattern on the bed cover. "Something did happen to me though. Um..." I swallow. "You know how a while back, the police got that anonymous call about a woman being attacked on Fort Street?"

Mom gasps while Dad sits up, alert with an intensity that's kind of intimidating.

"W-well, I was coming out of the church and these two guys grabbed me and dragged me into this alley." My voice starts to quiver.

Dad's death glare is so not helping. I know it's not directed at me, but it's still hard to talk around it.

"They were going to rape me, but then Vincent Mancini showed up and he saved me. He beat those guys and they scampered. He was really nice and kind, and he drove me home and made sure I was safe. I think he was the one who called in the anonymous tip to the police."

Mom hasn't made a sound since her gasp. Her skin goes sickly pale as she closes her eyes and whispers, "Thank God you're all right."

"Why didn't you tell us this before?" Dad's voice

is thick with emotion.

I glance at him then back down at the covers. "Because they didn't hurt me. They never got a chance...thanks to Vincent. And then I heard you talking to Mom and the two guys got caught, and even though it was for drug possession...they weren't a threat anymore. I was worried if I told you that you'd never let me see Rahn again...or even let me out of the house. The night it happened, I couldn't handle the thought of some kind of interrogation. You can be scary sometimes, Dad. Especially when you're upset."

Dad looks pained, scrubbing a hand down his face and huffing. "I know I come across as hard sometimes, but the thought of you girls getting hurt terrifies me."

"So you hide it behind this gruff mask." I smile.

His expression softens for a moment.

"You're not the only one who does that." I give him a pointed look. "Things aren't always what they seem. I thought Vincent was this intimidating bad boy, but he was really sweet and protective. He saved me."

"Okay." Mom clasps her hands together and totally misses my point. "So you haven't been back to St. Michael's again, have you?"

"No," I grumble. "You wouldn't let me after that first guy was caught. You were worried."

"And rightly so!"

"Yes." I nod. "But just because one bad thing happens doesn't mean I should hide away from the world."

"Is that why you're telling us this now? Because you and Rahn have some humanitarian trip planned? You want to head to some war-torn country and risk your lives, don't you!"

"Mom." I hold up my hand to calm her. "I'm telling you because I don't want to lose your trust. I'm telling you because I want you to realize that I was saved by someone everyone assumes is bad."

Dad huffs and crosses his arms. "Well, I am grateful that Vincent stepped up, but that still doesn't mean I want you hanging out with him...or spending any more time in that part of town."

"He's not a bad person. There are a lot of good people who live out that way."

"Even so, there are a lot of bad people who live out there too. The Mancini family is dangerous, and if you were hanging out with that boy, it'd make you vulnerable. I'm sorry if you don't like that answer, but I don't care if that kid has a heart of gold. You are not to become friends with him."

"And you're not going back to that church," Mom adds with her *don't even try to argue with me* look.

I don't bother hiding my disappointment. My plan is totally backfiring. I thought if they heard what

Vincent did for me, they'd soften up a little.

Dad's scowl catches my eye as he leans in to study my expression. "You haven't been hanging out with him already, have you? Where were you tonight?"

Taking on Mom and Dad together was a bad idea.

I look between them, knowing the truth will decimate the rest of my year. Now is not the right time to tell them that I'm falling in love with a Mancini.

A thrill skitters through, memories of Vincent's soft confession warning me to protect what we have.

Looking Dad straight in the eye, I lie. "I was with Rahn, and we may have talked about some ideas for the future, but at this stage I'm not planning a trip to some war-torn country." Mom snickers as I rise from the bed and walk to the door. "Again, I'm sorry for being late. I won't lose track of time again."

"Good night, sweetie. We love you." Mom blows me a kiss.

"Love you too," I murmur before slipping out the door and hightailing it to my room.

I seriously don't know if I've done more damage or good tonight. Mom and Dad will no doubt stay up for another hour dissecting and processing the fact that their daughter was nearly raped, and completely ignoring the fact that I was saved by a warrior. A *good* human being.

As I get into my pajamas, I relive the conversation,

wondering how I could have played it differently, trying to find ways that I could turn this around. Maybe it's going to be a case of dropping little nuggets of gold as the weeks roll by.

Vincent did this. Vincent did that.

He's a hero. He likes to help people the way I do. I'm getting to know him and we have more in common than you think. We've spent hours writing each other notes and talking about stuff. He's a gentleman. He has a kind heart.

He thinks I make him a better person, but he has no idea how brave I've become. How strong I want to be, for him.

Yes, he may be a Mancini, but he's not dangerous to hang out with.

His brother's innocent, and even though his uncle and cousin are jerks, he won't be under their thumbs forever.

Slumping onto my bed, I brush my finger over my lips. The thought of Vincent's kisses makes my body buzz. Being wrapped in his arms is a feeling I'm not willing to give up. I need to fight for this guy.

I need to figure out a way to convince my parents that being by Vincent's side is the safest place in the world.

#28

VINCENT

The Danger Zone

I think about Chloe the whole way home, reliving our conversations and kisses...the way she said she thinks she loves me.

I've never felt this way before—overpowered by this emotion that's all-consuming, energizing... inspiring.

I hope one day she finds the courage to talk to her

parents about me. And that I find the courage to face whatever that might mean. She's a girl worth fighting for, I know that much.

My lips twitch with a smile that stays in place as I pull up to the house and get out. For some weird reason I feel like humming. What the hell is wrong with me?

I snicker and shake my head, twirling my keys around my index finger as I lope up the front steps and into the house.

Much to my annoyance, Enzo is still up. He's in his lounger, staring at the TV while he sucks on a cigarette and nurses a bottle of vodka.

His glassy eyes and languid body tell me everything I need to know.

The bastard's drunk.

I hate it when he gets like this. He's impossible to reason with, and his violent tendencies really shine through.

Without acknowledging him, I creep past, hoping he won't even notice me.

But of course I'm not that lucky.

Of course Diego has to stride into the house after me with this cocky grin and a dark, dangerous look in his eye.

I frown, instinct telling me to put my game face on.

Swiping a finger under his nose, Diego swaggers

over to me. His triumph is unnerving and I wish he'd just say it already. What the hell has he got on me?

Diego waits until he's an inch from my face and can stare me right in the eye.

I meet his gaze, desperately trying to read it.

"Thought you said she was no one." His voice is low and gravelly.

Shit.

I swallow, but keep my eyes locked on his. "What are you talking about?"

"The blonde, the girl you just drove home."

"What?" Enzo spins in his chair.

Fuck!

I shrug, hiding my unrest behind a confused frown. "What girl?"

"Don't lie to me." Diego points in my face. "I watched you drive her home. I followed you."

How did I not see that?

Am I frickin' blind?

"Diego, back up." Enzo gets out of his chair and staggers over to us.

I'm aware that it's two on one with a pissed-off cousin and a drunken uncle. This could hurt, but there's no way in hell I'm telling them anything about Chloe.

"What girl?" Enzo slurs.

I shake my head. "I don't know what he's talking about."

Diego fists my shirt and slams me back against the wall. "Do you think I'm fucking blind? I just followed you to her house, man! It's the girl from the fair. The one you said you didn't know. The one you've been lying to us about. Now, who the hell is she?"

I wrestle him off me, pushing him back with a sense of urgency that's making me stronger. "Why do you even care? So I took some lost girl home. Big deal."

"You lied about her. She must be a big deal."

"So?" I push Diego back when he comes at me again.

"So, we want to know who she is." Enzo's glassy eyes narrow. "She your girlfriend?"

"What difference does it make? Why do you even care?"

"I care because you lied about her. Who is she?"

I shake my head and look to the floor. Like I can admit she's the daughter of Chief Barlow. Like I can tell them that I'm falling for her.

"Okay, fine." Diego crosses his arms, his smirk back in place. "You don't want to tell us, I'll just pick her up and ask her myself. I'm sure I can think of some ways to get that pretty little thing talking."

Molten fire spurts through my core. Anger blasts in my chest as shaky breaths start to spurt from my nose.

"Hey, maybe I can convince her that she's

hanging with the wrong Mancini. I can show her what a real man looks like." Diego licks his lip. "I wouldn't mind a taste of that honey. I bet she's extra sweet, isn't she?"

And the rumbling volcano erupts.

With a thundering roar, I launch myself at Diego and let my fists fly.

His eyes bulge as he falls back, and I get a few decent punches in before he gets over his surprise and starts hitting back. I don't let up, even when Enzo gets in on the action.

I'll be black, blue and aching by the morning, but I don't give a shit.

They are not touching my Chloe.

#29

CHLOE

A Night to Remember

Vincent hasn't been at school for the last few days. I'm really worried about him. I want to catch the bus back to Fort Street, or use the car to go check on him, but I know showing up at his door is a really bad move.

I wish I could tell Dad the truth and get him to go and check that Vincent's okay, but then he'll know how much I care about him and I'm trying to avoid permanent grounding right now.

After the last few days, Dad's practically feral with anger.

Uncle Conrad stole our stuff and took off without a goodbye. Max kind of alluded to the fact that he had some gambling debts, but it was a whispered conversation out of Dad's earshot and I didn't get too many details before Max skittered back to her room.

The tension in our house is unbearable.

Mom's pissed off with Dad for letting Uncle Conrad stay so long and going on about how she knew something like this would happen. Dad's pissed off with his brother for betraying us so badly. Max is hurting that her favorite relative has skipped out, plus she's…

I glance at my older sister, sitting on the bench with this hard, tormented look on her face.

We're currently at the last game of our season, the one that will decide if we get into the playoffs or not. It's a big deal. Dad's brought a scout over from Ohio University for the sole purpose of watching Max and recruiting her.

There's just one monumental problem: Max doesn't want to be here.

Her heart and mind are with Velocity and the Summer Rock Festival audition they're supposed to be doing right now.

She needs to be there with them, but instead she's stuck here with us.

Coach tells her she's up next and she moves like a robot, putting on her helmet and grabbing the bat. She's been edgy all day, but since the last inning she's seemed to shift into a new zone. This weird kind of emotionless autopilot.

Crap, she really shouldn't be here.

"Okay, good play. Good play!" Coach shouts and applauds Kingston's bunt while Max shuffles to home plate.

"Yeah, Maximus!" Dad shouts from the stands. He's working overtime to impress the scout. I've never seen him so friendly and jovial.

Max taps her bat on home plate, and my stomach jitters with nerves.

"Strike one!" the umpire shouts.

Maddie hisses beside me, as anxious as I am.

"Come on, Maximus!" Dad claps his hands. "You can do better than that!"

I frown at Dad, wishing he'd shut up. Like Max needs that added pressure right now.

"Strike two!"

"Ouch," Maddie murmurs, standing up as Max slumps her shoulders. "She really needs to get her head in this."

"How can she when her heart's somewhere else?"

Maddie glances down at me, her expression

pained. I think it's kind of hurting her that Max wants to give up on baseball. She's always loved how kickass her twin is, but maybe Max is kickass at playing guitar too. Velocity wouldn't have asked her to join if she wasn't. We can't make Max feel bad that she's passionate about something other than baseball. Just because she's amazing doesn't mean she should have to do it for the rest of her life.

The pitcher winds up and I hold my breath until I hear that sweet *thwack* of the bat smashing the ball. Letting out a surprised laugh, I smile as the ball arcs through the air—a sweet homer.

"Yeah!" Maddie raises her arms, laughing when Holden jumps over and lifts her off the ground in a hug.

"That's it, Max!" Holden hollers and claps with the rest of the team.

I study my sister closely as she runs around the bases. She's concentrating, determined, but as she hits home plate, I can tell by the look on her face that she's not into it. She hit the homer for Dad... not her.

Her lips are drawn in a tight line as she storms off the field, ignoring all the congratulatory pats on the back.

As soon as she's behind Coach's back, she throws her helmet off and starts shedding her gear.

"What are you doing?" I ask.

She glances over her shoulder to make sure Coach

isn't watching.

"I've got to go."

"What?" Holden steps up, having heard her soft comment.

She winces at him. "I shouldn't be here, and I should have been honest about that a long time ago."

"But you're so good," he whispers.

"My heart's not in it." She blinks, her voice thickening with emotion.

I share a quick look with Maddie, who hides her disappointment behind a kind smile. Gliding her arm about Max's shoulders, she gives her a little squeeze and then sets her free. "It's okay, sis. We've got you covered. Just go."

"Yeah." I grin. "Go for it."

"Thank you." She practically sobs the words before kissing Maddie's cheek, then mine.

I giggle and shunt her behind me, putting on an innocent smile when Coach turns around to see what we're doing.

"Max just needs the bathroom." I point over my shoulder at my retreating sister, who is full-on running after her heart and a completely new dream.

Wow. I don't think I've ever been so proud of her.

The amount of courage that must take. She's defying Papa Bear right now. There are going to be big repercussions.

It makes me think of Vincent and how I shied away from the entire truth the other night when I told my parents about what a good guy he is.

I wonder if I'll ever find the strength to really lay it out straight.

I'm in love with Vincent Mancini, so deal with it.

The idea makes a shaky laugh escape me.

"I know." Maddie nods, totally oblivious to what I'm really thinking. "The aftermath for this thing is going to be huge."

"We're going to get yelled at," I murmur.

"Oh yeah, that vein in his forehead is going to bulge big-time!" She raises her eyebrows and all I can do is let out another jittery giggle.

Maddie was right. I've never seen Dad's vein pop out that far. He is fuming, and since he shoved us in the car, demanding we take him to Max's location, he hasn't uttered a word.

I can't decide which is scarier—Dad's bellowing outside the locker rooms once we admitted that Max had taken off to Brazenwood to play guitar with her boyfriend Cairo Hale, or his stony silence since.

In an eerily calm voice, he instructed Mom to take

our yellow Camry home and then ordered us into the back of his car. I don't know why our Camry was still in the parking lot. I figured Max would take it to get to the club, but maybe she hitched a ride with a friend or something.

My confusion has been overrun by nerves. I can ask her when we get to the club...if Dad will let me.

I glance at Maddie and we cringe at each other.

I didn't expect Dad to drag us along too, but I guess we're partly responsible. We lied to get Max out of the game, and we even tried to lie when Dad first found us, saying Max was sick. It took him two seconds to see through Maddie's lame attempt and before I could even speak, she was confessing everything in this fast, nervous clip.

We're over halfway to Brazenwood now. Oh man, it's going to be like a freaking fireworks display when Dad walks into that club and finds her. I feel sorry for Max already. And poor Cairo's going to get it too. Yeah, Maddie confessed that little tidbit when Dad was towering over her, yanking out the truth like an expert interrogator.

Dad's phone starts ringing. He grabs it off the dash, his face contorting as he answers it.

"You have some serious explaining to do!" he yells.

I flinch and Maddie reaches for my hand, giving it a reassuring squeeze.

"Oh, I am already on my way," Dad grits out, then glances over his shoulder. "Yes, Maddie and Chloe have been very helpful. I've even brought them along for the ride so I can blast you all together."

Maddie and I shrink back into the seat as Dad turns to face the road.

But then he goes still, the anger in his voice evaporating. "Are you okay?"

Fear spikes through me and I bolt up straight. Dad's tone is off. It's that cool, calm one he sometimes uses when he's really scared.

"Max, what's going on?" Dad winces like he's just been punched in the stomach. "Max? ... Max! ... Shit!"

He throws the phone onto the passenger seat and floors it.

"Dad is everything okay?" Maddie leans forward in the seat.

"When we get to the club, you two need to stay in the car. Got it?"

"But why?"

"Maddie, just do as I say."

There's that fear again, that gruff mask he wears when going into battle.

"I will. I just want to know what's going on."

"Your sister's got herself into some trouble. This is what happens when you lie and go off and do things you're not supposed to do!"

His words make me cringe as we speed into Brazenwood. I really need to tell him about Vincent. Not tonight, of course. I value my life, and his. I imagine after this that Dad will not be in a very charitable mood when it comes to matters of the heart.

As soon as we reach the club, Dad finds a parking space across the street and repeats his order for us to stay in the car.

Maddie and I nod, anxiously watching him cross the road.

"What kind of trouble?" Maddie softly asks.

"I have no idea." I lean around her so I can get a better look at the club. The *Escapar* sign is glowing in red neon above the entrance. It's written in this cool scrawl-like writing. It's obvious the club is new. Everything about the place has a cool, modern edge to it. People are milling outside the club, a large line forming, but Dad walks right to the front and is allowed in without a hitch. I don't know what he said. He didn't even flash his badge and they moved aside for him.

I frown and study faces while we wait. It feels like an eternity.

"Is that Cairo?" Maddie nudges me with her elbow. "Look, there!"

She points out the window as Cairo and the rest of Velocity squeeze out of the club. Mr. Hale is there too, and that must be his wife, Mrs. Hale. They all look sick with worry.

"What the hell is going on?" I whisper.

"I don't know, but screw waiting in the car." Maddie shoulders the door open and we race across the street to get some answers.

Cairo doesn't even see us until Maddie's beside him, demanding his attention and a whole heap of answers.

"She followed your uncle Conrad. He was being dragged out the back by these two guys. I don't know what's going on, but..." His expression is pure agony and my insides are reeling.

Uncle Conrad's back? He was dragged away?

What the hell is going on?

Wrapping my arms around my waist, I shuffle from foot to foot, my imagination turning from one ugly scenario to the next. Thank God Dad has gone in to fix this. Worry nearly eats me alive until I'm distracted by a short Latina woman who struts out of the club with a plastic smile on her face. She's in stiletto heels and a dress that leaves nothing to the imagination. Her dark hair is perfectly arranged, as is her makeup. She looks like a model...and something about her is so familiar, but I can't think where I've seen her before.

Cairo storms toward her. "Where is she?"

"She's coming. Her father is bringing her out.

Everyone is fine. Everyone is happy."

Maddie scoffs. "I highly doubt that."

The woman gives her a tight smile before leaning forward and saying something I can't hear.

Cairo's face contorts with anger. "I don't know what the hell goes on back there, but if she even has one scratch, I am making it a big deal."

"She's safe, so don't worry." The woman's voice takes on a hard edge as her eyes flash with warning. Then as if a switch has been flicked, she pastes on a charming smile and waves us a cheerful goodbye.

"Who was that?" I ask, staring after the woman as she struts back into the club.

"That's Luisa Garcia." Cairo scrubs his face with a sigh. "Her brother and husband own this club."

"I take it she's in charge of marketing." Maddie's voice is dry and unimpressed.

I glance at my sister and then look back to the club. Where have I seen that woman before? It's bugging me that I can't place her.

"There they are." Maddie jolts away from me, running across to our family.

"I told you to stay in the car!" Dad thunders.

"Yeah, right." Maddie brushes past him and yanks Max into her arms.

My poor sister looks lost and petrified. I know that expression. I felt it the night I was nearly raped. Alarm jolts through me and I race across to her, wrapping my arms around both my sisters and clinging tight to create a fortress around Max. I don't know what the hell went on in that back room, but I'm nearly quaking with relief that Max made it out okay.

"Girls, get in the car!" Dad barks, but we all ignore him, still locked in a group hug that's surging with unspoken emotion.

Cairo appears behind me, squeezing past so he can get close to Max and run his hand down her back. He leans his forehead against the side of her face and my heart melts. It's so sweet. It makes me think of Vincent.

I want to see him so badly right now. I want to make sure he's okay. I want to tell him about tonight.

Maddie and I pull away so that Cairo can hug her properly, but he doesn't even get his arms around her before Dad ruins it.

"Get away from her." He yanks Cairo back. "You are not to touch my daughter again."

"Dad—" Max tries to intervene, but her argument evaporates when Dad points at her.

"You walk to the car and you get in. You don't talk, you don't look over your shoulder. You understand me?"

She looks devastated as she skims her eyes over Cairo, then nods and shuffles away. Maddie and I flank her, resting our hands on her back and guiding her to the car. She pulls in a shaky breath and as soon as we're in the back seat blurts, "I'm sorry to drag you into this. I didn't mean for it to…"

Her voice is cut off by this dry sob that tears at my heart.

"They've got Uncle Rad," she sobs.

"What?" I whisper, but don't have time to find out the truth before Dad slams into the car.

This creepy silence descends as Max shrinks in on herself. I glance over her shoulders to catch Maddie's eye. Even she doesn't have the nerve to speak right now.

But I'm dying to know what Max meant about Uncle Conrad.

Who's got him?

Dad pulls away from the curb, muttering to himself, until he finally explodes.

"You could have been killed, Max!" He slaps the wheel and I can't help flinching.

Max could have been what?

She whimpers and pulls in this raggedy breath. "Uncle Conrad came back to help make things right. He gave me a ride to the club, not knowing that the guys he was running from were going to be there." She sniffs and wipes the tears off her face as she looks between me and Mads. "Those gambling debts have caught up with him, and now they've got him! And they won't give him back until Dad's paid the money!"

Maddie gasps, and all I can do is gape at my sister. This is unreal.

"It's okay, girls. I'm going to make it right." Dad's deep voice is so sure and confident. "Uncle Conrad will be safe and sound by 8:03 tomorrow night. Believe me."

I lean back in my seat, tuning out Dad's assurances while I try to process the fact that my sister could have been killed tonight and my uncle is being held hostage until my father can pay for his release.

Holy crap! This is heavy.

As we head for home, my mind jumps back to that woman outside of the club. Luisa Garcia. Does she have something to do with all of this? She came out assuring Cairo that everything was fine. Was she covering for her brother and husband, who own the club? How does she fit into the chain?

Man, something about her is really bugging me, and I don't think I'll be able to rest until I figure out who she is and how I know her.

#30

VINCENT

How Not to Break Her Heart

Fighting with Diego was stupid. It gave away the fact that Chloe's important to me.

Diego and Enzo beat me until I couldn't fight back anymore. My body was radiating with pain and all I could do as they dragged me to my room was let out a whimpering moan. I woke up the next morning handcuffed to my bed. They were going to keep me in there until I fessed up. No food, no water until I told them who Chloe was.

I had no choice if I was going to keep her safe, so I told them the reason I wanted to keep things quiet was because she's Chief Barlow's daughter.

"He doesn't know about me and we want to keep it that way."

I thought they'd be livid, but instead they both laughed and told me we could use it to our advantage. I can use Chloe to keep tabs on her old man and report back any new investigations. I can be a spy.

So I guess that means I have to break up with Chloe.

Which is why I've been avoiding school. I could have gone back on Friday, as I can hide most of my bruising beneath my clothes, but I just haven't been able to face her. I don't know how to look her in the eye and tell her we shouldn't be together.

Shit, I'm dreading it. But I'm not spying on her family. I'll break it off today and tell Enzo she dumped me. Selena's been covering with the school, calling in sick on my behalf, but I can't keep hiding forever.

I have to get this over with today. I'd rather drink a

vat of acid, of course, but I don't know what else to do. My family is dangerous and I won't have her caught up in that mess.

I walk up the front steps of Armitage High. My feet are lead weights as I shuffle to the office and hand over the doctor's note Selena forged for me. The receptionist reads it and nods before giving me a pained, sympathetic smile.

"I'm glad you're feeling better." Her eyes tell me that she knows I didn't really have the flu. Her sad smile tells me that she knows I'm hiding bruises beneath my clothing and that the fading scratch on my cheek wasn't just the accident I'm going to claim it to be.

"Thanks." I move out of eyeshot quickly and head back into the hallway.

I don't want her sympathy, and I don't want her calling the cops about it either. They never do anything anyway, so what's the point? The one time Nick wasn't there to stop Diego going after me, he reported it to the police the next day. They popped by the house to have a chat with my uncle, who paid them off. The second they left, Nick got the beating of his life. He fought like a tiger and managed to do a little damage, until Uncle Enzo threatened to go after me again. Nick told him he'd kill him if he did.

Uncle Enzo just laughed and got Diego and the boys to hold Nick down so he could finish what he started. Nick and I were laid up for a week. But as soon as we were presentable and able to walk around without wincing, he put Nick back to work and sent me off to school with a warning to keep my mouth shut.

"It'll only be worse if you tell."

I've always heeded that warning.

Shuffling down the corridor, I flick my collar up and hunch my shoulders, keeping my glare on so that no one will talk to me. My stomach is sick with nausea as I try to work out what I'm going to say to Chloe.

This is going to kill me.

Rounding the corner, I spot her. She's standing next to her sisters, looking pained and worried. My insides jerk to attention.

What's happened to put that look on her face?

She's rubbing Max's back, obviously giving her some kind of speech to encourage her sister. I frown. Did that Cairo dude dump her? Chloe told me they were together, but it was a big secret.

I want to catch her eye, to find out what I can, but then I don't want her to see me. It'll just rush the breakup forward to now and I'm still not ready.

Spinning on my heel, I take off down the hall, hoping she doesn't notice me.

"I heard her dad's grounded her for the rest of the year." I catch a trail of gossip as I head for my locker.

"She skipped out on the game and went to that

new club in Brazenwood."

"Oh man, I heard their dad screaming at them, and then they had to go with him to collect Max."

I close in on my locker and catch one more piece of the puzzle.

"I'm surprised he didn't arrest Cairo Hale. He was so angry."

What the hell is going on?

I glance up and notice Roman Sanchez. He's looking kind of glum as he shuffles past me, and I forget my locker and follow him. As soon as he hits the stairs, I thump after him. Glancing over his shoulder, he spots me coming and scowls.

"What do you want?"

Before he can get any farther, I grab his shirt and haul him down the last of the stairs and around the corner. Pushing him back against the wall, I keep him in place with my arm across his chest and demand some answers.

"What happened this weekend?"

"I'm not saying shit until you back the hell off, man. Let me go." His scrawny arms wrestle me off him and I step back.

Tugging his shirt straight, he gives me another heated glare.

I step back into his space with a look of warning and he raises his hands. "All right. Chill out."

"What happened?"

"I take it you're referring to the Max gossip circulating. Why do you even care?"

"Tell me what happened," I growl.

Roman sighs, running a hand through his hair before quickly mumbling out the truth. "Velocity had an audition at this new club in Brazenwood and Max skipped out on an important baseball game to be there. Her dad went nuts, and it only got worse when her uncle was dragged out back and beaten because he owes the owner big bucks."

"Mendez?" I frown.

"Nah, the club's owned by some Santiago guy. Came across from Reno. He must have some kind of understanding with the Mendez brothers or something, because I didn't see any of them around."

I scowl, my insides twitching as I think of Nick and the stuff he used to do in Brazenwood. He never told me who he was working for, but I always assumed it was for the Mendez brothers. What if it was someone else?

"Is Chloe okay?" I mutter without thinking.

"Chloe?" Roman frowns. "It was Max who got dragged into it, trying to save her uncle. In the end her dad showed up, and all Cairo's told me is that deep shit went down and Max's dad had to pay for his brother's release. He's now been shipped to Florida and she's on lockdown until graduation."

My eyebrows flicker with a frown. "Is she okay?"

"They're both pretty gutted, but everyone's safe, yeah."

"Did the family get threatened?" My insides ping tight. The thought of Chloe getting mixed up with those assholes sends genuine fear spiking through me.

"Barlow dealt with it. Apparently everyone's in the clear, but that doesn't change the fallout, you know?"

"Yeah," I sigh, my shoulders slumping.

"Why do you even care?" His brown eyes try to read me.

I back away from him, shoving my hands in my pockets and growling, "I don't."

He can probably see right through my big fat lie, but I walk away before he can analyze me. Shit. I shouldn't have asked him anything. Chloe could have told me what I wanted to know. But I'm going to be busy breaking up with her when we chat.

Fuck!

I don't want to do it, but the shit that went down this weekend is just another reason to. Chloe needs to stay away from me and out of Brazenwood. Her father putting Max on lockdown is probably the safest move. I kind of hope he does it for Chloe too.

I hate the idea of her being anywhere near that kind of danger.

"Vincent?"

I jerk and glance to my right. Chloe's standing at the bottom of the stairwell, her blue eyes glistening as she drinks me in.

The expression on her face stuns me and I can't move for a moment.

She's so freaking beautiful.

And I don't deserve that relieved smile on her face.

Jumping off the stairs, she rushes toward me, taking my hand and pulling me into the private alcove where we've met before. As soon as we're safely tucked away, she wraps her arms around my shoulders and clings tight.

"It's so good to see you," she murmurs against my neck.

I want to pull her close, envelop her in a hug that shows her what I'm feeling.

But I can't.

Rubbing her side, I gently step back.

She gazes up at me, her expression confused and curious. "Are you okay? Where have you been all week? I've been worried sick. They didn't hurt you again, did they?"

"I'm fine," I rasp, gently plucking her hand off my face as I try to distance myself.

She's making it damn hard.

I love how much she cares about me.

I don't want to let that go.

But if I love her, then I have to.

"I wanted to see you so badly yesterday. I nearly drove across town to try and find your place, but... Max needed me, and my parents are being super strict about letting us leave the house. My dad had..." She shakes her head. "I have so much to tell you."

My expression crumples with despair.

I want to hear it. I want to be transported to that pile of musty sheets in the greenhouse and sit with her all day so she can tell me everything in detail.

But not even the greenhouse is safe anymore.

I feel like nowhere is.

"Vincent?" Chloe touches my face again. "What's the matter? Talk to me."

"I can't." I clear my throat, hoping to strengthen my voice. "This isn't going to work."

"What isn't?" Her face puckers with confusion.

I look to the floor between our feet and manage to croak, "Us."

"What?" She jolts with surprise.

"I shouldn't have told you I loved you. I just got caught up in the moment and I said it because I wanted to make out with you." I rush through my rehearsed speech. It sounds wooden and turns me into the world's biggest asshole. "But I was wrong. You're not the girl for me, and I'm sorry for leading you on. I—"

"You're lying." She cuts me off, crossing her arms and staring at me with eyes that are rapidly filling with tears.

Shit. Chloe, don't cry.

I clench my jaw and look at the wall. "I'm not lying. It's better if we're not together."

At least that's the truth… in some ways. Not being with her keeps her safe.

I glance at her, waiting for her next argument.

But all I can see is trembling lips and a bunched chin. She's fighting the tears as best she can, but she's going to lose.

"Please don't do this," she whispers. "Vincent, you don't—"

She reaches for me, but I flick her hand off my arm. "It's over, Chloe. It never should have happened in the first place."

I'm trying to sound harsh to make my point, but it only hurts more.

The ache in my chest is going to annihilate me, so I dive out of that alcove and head for the stairs.

I nearly make it.

But then I catch her sob.

It's a heart-wrenching, pitiful sound that matches the silent cry ripping through my chest.

I grip my head and mutter to myself, "Do the right thing. Fucking do the right thing."

But I can't.

I can't walk away from that cry.

Closing my eyes, I battle it out in my chest and slowly rotate on my heel. Shuffling back down the hallway, I find Chloe against the wall, her hands covering her face. She whimpers into them, the sound a pure kind of torture that hurts worse than Diego's fists.

I lean my shoulder against the wall and softly murmur, "I'm such a fucking liar."

She goes still, then slowly drops her hands. Her face is streaked with tears that I can't help but brush away with my knuckles.

Her blue eyes are bright with confusion and I dip my head, humiliated by my own weakness. "I'm trying so hard to do the right thing. I *should* walk away and leave you the hell alone. But now that I'm actually trying to do it, I can't." Cupping her cheek, I flash a little of the agony I'm feeling. "I love you, Chloe. I love everything about you, from that stubborn streak of yours that I'm sure will drive me crazy, to that beautiful heart, which I want to own and cherish for as long as I can."

Her lips pull into the smallest of smiles.

"You wouldn't smile if you knew what an asshole I was. If I were a good guy, I'd dump you and walk away. I'd do everything in my power to keep you safe. But I can't listen to you crying, and I can't walk off making you believe that I don't love you."

"I love you too," she whispers, lurching into my arms.

This time I hold her. I wrap my arms around her and we cling to each other.

She brushes her fingers through the back of my hair and the resolve I was trying so hard to stick to crumbles to dust. I won't be able to pull a stunt like this again.

I don't know what the hell I'm supposed to do, but somehow I have to keep this girl safe while not breaking her heart.

Splaying my hand across her back, I glide it up her spine until I'm holding the back of her neck. Her skin is soft and warm beneath my fingers and I'm not sure how I'll let her go. I wish the universe could suck us up to space—somewhere safe and private where I could tell her everything and we could find our way forward.

I wish I could take her hand and sneak out of school and then just drive until we're in the middle of nowhere, safe from everything that's trying to pull us apart.

But reality doesn't work that way.

The bell rings, reminding us that we're still juniors at Armitage High. That I have no money to support her or look after her. That driving to the middle of nowhere will achieve nothing in the long run.

Chloe pulls out of my embrace. Holding my

cheeks, she drinks me in with a sweet smile. "I don't know why you just tried to do that, but I'm guessing we need to talk."

"Yeah," I rasp.

She glances down the hallway. "Dad's on high alert, and I can't afford to skip class right now."

"It's okay. I know." I brush my lips against hers. "But we can't meet on my side of town anymore. It's too dangerous." I wince.

The worry skittering across her face fills me with a mixture of warmth and fear. She cares so damn much about me. I don't deserve it, but I don't know how to walk away from it either.

"We'll find a way." Her smile tries to break through my anxiety. "I don't know how yet, but one day I'm going public with you, Vincent Mancini, and everyone's going to know how much I care about you."

She rises to her tiptoes, owns me with a short, searing kiss and then races off to class. I flop against the wall, watching her blonde hair fly, and all I can manage is a giddy, euphoric laugh.

It's surreal.

This whole thing.

I don't know whether I'm a fucking idiot or the luckiest guy on the planet.

Maybe both.

#31

CHLOE

A Thought

Vincent trying to break up with me was just weird.

For a second, I seriously thought he meant it, and my heart had never hurt so badly in my life. I was all set on telling him my news about the club and Max and that woman I'm trying to remember.

But then he totally distracted me by lying.

And then he came back and told the truth.

I feel kind of wrung out. This weird blend of elation and confusion.

He must have tried to dump me for a really good reason and I'm desperate to find out what it is, but with Max going through her crisis and my parents on full alert right now, it's kind of hard to move.

Vincent and I need some decent time together so we can talk this all through. I have to know what went down at his place last week. I need to figure out why he was trying to distance himself.

His family must have said something to him to make him scared. Shit, I have to get him out of that place.

Drying my hands on the dishtowel, I leave Mads to finish up the dishes and walk to my room. I need to get my homework done, although it's going to be freaking impossible to think about Biology when all I want to do is figure out Vincent and how to set him free.

I want to be with him.

I want to rescue him.

I want Dad to see him for who he really is.

Opening my laptop, I start searching Nick's case again. I have a bunch of searches in my Google history and go through some of those, rereading the articles and trying to find nuggets of truth within the lies.

"Hey, Chloe."

I jump a mile when Dad greets me. Slapping my laptop closed, I give myself away without thinking. Dad's eyebrows dip together as he moves from my doorway and further into my room.

"What are you doing?"

"Homework." I blink, then cringe.

I am so not getting away with this lie right now.

And with everything Max has been doing, Dad's not letting a single thing slide.

Stopping by the edge of my bed, he points to my laptop. "Open it."

"Dad..."

"Open it!"

With a soft huff, I do as I'm told and spin the computer so he can look at my screen.

He perches on the edge of my bed and quickly scans the front article before shooting me a dry glare. "You still on this?"

"I'm sorry." I shrug. "But I just can't seem to let it go. Nick Mancini is innocent, I'm sure of it."

"Chloe." Dad kind of groans my name while rubbing his forehead the way Max does when she's stressed. "Why won't you just believe me when I tell you the Mancinis are bad?"

"And why won't you believe me when I tell you they're not *all* bad?"

"Just because Vincent saved you that night doesn't make his brother innocent! I can show you

260

the case file. The evidence is substantial and pretty damning."

"I think the case files have been fudged. I think it's one big cover-up. Just like the way Luke set up Vincent."

Dad huffs and lets out a hard snicker. "Luke tried to set Vincent up for stealing. It's hardly murder."

"It's still a crime. It's still injustice!"

Dad looks tired as he sags forward, resting his elbows on his knees and shaking his head. "We don't always get justice, Chloe. And I told you, I can't reopen a case unless I have a decent reason to."

"And that's what I'm trying to find for you."

He snaps up straight and turns to me. "You stay away from this. You're not a cop, and I don't want you getting in trouble."

"If you think I'm wrong, then there won't be any trouble," I retort.

His eyes narrow to a glare that's strong enough to make me apologize.

"I'm sorry, okay? Something just feels off and I can't turn my back on it."

"Please try." Dad's expression bends, the hardness being melted by a look of desperate pleading. "I need my family safe, and after everything Max and Conrad went through this weekend, I just need you to drop this for a little bit."

Closing my laptop with a sigh, I splay my fingers

over the gray machine and look at him.

"So you're dropping it?"

I shrug. "That's what you want me to do."

"But will you?" He leans in, studying my expression.

I tip my head, softening my gaze and talking quietly. "Dad, I know you're hurting right now. Max giving up baseball, Uncle Conrad...all these people lying to you. People you thought you could trust. But can I make a point that you'll probably hate?"

His eyebrows dip into a sharp V.

"Maybe none of them would have lied if they weren't so worried about your reaction. Maybe...they would have come to you for help instead."

"Are you trying to say I'm some kind of scary beast or something?"

"Sometimes," I whisper so softly that maybe he can't hear me.

He does.

I can tell by the look on his face.

Reaching for his hand, I curl my fingers around his and smile. "Dad, I love you. And I know how much you love us too, but you can't keep putting your dreams and expectations on Max this way. You can't do that to any of us. These are *our* lives. And I know you want to protect us, but you can't do that forever. You need to let us figure out our own mistakes, work out our own dreams."

"I'm letting you follow your dreams," he mumbles. "You want to save the world. I'm all for that."

I grin. "And what if I fall for someone you don't think is good enough for me?"

"You mean how Max has fallen for Cairo? And apparently there's nothing I can do about it!" he spits.

"Well, Dad, there isn't. They like each other, a lot, and if you just gave the guy a chance, you'd see how good he and Max are together. He'll take care of her, you know?"

"I thought that was my job," Dad mutters.

"It was, but she's not your baby anymore. None of us are."

Dad cringes, his jaw working to the side as he tries to take in this weird role-reversal. I'm kind of reeling too, but it's one of those golden moments I have to snatch and hold for as long as I can.

I'm basically lecturing my father and he's listening.

Who knows where this could lead?

If he buys into this conversation, it could open up a whole new world where Vincent Mancini might not get judged as Satan the second he walks through my door.

"Chloe..." Dad squeezes my hand with a sigh. "While you're under my roof, whether you like it or not, you are my responsibility. And you may not be babies, but I love you and care about you enough to protect you. So if you're trying to help Max get out of her grounding, it's not going to work. I'll let her play guitar for this prom thing, but she still has to be taken to and from school, and her weekends will be spent playing baseball or hanging out here. I'm not changing my mind on that."

I nod.

"And as for you, leave this Mancini thing alone. If you're right and it is some big cover-up, then it could lead to trouble. And I never want to walk into another situation where my daughter's life is threatened. Do you get me?"

"Yes, Dad."

"Paying that Santiago guy was one of the hardest things I've ever had to do. I want that asshole to go down. And maybe once I've dealt with him, maybe then I'll spare a thought or two for Nick Mancini, okay?"

His little speech gives me hope and for a second I have the fleeting thought that maybe I should tell him everything I already know. Tell him what Vincent and I got up to over Spring Break.

But instinct warns me to shut the hell up. Dad's just held out an olive branch that will snap in half the second I admit to sneaking around.

He'll compare me to Max and what she's gotten up to. He'll picture me in *Escapar* with that Santiago guy and his fear will have me on permanent lockdown the way Max is. We already have to ask for permission every time we leave the house. Both my parents are asking for every last detail before we walk out the door.

I guess I can understand why. That night at the club must have scared the crap out of Dad.

The look on his face as he thundered out of there with Max.

The club.

Outside the club, with that woman I still can't figure out.

Her beautiful face flashes through my mind—her dark hair, perfectly shaped eyebrows, flawless makeup...the beauty spot on her upper lip.

My insides ping as a voice flitters through the back of my mind.

"She even had a beauty spot on her upper lip."

Who said that to me?

"Now get on with your homework." Dad leans across to kiss my cheek before lumbering out of the room.

As soon as he's cleared the door, I whip my laptop open and start a new search: *Luisa Garcia Escapar Brazenwood.*

A photo pops up of the petite woman dwarfed between two tall men. It's an article about the Summer Rock Festival auditions and how Tomas Santiago and his brother-in-law and business partner,

Donny Garcia, are hosting the event.

I enlarge the image and squint at the screen, spying the black spot on her upper lip. I can picture someone tapping her upper lip as she describes it to me.

"Camila." I gasp as the thing I've been trying to remember since Saturday night finally pops into my conscience.

Todd McCrae's girlfriend described Luisa Garcia in detail when she told me about the lovely female detective who looked like a model and even had a beauty spot on her upper lip.

The woman who came and took away Todd's stuff was no detective.

That was the sister of Tomas Santiago—the guy who threatened my family.

I have another dot. Another piece of the puzzle.

Now I just need to figure out how it all fits together

#32

VINCENT

It's Time to Talk

I'm weak, but I'm happy.

I'm living in a constant state of worry, yet all I have to do is catch one of Chloe's smiles and I'm brought home again.

I should have broken up with her.

But I couldn't.

And so I'm trying to make it work.

We still need to have our big talk. I have to tell her what Enzo is expecting of me, and she needs to give me the full rundown of Max's horror at the club in Brazenwood.

It's kind of impossible to find the time at school. Students are everywhere, always watching. We can't exactly talk in Biology, and sneaking away to that alcove only gives us enough time for a quick chat, nothing serious.

Chloe's been sticking close to Max this week. Her big sister's needed the support to tell her parents what she really wants. Apparently she's calling a family meeting tonight and she's freaking out. Chloe has to be there for backup.

Her sisters still don't know about our relationship and Chloe's obviously not prepared to tell them yet. I kind of don't want her to. This secrecy provides a certain amount of cover until everything blows over and we can figure out how to tell the world we're together.

Will that ever happen?

Are we dreaming?

I have no idea how I'm going to get Enzo off my back. He currently thinks I'm working Chloe for any new information. I've fed him a couple of half-truths to keep him happy.

Chief Barlow's attention has been captured by a new guy in Brazenwood—some Santiago dude. It was enough to make Enzo smile.

"He won't get anywhere in Brazenwood, but if it keeps his beady eyes off us then all the better."

He sniffed an arrogant sniff and chuckled before walking out of the room to call his half-brother, Geri.

I don't know what the hell he's up to, and I don't want to know. He'll definitely take advantage of the fact that Chief Barlow's distracted.

Shit, I wish I didn't know him. I wish he wasn't my family.

Stalking to my locker, I glare at the two girls loitering in front of it until they scamper away.

With an irritated huff, I fling it open and then my insides simmer to a soft glow as I reach for the white piece of paper.

I'm not sure how much longer I can go without having our talk.

Can you meet me on Friday night or the weekend?

Rahn said she'll cover for me.

I can catch the bus somewhere. Just give me a time and place.

I have so much to tell you. Please don't make me wait much longer.

Love you xx

C

Scrambling for a pen, I rip a sheet of paper from the back of my closest book and write back.

Friday night. I'll be there.
I hate you catching the bus though. Can I pick you up from Rahn's place or is that too risky?
Can't wait to hang out.
I miss you xx
V

Rahn's place is kind of risky. I'll sneak out of her room and run down the street. There's a bus stop at the corner of Stanton and Emery. I'll wait for you there.

Maybe we can head somewhere out of town so I can tell you everything...and catch up on all the kisses I've been missing.

Is eight okay? xx

C

I'll be there.
And I know just the place.
Kiss you soon xx

V

#33

CHLOE

A Bus Out of Town

"Thank you so much for covering for me." I squeeze Rahn in a tight hug, knowing how much this means. My parents grilled me before I left the house, wanting to know exactly what Rahn and I would be up to. She played along like a champ when she came to pick me up.

Her tiny fingers dig into my hoodie as she hugs

FOUL PLAY

me back. "Be safe, okay?"

"I will be." I lean back with a smile. "He's picking me up from the bus stop at the end of your street. It's going to be fine."

"Do you know what time you'll be back?"

"Not sure yet." I wince. "We seriously have a lot to talk about."

Her lips curl into a half-hearted smile. "I'm pretty sure you're not just going to be talking."

I can feel myself turning red and dip my head to hide the warm current buzzing through my veins.

Rahn snickers. "You know you've got it bad, right?"

"Yeah." I give her a dreamy smile. "I've got it real bad."

"And I'm pretty sure he does too. I caught him looking at you the other day in Biology. He had the sweetest expression on his face." Her brown eyes search my face and it looks like she's trying to smile, but she can't quite muster one. "You know I wouldn't be helping you if I didn't..." She shakes her head. "I can just sense how much you mean to each other. The way you talk about him gives everything away."

"I only tell you." I grip her wrists. "Thank you for letting me be honest. Thank you for keeping my big secret. And I'm sorry if you feel like I've taken advantage of our friendship or..."

She lets out a short sigh. "I have to be honest,

sometimes it's felt like that."

My insides squeeze with guilt, my dreamy expression disintegrating. "I'm sorry. Rahn, I'm so sorry."

She raises her eyebrows. I can tell she appreciates my apology when a slow smile forms on her lips. "You love him, and I'm pretty sure he loves you. I can't stand in the way of that. So, even though I wish you were staying to hang out with me tonight, I understand. Just don't forget about me. You're the nicest friend I've ever had, and I don't want to—"

"I could never forget about you!" I pull her into a fierce hug. "You're the nicest friend *I've* ever had, and I love hanging out with you. I just can't wait for the day when we can all hang out together. I don't like sneaking around and hiding."

"I know. I wish you didn't have to. From what you've told me, Vincent is a sweetheart, and I want the world to see that."

"They will." I nod. "One day, everyone will know how amazing he is. And tomorrow, after my baseball game, I'm coming straight back here to spend the rest of the weekend with you. We'll paint our nails and—"

"Talk about Vincent." Rahn rolls her eyes.

"No." I giggle and lightly slap her arm. "We don't have to talk about him at all."

"Oh yes we do. I'm going to need specific deets

about tonight. There won't be enough time in the morning." She winks at me, confirming what an amazing person she is.

I beam her a grateful smile and she laughs at me.

"Seriously, Chloe, your love for the guy fuels my hope. One day I'll find someone who makes me smile the way you do when you're talking about him."

My eyes glass over for a second, my huge grin speaking for me.

Rahn giggles and pulls me into another hug before guiding me to her window. "Get going, you romantic sap."

Before slipping out, I spin back to double-check. "Are you sure you won't get in trouble for this?"

"The boys are asleep and my parents are zoned out in front of a movie. Dad wouldn't come in here if his life depended on it and Mom's too tired to move. We're seriously in the clear."

"Okay." I give her a relieved smile. "Don't wait up."

She giggles. "I can't wait to hear every little detail."

I let out a giddy laugh before jumping out the window. I land with a soft thud in the grass and sneak away from the house.

The bus stop is just down the road. It's well lit, and I don't feel nervous as I wait for Vincent's car.

In fact, I'm excited for the first ten minutes, but the

feeling starts to fade the longer I wait. After half an hour, a bus and no blue car, I'm starting to worry.

Where is Vincent?

Crap, I hope his family aren't being assholes.

Have they hurt him again?

I worry my lip and wait another thirty minutes until I'm absolutely convinced he won't show.

I so badly want to catch the next bus to his place, ask around until I find his house, then knock on the door until they let me see him.

But that won't fly.

It's the last thing Vincent needs right now.

Tears sting my eyes. I glance down the street and contemplate going back to Rahn. She'll give me a hug and listen to me cry.

I'm gutted. Vincent and I never really get to see each other and this would have been the perfect night to tell him about Luisa Garcia and everything that went down at that club in Brazenwood.

I'm desperate to hear about his home life and why he wasn't at school that week.

I want to be a part of his life. I want him to be free to tell me anything.

A bus approaches and I step back from the curb until it pulls to a stop. A tired woman with short brown hair steps off and glances my way before turning down the street. Next comes an elderly man. He's taking his time on the steps and I nearly offer to help him, but I'm distracted by the bus destination sign that switches from Armitage to Cullington.

Cullington.

Club Matrix is in Cullington, and my research has told me that Luisa Garcia's husband owns Club Matrix too. I wonder if I could find any new information there?

I wonder if Luisa will be there tonight. If I bumped into her, would she answer a question or two?

Probably not.

I should just walk back to Rahn's place, but...

What if there's some evidence at the club? Someone else I could talk to?

This might be my only opportunity. Rahn's covering for me. I'm not on a curfew.

I'm—

"Last run for the night, honey. Are you getting on?" The bus driver gives me an impatient look.

It takes me less than a second to decide, and before I can think better of it, I jump onto the first step and pull out my wallet.

It's a pricier ride than usual because the bus is heading out of Armitage. It was an initiative pushed through by our town council. They worked in with the Cullington town council and arranged for a bus service in Armitage to help out some of the poorer families who couldn't afford to own a car. It also includes an early morning and late evening commuter bus that takes workers to and from Cullington. Being the bigger city, Cullington has more work available, but Armitage has the cheaper housing, so it's mutually beneficial for both towns.

Paying my fare, I walk to the back of the bus while the driver heads out of town.

It's not until we're taking that final turn out of Armitage that it starts to sink in how reckless I'm being.

How the hell am I supposed to get back?

Hopefully Uber will save my ass. It'll be a really pricey fare, but quite possibly worth it.

I might as well use my cover for something useful, and what's more useful than checking out a certain club that could unearth a bunch of answers? Dad made us swear we wouldn't go anywhere near that club in Brazenwood again.

But I'm not going there.

Even so, Dad will kill me if he finds out.

And there's a strong chance Vincent will be pretty pissed too.

But it's for a really good cause.

The sooner we get Nick exonerated, the better. Vincent needs his brother and tonight, I need to unveil another layer of truth that might help in setting the guy free.

Dad needs proof before he'll reopen the case. Well, I'm going to find him some.

#34

VINCENT

No Way Out

The handcuff around my wrist and bedframe both rattle as I fight my imprisonment.

Shit! Shit! Shit!

I can't believe this is happening right now.

Chloe will have been waiting at the bus stop for me and I never showed. Standing there in the dark, vulnerable and alone, thinking I don't care enough about her to show up.

Fuck!

Desperate tears scorch my eyes, but I ward them off with a sniff.

I want to kill Diego.

Straining against the cuffs, I let out another roar as pain fires through my wrist and I relive the moment I was put here…

I was cocky enough to spin the keys around my finger as I walked for the front door. I was about to get some one-on-one privacy with my girlfriend. We'd talk, I'd hold her, she'd kiss me. It was impossible to dampen my mood.

I nearly made it too.

My hand was on the freaking doorknob when Enzo stopped me.

"Where are you going?"

"Out," I mumbled, yanking the door open.

But then Diego and Rex were there, slamming it shut again. Diego's dark eyes glinted with amusement as he eyed me up and down.

"You going to see her?"

I glared at him before staring back at the door. "You told me to spy, didn't you?"

Enzo snickered behind me and I caught Diego looking at him out of the corner of my eye.

Dread surged through me, unease cloaking me

like a rain cloud.

"I'm coming with you," Diego told me, like it was no big deal.

"Like hell," I muttered, my voice dark with anger.

"I won't get in the way." He gave me a sly smile. "I just want to see what she knows."

I turned, eyeing up Enzo and trying to put on the best frickin' show I could. "You think I'm lying to you?"

"He'll just watch from the background." Enzo shrugged. "No big deal."

"Forget it." I walked away from the door, figuring I'd sneak out the bathroom window.

Diego grabbed my jacket and pulled me around. "What's your problem, man? I'll just be watching."

I flicked him off me and growled, "She won't say anything if you're there. Why would she trust an asshole like you?"

My insult definitely stung, but he clenched his jaw and gave me a tight smile. "I'll hide in the shadows. Shit, I'll even close my eyes when you're having your way with her."

My fingers curled into a fist.

"We just need to know that you're doing your job." Enzo slid his hands into his pockets, looking so calm and in control.

It was completely opposite to the volcanic eruption in my chest. Rage was on the cusp of breaking free, but I had to keep it together for Chloe. I'd never make it out of the house otherwise.

Gritting my teeth, I managed a controlled reply. "I'm not going if you are. I can't act casual if you're watching me. I don't care where the hell you hide. I either go alone or I don't go at all."

Diego and Enzo shared another chilling look and I knew my number was up before they even grabbed me.

I fought and yelled, "Don't touch me! Get your fucking hands off me!"

I screamed and kicked the entire way to my room, making all three work up a sweat in order to contain me.

I was fuming, but was at least comforted by the fact that I could sneak out of the bathroom window in about half an hour. I was pissed that I'd be late, but I was pretty sure Chloe would wait for me. She's that kind of girl.

"You're a lying little shit." Diego shoved me back and I stumbled over to my bed. "Where's your family loyalty, huh?"

"Why the fuck would I be loyal to you?" I stood back up, facing him head on.

The question scored me a punch in the face, but it was a slight misfire and didn't really hurt. I was tempted to launch myself back at him, but Rex was right there and I'd have no chance in hell of getting to Chloe if they beat me again.

Enzo stood in the doorway, studying me with the kind of look that tempered my rage and replaced it with a healthy dose of dread.

His lips twitched in thought and then he crucified me by muttering, "Cuff him."

"No!" I surged forward, trying to run between them. But Diego was on me in a second, wrestling me back to my bed. Rex grabbed my other side, making my fight worthless.

I roared as Diego pinned me down, digging his knee into my chest while Enzo yanked my wrist up to the bedframe. I struggled and strained against him. I made him work for it until that sickening click of metal sealed my fate.

"You fuck!" I screamed at him, tugging against my restraints.

"You don't want to go out. Fine. You stay here. Maybe these guys can go instead. I'm sure they'd love to find out whatever secrets she has to tell you."

My nostrils flared, desperation firing through me. I tried to hide it by smashing my teeth together and keeping my rage in check.

"Where were you meeting her?"

I shook my head and he slapped me hard.

"Tell me where she is."

"I hate you." I looked him in the eye so he knew I was telling the truth.

He gave me a smarmy smile before turning to his son. "Start at the greenhouse."

"No!" I roared, figuring I may as well play on it. If I acted desperate enough, then they'd assume that was our meeting place.

It could potentially get me beat later, but at least Chloe would be safe.

Diego hasn't gotten back yet. He'll probably bust open the door, saying she wasn't there and demanding more goods, but I'm not giving him shit.

It's been over an hour since I was supposed to meet Chloe. She would have given up by now and will hopefully be tucked safely inside Rahn's house.

She'll be sad I didn't come.

Hopefully I can get out in the morning. Maybe Selena will take pity and sneak in here with the key.

I don't care if it's a risk, but I'll get away to find her. I just need her to know that I still care. That if I could, I'd be by her side always.

Closing my eyes, I thump my head against the pillow and stare into the darkness, wishing a hundred times over that I'd never been born a Mancini.

#35

CHLOE

A Shocking Theory

The walk from the bus stop to the club is about ten minutes. I walk damn fast, looking over my shoulder as I go.

This is seriously a bad idea. I shouldn't be doing this on my own.

But I'm here now.

I'm in this.

I can't turn back before at least checking out the club.

Lining up behind a group of girls, nerves skitter through me as I glance up at the club sign. The green neon glows against the dark background.

I hope she's here. I hope my effort is worth this.

The bouncer raises his barely there eyebrows at me. "ID."

I glance up at his dark, round face, instant dread pooling in my stomach.

Shit! I don't have a fake ID.

With a sweet smile, I pull out my license, expecting a cool rejection, but instead he tips his head for the door.

I stand there, kind of surprised, until he starts laughing at me. "If you're waiting for a stamp, I'm not giving you one."

"A stamp?"

"No stamp, no liquor."

"Oh." I smile. "Well, that's okay. I wasn't planning on drinking."

"Then go on. Get in there. The dance floor's waiting." He winks. "Anyone gives you trouble, you come see me."

"Thanks." I grin and slide past him.

Strobe lights are flickering as I edge into the crowded room. The thick bass pumps right through me. "Move, Shake, Drop" is impossible not to dance to and my hips wiggle a little as I ease my way around the edge of the dance floor.

I'm scanning the crowd the whole time, looking for a short Latina woman in tight clothes with perfect makeup and a beauty mark on her upper lip.

Stopping near the bar, I rise to my tiptoes and scan the crowd again. The strobe lights are off and there's now a red hue over the crowd. I can't see Luisa anywhere, although it's going to be kind of impossible to spot her like this. I need to get in there and start circulating. Hopefully, if she's here, I'll bump into her.

Or I'll spot something else that might trigger another clue.

Luisa obviously knew Cairo, the way they were talking to each other, so if I'm lucky enough to see her, I'll drop his name to make a connection and then try to pull her into a quiet corner for a chat.

I'm still not sure exactly what I'll say to her or how I'm going to ease into my questions about why she pretended to be a detective.

Should I even ask her that? Is that too confronting? Will it make her back off completely? Or kick me out of the club?

I worry my lip as I try to figure out the best way to approach this.

"What are you so worried about, sweetness?" A guy I don't know appears beside me.

He's tall and lean, with an angular face and short blond hair. His blue eyes are glassy with a mixture of alcohol and lust. I swallow and inch away from him.

"Where you going?" He jumps in front of me. "Do you want to dance?"

"No thanks." I shake my head and try to smile at him. "I'm just waiting for my boyfriend."

He clicks his tongue and looks over his shoulder, but still doesn't give up.

Dammit.

His breath is warm and repulsive as he gets in my space. "What's he doing leaving you standing all alone here?"

"He's in the bathroom," I grit out and quickly muscle my way into the crowd.

Shit, I hope he doesn't follow me.

Glancing over my shoulder, I spot his head above the crowd and roll my eyes.

He's not going to let me get away that easily and will no doubt keep up his little flirt-a-thon until my boyfriend shows up.

Which is never.

The thought sits like a rock in my belly.

I'm positive Vincent's been held up by his asshole relatives, and that's why I need to be here, proof-hunting.

Finding a sheltered corner near the bathrooms, I stand on a step that leads to an emergency exit and scan the club again.

By the time my gaze has swept the floor, Mr. Blue Eyes has spotted me and is working his way over with a drink in each hand.

Shit! He obviously doesn't buy my boyfriend story and is now set on getting me drunk too.

With a little huff, I glance over my shoulder and spot the exit sign. It's for emergencies only and if I pop it open, some kind of alarm will no doubt go off.

Crap, I wish Vincent were here. He wouldn't let anyone near me.

I love how protected I feel when I'm around him.

Blue Eyes is getting closer.

What am I supposed to do?

Jumping down from my spot, I weave around the tables and consider making my way to the bouncer at the front door, but then I spot an archway to my right. It probably leads backstage. If I can duck in there without the guy noticing me, he can spend the rest of the evening searching the club and maybe I can sneak out some back staff entrance or something.

Running for the black archway, I duck through it and keep walking until I reach backstage.

I pause at the end of the corridor, wondering which way to turn when low chatter catches my ear.

I'm probably not supposed to be back here, so rather than pretending to be lost and heading back out to the club, I duck behind the first door I can find.

It's white and has a big PRIVATE sign on the front, but there's no light coming beneath the door, and I'll only be in here a second. It's not like I'll disturb anyone.

Clicking it shut as quietly as I can, I wince and rest my forehead against the wood. I'll wait two minutes before sneaking back into the corridor.

Seriously, this is not going at all how I planned.

Not that I really planned anything, I just spontaneously jumped on a bus and came here. I'm an idiot. How am I going to explain this to anyone?

Rolling my eyes at myself, I lean my ear against the wood to try to hear if the coast is clear, but I'm distracted by a noise behind me.

Glancing over my shoulder, I gaze into the shadowy darkness. I must be in some kind of office. I can make out a desk shape, and that thing to my left might be a couch.

A light from the room next door pops on and I flinch as it streams through the square window in the adjoining door.

There's a soft giggle and then some kind of whispered conversation. The woman sounds Latina. I can't hear what she just said, but I don't miss the husky reply from a voice that sounds totally familiar.

Where do I know that voice from?

I creep toward the light, curiosity drowning out

the cautious warning in the back of my mind.

"You hungry?" the woman asks.

"Only for you." The man's reply is followed by a playful growl that elicits another giggle.

I'm at the window now. I shouldn't peek. I shouldn't look.

But I know that voice.

Resting my fingers on the edge of the frame, I slowly shift my weight until I can see clearly into the room.

It's a small space with another couch and a desk— seems like the mirror image of this room.

There's a woman sitting on the edge of the big black desk, her legs spread to accommodate the man standing in front of her.

They're making out—the heated kind that will lead to sex.

I'll be leaving before that happens, but I just want to get a look at their faces. He's kissing her neck, causing her to moan and dig her manicured nails into his dark hair.

I swallow, my breath hitching as she tips her head back, and I see Luisa Garcia. Even though I can't see her entire face, I can tell it's her.

The man glides his tongue up her neck, sucking the end of her chin, before standing tall to shed his jacket.

Holy shit!

It's Milo Carter.

Mayor of Armitage.

Holden's dad.

Mr. Family Values.

He's about to have sex with a married woman...who isn't his wife. And from the way they're acting with each other, this isn't the first time.

I'm so shocked I can't move. My eyes are bulging big-time as I gape at the couple about to get it on.

And suddenly a thought hits me.

Maybe I'm not the only person to witness this.

Maybe a certain reporter saw something he shouldn't have and was going to write all about it in the *Armitage Gazette*.

News like that would crucify a mayor.

News like that needs to be squashed...eliminated.

Erratic breaths punch out of me as I try to wrap my head around my theory.

I'm right. I've got to be right.

Todd McCrae told his girlfriend that he was sitting on something big. This is huge. Was he going to blackmail the mayor?

Did they kill him in anger and then try to cover it up?

Or were they waiting with their guns at the ready? *Nick's* gun at the ready.

Mayor Carter would have the money and power to squash an investigation, and with ties to someone like Luisa Garcia, and her brother Tomas Santiago, they could easily make this thing go away, while setting up Nick Mancini at the same time.

Holy crap!

I have to call Dad.

My hands are shaking as I rip the phone out of my pocket. With trembling fingers, I try to dial my father, but can't even unlock my phone screen without dropping it.

I scramble to catch it before it hits the floor, but all I manage to do is tip the edge of it so it flings sideways and hits the metal paper basket with a loud *thwack*.

Silence follows the unexpected sound and I crouch down against the door, hoping if I stay quiet enough that no one will investigate.

I wait it out, praying my breathing isn't too loud. There's a shuffling on the other side of the door. Neither of them has said anything.

Are they walking out of the room?

My nerves get the better of me and I slowly stand, glancing into the window and letting out a scream when Milo's glare greets me head on.

Stumbling back from the door, I try to make an escape but he's after me in a second, grabbing my waist and pulling me off my feet.

I scream again but he muffles the sound with his hand.

"Shut up," he growls in my ear.

I struggle against him, kicking my legs, determined not to be frozen by fear this time. There'll be no Vincent to rescue me, but I'll fight like a wild cat to get out of this place.

Flailing my legs, I struggle for release as Mayor Carter drags me into the lit office.

"Shut her up." Luisa glances at the door, urgent fear stark on her face.

"I'm trying." Mayor Carter grunts, then roughly releases me. I hit the floor on uneven feet and stumble backward.

My hip whacks into the chair, throwing my balance. I fall with a gasp that is cut short when my head hits the edge of the desk and my world turns an instant shade of black.

#36

VINCENT

An Unwanted Visitor

Selena freed me this morning. She got Enzo's permission, of course.

He would have locked me up all weekend, but Selena has a special way of softening the guy and I've been released in order to go and collect protection money from the Porters and Mr. Giovanni.

I hate this job, but after my fight last night, I have

to do as I'm told or the trouble will only get worse.

Diego came back from the greenhouse in a rage. I managed to convince him that Chloe must have left, or maybe she saw his dumb ass and took off before he saw her.

His eyebrows flickered with a frown and then Enzo was there asking him if he was subtle about it.

Diego couldn't reply which means he hadn't been subtle at all.

That started an argument between the two of them, and I was left cuffed to the bed to wallow in my anger and misery.

I'm still feeling like shit this morning, but I'm heading to Chloe's side of town. Enzo took my keys, so I'm car-less until I return with the protection money. I don't care that I'll be late. I'll find Chloe first, apologize, and then go do my freaking jobs for Enzo.

Shuffling to the bus stop, I kick the ground and scowl at the lady who's staring at me. She frowns right back and shakes her head like I'm a naughty boy who needs a little discipline.

I roll my eyes and glare at the sidewalk.

"Vincent!"

The voice makes my head pop up.

At first I think it's Chloe, but my insides ripple with confusion when I spot Rahn dashing across the street toward me.

What the hell is she doing here?

I glance past her shoulder and squint, trying to see if Chloe's in her car, but Rahn's alone.

Did Chloe send her?

Is she bringing some kind of breakup message?

"What are you doing here?" I snap, as soon as she's within earshot.

"I'm looking for you." Her glare is intense and out of character. Rahn's always so happy, but right now she looks as though she wants to murder me. Shit, Chloe probably spent the night crying in the bed beside her. She's here to lecture me and tell me I'm not good enough for her friend.

I clench my jaw and stare at the ground. "Look, I'm—"

"Where's Chloe?" Rahn cuts me off with a shaky voice.

My head snaps up. "What?"

"I was her cover story so you guys could hang out last night. She was supposed to be back at my place before everyone got up so we could wake up together and look legit. She's due home at ten this morning. They have a baseball game today. So, where is she? Vincent, *where* is she?"

"I don't..." My air supply is cut short as I try to take this in. "I didn't get to see her last night. I couldn't make it."

Rahn's already pale skin turns a sick shade of gray, her anger giving way to all out fear. "Oh my gosh.

She… But she left to see you. She was going to wait at the bus stop for you."

"She didn't come back to your place?" I grab Rahn's shoulders, holding myself steady as she breaks me in half.

"No," Rahn whispers.

"Did you call her?"

"Yes, I called her! I've been trying since I woke up at six. Why do you think I drove over here?"

I can't speak as I shake my head and look around.

I'm trying to think, but it's impossible when fear is pulsing through me like a strobe light.

Did Diego actually get to her?

Was he lying last night when he said she wasn't there?

I'm going to kill him. If he's even breathed near her I'm going to fucking kill him.

#37

CHLOE

A Justifiable Death

My head is killing me.

I don't want to open my eyes and acknowledge the pain.

I just want to float back into oblivion. Things don't hurt in that black abyss. They're not scary either.

Squinting my eyes, I creep them open and the fear that pummeled me seconds before I blacked out

299

returns full force.

My breath hitches as I take in my surroundings. Things are still kind of blurry and blinding as my eyes struggle to focus.

Something is hurting my mouth. I wriggle my jaw and figure out that I'm gagged.

My head hurts. I reach up to investigate what feels like a lump on my forehead but my hands are tied behind my back.

I gasp and wrestle against the hard plastic tie, but that only causes more pain.

Letting out a soft whimper, I wriggle on the hard wooden floor, trying to get my bearings.

I remember Milo Carter and Luisa Garcia kissing. I saw them.

And then I dropped my phone.

I ran.

He caught me.

And then I can't remember.

I must have fallen and hit my head.

Forcing a breath through my nose, I will my erratic heart to calm the hell down.

I need to figure out where I am.

Using the wall behind me, I nudge myself up to a sitting position. My body is aching from spending the night on the floor. Blurry dark images flash through my mind.

My limp body bobbed up and down as someone

carried me over his shoulder.

I was placed on the floor and then I drifted away again.

I rotate my wrists in an effort to ease the cutting plastic, but it only makes my skin hurt more. My shoulders hurt from being forced into this position for too long.

A band of pain is wrapped around my head, but my vision has started to clear.

I can make out the room now. Light is streaming in from a skylight above me. It must be morning.

Shit. I have to get out of here.

Rahn will be crazy with worry. And then my parents are going to find out what I did.

I want my dad.

I want Vincent.

Sniffing at my self-pity, I try to focus back on the things I can control…like figuring out where I am.

The club. I caught the bus to the club last night.

I went out back. I saw what I saw.

And they've taken me somewhere.

I scan the sparsely furnished room. There's a black leather couch in the corner with a glass coffee table in front. Closets line the wall in front of me, and the only other thing of note are the empty coffee mugs on the table.

Did they sit here watching me while I was passed out? Sipping on their freaking coffees?

I close my eyes to ward off the creepy chills climbing my spine.

I feel sick.

Tears threaten to blur my vision, but I quickly blink them away. I need to think. I need to get to a phone and call for help.

I might not know where I am, but I can tell them where I was.

Pushing my back against the wall, I inch my way up like a caterpillar until I'm on my feet. My ankles are tied so I'm going to have to jump to the door. I'll try not to make too much noise.

Pulling in a breath, I steady myself and make a little leap forward, but as soon as I land my world tips sideways and I'm crashing to the floor. I manage to stick out my elbow and stop my head from hitting the wood, but pain radiates up my arm.

I groan and roll onto my back, which hurts so I push over onto my side again and go still when I hear voices outside the door.

"Well, we have to think of something! We can't just leave her here!" a woman snaps.

It must be Luisa.

"I'm not killing her."

"Milo, she has to go. She's seen too much."

"Can't we just pay her off...or scare her into silence?"

"Because it worked so well last time?" Luisa's

voice pitches. "That turned into a complete mess."

"Only because you pulled the trigger."

"We knew that might be a possibility, that's why we covered ourselves. He was asking too much, and I didn't trust him not to take our money and then publish the story anyway! You've seen the photos. They'd destroy us. Your career would be down the toilet, not to mention the fact that my husband will kill me if he knows what I've been doing with you. We killed McCrae for our own safety, and we got away with it."

"It's not going to work like that this time!" Milo argues. "I can't kill Barlow's daughter. He's nothing like Tannon. He will not stop looking until he finds her killer, and he will dig for all the right evidence. He'll bring in support from the FBI if he has to. That guy cannot be stopped. He can't be scared off or paid off."

"You never should have offered him that job," she clips. "I told you it was a mistake."

"Yeah, well, he seemed kind of power hungry, hating his current job. You know the council was putting pressure on me to find someone new. We needed stability after the murder and I wanted to be the guy to supply it. The election's coming up soon and I need to look good. I thought he'd be easy enough to manipulate. I did him a favor, he owed me one. But he's turning out to be way more by the book than I expected. He wasn't like that in college, I swear." Mayor Carter huffs. "The point is, we can't kill his kid."

"So what the hell are we supposed to do?" Luisa sighs and rubs her forehead—I can tell by the way her shadow is moving.

Suddenly the door bursts open.

I shut my eyes, relaxing my body so it looks like I'm sleeping.

I'm woken by a sharp shake to the shoulder. I gasp, my eyes pinging open.

Milo gazes down at me, his expression unreadable.

He's not glaring. He doesn't look angry or scared.

In fact, his lips actually curl into a smile.

"Morning," he greets me softly.

I frown at him.

"Sorry about last night. You fell and bumped your head. I tried to catch you."

My eyes narrow into a glare so he knows I think he's a big fat liar.

He pastes on a politician's smile and helps me sit up. With one swift move, he swoops me into his arms and plops me onto the leather couch.

"You comfortable?"

I give him an incredulous look, which makes him shuffle in his seat and run his fingers over his bottom lip. His movements are twitchy and nervous.

"Chloe, I'm going to take the gag off your mouth. If you scream, I will have to hurt you. Do you understand?"

Fear tries to cut off my air supply and all I can manage is a stiff nod.

Easing the gag down my chin, he lets it rest around my neck while I open and close my mouth a few times.

Sharp steps pull my attention to the door. Luisa is outside. I can tell by the staccato rhythm that she's pacing.

"Tell me what you remember about last night." Mayor Carter's voice is soft and easy.

I sniff, trying to figure out what to say. I don't know where he's going with this and I'm not sure if it's safer to lie or tell the truth.

His hand lands on my knee, his large fingers enveloping my leg. I flinch beneath his touch, but he grips a little tighter, flashing me a desperate look— *do as I say, dammit!* When I still don't respond, his brow flickers with annoyance and he squeezes until pain is shooting both up my thigh and down my shin. "You need to tell me the truth. It's important I know what you remember."

I cry out beneath his grasp and the truth tumbles from me before I can stop it.

"I saw you kissing." My voice is strangled by my discomfort. "You're having an affair with Luisa

Garcia!"

"Okay." Mayor Carter eases his grip but keeps his hand in place. "I'm sure you can understand how highly sensitive that information is. If we let you go back out into the world with this knowledge, would we be able to trust you to keep it to yourself?"

Really? He's trying this?

His cool gaze lands on me, demanding simple compliance.

But what will that mean?

Freedom for a second, but then I'll spend the rest of my life looking over my shoulder, because there is no way a man like this is going to let me walk away with the kind of knowledge I have and not keep an eye on me every step of the way.

It also means that these two will get away with Todd McCrae's murder while an innocent man does *their* time in jail.

I can't live with that.

Nick's innocent. He deserves freedom. Vincent deserves his brother back!

But if I say no, what's going to happen to me?

"I'm sure I can think of some really good incentives to keep you quiet."

"I can't be bought," I rasp, glancing at his hand on my knee and hoping it won't hurt me again.

Mayor Carter huffs, rubbing his sweating forehead with shaky fingers. "So you'd prefer to be threatened, then? Okay, well, I'm sure I can think of numerous ways to destroy your family's life."

"You can't threaten me either," I interject before he starts listing them. "If you want me silent, then you'll have to kill me, and good luck with the wrath my father will rain down on you when he finds out what you've done. You two are murdering liars and I will do nothing to help you keep your secrets. You deserve to rot in jail and Nick Mancini deserves to walk free."

I don't know how my voice has so much strength right now. Maybe it's just pure conviction. The fire raging inside of me will not be contained, and as much as it will hurt my family to lose me, I'm not staying silent.

If my death can bring these two killers to justice then so be it.

Yes, I'm terrified.

But I'm also one hundred percent justified.

Mayor Carter's lips bunch into a tight line, breaths spurting out his nose. "You are a fool." His voice trembles. "Do you understand what you're making me do?"

"I'm not making you do anything. Give it up now. Return me and serve your time. That's your easiest way out of this. Everything else is going to either eat you alive or get you killed."

His eyes flash with warning, but I'm on a roll so I

lay down one more card before he can shut me up.

"You know you can't get away with this. You can't lie forever. The truth will come out one way or another. Do you honestly want to be convicted for killing an innocent teenage girl? How are you supposed to hide it? How are you—"

With a growl, he yanks my gag back into place before giving me a hard shove. I flop back against the couch, my already tender head aching as it hits the leather.

Storming to the door, Mayor Carter spins and points at me. "Making me kill you is a stupid move!" His panic-laced voice reverberates throughout the room. "I didn't go down last time and I won't go down again!"

He slams the door so hard the walls vibrate.

The strength that's been holding me together suddenly disappears. Fear tries to cut off my air supply as I wrestle against the gag and my constraints.

I'm going to die.

I just signed my own freaking death warrant.

And yes, it's for a very good cause, but that doesn't change the fact that I don't really want to stop living today. My death is going to hurt the people I love.

I need to get out of here.

I need to get back to them.

#38

VINCENT

The Wrong Lead

"I have to go," I mutter, spinning away from Rahn and heading to my place.

"Wait! Where?"

"Don't follow me," I call over my shoulder when I hear scuttling feet behind me.

She ignores my request and keeps coming.

I roll my eyes and pick up the pace, hoping to lose

her around the next corner, but I'm jolted to a stop by the very person I'm after.

"Diego!" I roar, sprinting straight at him and tackling him off his feet.

He lands with a surprised thud. It takes him a moment to register what the hell I'm doing and he misses his first block.

My knuckles crunch into his cheek before I grab his collar and shout in his face, "Where is she?"

"Get the fuck off me!" He wrestles against me, powering a fist at my face.

It hurts, but not enough to let him go.

I taste blood and lick my split lip.

"I'm not letting you go until you tell me what you did to her."

"I don't know what the hell you're talking about," he shouts, struggling to free himself. I dig my knee into his chest and grab his hair.

"If you've hurt her, I'm going to kill you."

"I haven't even touched her," he roars. "I couldn't find her last night! Get off me!"

His struggle is growing stronger as his rage builds to a boiling point.

Thumping him back down against the sidewalk, I throw all my weight into keeping him still while I glare at him.

His brown eyes glare back and I can tell he's not lying.

There's no arrogant smirk, just outright confusion and pure rage.

Shit. He hasn't seen her.

He doesn't know where she is.

Which means I have no idea either.

And no easy way of finding her.

Shock makes my muscles slack.

I release my cousin, standing tall and taking a step back while he scrambles to his feet. He's not used to being beat by me, and he'll make me pay for humiliating him.

Lunging forward, he comes at me with his fist and I give him a free right hook.

Rahn gasps while I stumble back and catch myself against a concrete wall.

"You're fucking crazy!" Diego swipes a hand under his red nose. "Dad's going to end you for this."

I ready my fists, but Diego takes off, running home to Enzo. I tip my head back and swallow past the boulder in my throat.

Diego wasn't lying.

So, where's Chloe?

I fear for her more than whatever repercussions await me at home. I have to find my girl. I have to make sure she's safe.

But I don't even know where to start looking.

I gaze across the street, quickly calculating how

long it will take for my family to return and make me pay. I need to get Rahn out of here before she gets hurt.

Turning to face her, I point in the direction of her car. "You've got to go. Get back to your side of town as fast as you can."

"I'm not leaving without you." She shakes her head.

"What?" I frown at her.

"I need you to help me find her. Please. Just come with me." Her voice quavers as she wrings her hands and looks ready to burst into tears.

I can't just leave her to look on her own.

"Where are you going next?"

"Her place."

I shoot her a skeptical frown.

"Yeah, I know it's a long shot, but we have to try. I'd rather show up looking for her than call and send them into a blind frenzy. At least if we're there, we can help. We can...ask her dad for help."

Her expression is kind of agonized as she no doubt reads my mind.

Shit.

Chief Barlow. Yeah, he's going to love me for this one.

Rahn worries her lip while I swipe the blood off my chin and pat my split lip with the end of my finger.

"Here." She rustles around in her bag and holds

out a tissue pack. "You're going to want to clean up before you see him."

I sigh, taking the tissue pack and following Rahn to her car. We need to hurry before Enzo finds us, so I take Rahn's elbow and walk a little faster.

Her car alarm beeps as she unlocks it. Sliding into the passenger seat, I slam the door and ignore the nerves battering me from all sides.

I feel like I'm heading into a war zone and I'm not wearing one scrap of armor.

"You better floor it. I don't want them catching up and following us." I glance over my shoulder to check the coast is clear.

Rahn pulls away from the curb and does as she's told.

We speed back to her side of town while I fight off the storm that's taking me out. Dabbing a tissue against my swollen lip, I try not to give into the waves crashing over me.

I have to stay strong for Chloe. I have to face her dad, her family...do whatever it takes to find her.

I don't know where she is or what kind of trouble she's gotten into. All I know is that if I don't find her, my heart is going to disintegrate into a thousand pieces and I'll never be able to breathe right again.

#39

CHLOE

A Devious Plot

They've moved from outside the door, but I can still hear voices.

Sniffing at my tears, I pull in a slow breath, trying to calm my thundering heart and hear above my internal chaos.

Easing the air between my lips, I suck in another lungful through my nose and slowly start to regulate.

I tip my head to the side and strain to hear the conversation.

It's coming from somewhere to my left. Shuffling along the couch, I inch toward the murmurs until I find a good spot where the muffle becomes a little clearer.

I squint as I concentrate on making out the words.

"I know you don't want to do this … can't give you up … the only choice we have is to eliminate her."

"Who do we use this time? We can't…"

I miss the next part, frowning as Mayor Carter's voice drops too low for me to hear.

"My brother will help me if I ask him to. His money and threats worked last time … warned Barlow what he's capable of."

"Barlow paid him … debt settled. He's not going to push his luck … won't want anything to do with Chloe's disappearance … stupid to take on a cop like him."

"Well Donny's due back tomorrow … clean up this mess today."

"Her family will already be looking for her."

"So we need to move fast, then."

"What are you proposing?"

"We could just make her disappear…sell some kind of runaway story."

I flinch. *As if, lady!*

"It's not her style. The Barlow family sticks together. They're close."

I guess the mayor is a little more observant than I thought. Holden suddenly flashes through my mind, sending a piercing sadness right through my core. I can't believe his dad is plotting my death right now. Holden's going to be devastated.

"Well …" I lose Luisa's voice completely then. It drops down to a small whisper until a few seconds later it rises again. "Stop shaking your head. It worked last time! The setup went down just the way we planned it. We can do that again."

"Last time you stole Donny's phone to send that text! It was an opportune moment. Your husband's out of town right now, so we can't do that again."

"Maybe we could pin it on the Mendez brothers. Tomas has some solid connections in Brazenwood."

"Tomas won't want to get involved!"

"He's my brother! He loves me. He'd do anything to help me."

"And then he can hold it over you for the rest of your life. He'll want to know why you're trying to cover up another murder, and don't tell me you can use the same lie as last time! Besides, he works with Donny now. Aren't you worried it will slip out?"

"If Tomas knows how much I love you and how impossible Donny is to get away from, then he'll help me! We just need to find someone to pin it on."

"Who? Nick was an easy target. He already worked for Donny. You found his gun lying around, stole it, used it and it created the perfect setup. We barely had to think that one through."

"Well, isn't there some high school student we could blame it on? If we stage it right, we could say it was a date gone wrong or something. Does she have a boyfriend?"

My breath catches in my throat. High emotion is making their conversation loud and fast. But I'm not missing anything now.

I can hear every inch of their plan and I have a sinking feeling I know exactly who Mayor Carter is going to come up with.

"There's one student at Armitage High I'd quite happily pin it on."

"Are we talking about a certain Mancini?"

"It's the most believable choice, but how do we lure him in for a setup?"

"Let's try money…or maybe trick him into thinking we have some information about his brother. You said he was pretty cut up when Nick went to jail. If he thinks Nick's innocent, maybe we could present him with the *real* killer."

"I like it. That combined with his temper will be perfect. Let's get him in here, fire him up until he loses it, and then see how much damage he can do."

"Give him the right weapon and we'll get the

exact crime scene we need."

"You'll get him to do the killing?" Mayor Carter's voice dips.

"Maybe...if we sell the story right. He doesn't need to know that he's killing Chloe Barlow. All we need to do is mask her, sell the lie, and get him angry enough to pull the trigger."

No! Shit, no!

Tears burn as I once again start to wrestle with my bonds. I'm not letting them do this. They will *not* set Vincent up this way.

Surely he won't trust them. Surely he won't believe Mayor Carter.

But if he's desperate enough...

His emotions are going to be right on the edge after he bailed on me last night. He'll be eaten alive by guilt or frustration. And Mayor Carter's right. He does have a short fuse, but surely it's not that short.

Shit!

Rubbing my ankles together, I ignore the burn on my skin and fight to free myself.

#40

VINCENT

The Search Begins

We park outside the Barlows' house and both stare at the front door.

I wonder what's going on inside. It's only just past nine thirty. I desperately want Chloe to be in there, but I know she's not. I can feel it.

Sucking in a breath, I pop the door open and follow Rahn up the path.

Just before she knocks, I duck out of sight, pressing my back against the house.

"What are you doing?" she whispers.

"The second they see me, it's going to blow up. You might as well get a few words in before that happens."

She winces and then nearly jumps out of her skin when the door opens.

Rahn doesn't have a chance to say hello before Max is asking, "Are you okay?"

"Chloe's not home, is she?" Rahn's voice is so hopeful.

My chest constricts when Max tells me what I already know.

"I thought she was staying with you."

"Well, she was supposed to." Rahn winces.

There's a painful pause and then comes the question we've been dreading. "What's going on?"

"I was her cover. So she could go on a date." Rahn spits the words out fast.

"What date? Does Chloe have a boyfriend I don't know about?"

Rahn's skin pales like it did when I first saw her this morning.

I close my eyes and prep myself for the big reveal.

"Rahn." Max's voice is low. "What's going on?"

"She didn't come home last night." Rahn wrings her hands. "I waited up for a really long time but then just couldn't keep my eyes open. I was expecting her to sneak in, but when I woke up this morning she was gone."

"Are you telling me she spent the entire night with some guy?"

"No," I croak.

Max's head appears out the door, her eyes bulging when she sees me standing there.

"I was supposed to meet her last night." My face bunches as guilt and anguish spread through me like fatal viruses. "But I couldn't make it, and now she's disappeared." I swallow and look to the ground. "She had some stuff she wanted to tell me. We needed to talk and I was supposed to be there, but..." My air supply is cut off as my imagination annihilates me with possibilities. "I've got to find her. Please tell me she's in her room, because if she's not, I think something bad has happened to her."

Max dashes away from the front door without a word. The expression on her face tells me she believes us, and it's the longest minute of my life as I wait for her to come back.

Rahn sniffs and I glance up to see a tear trickling down the side of her face.

"Here." I pull the tissue pack from my pocket and hold it out. "It's gonna be okay," I rasp, but it's a lame attempt at comfort.

I don't know if it's going to be okay.

I'm pretty sure I won't survive if it's not.

A noise at the door makes me glance up and two Barlow sisters are now staring at me. Maddie's the one on the right; I can tell by the fiery look in her eyes.

"Where's my sister?"

"I just told you, Mads, they don't know," Max counters quietly.

"Tell me every detail." Her voice is icy as she looks between Rahn and me. "What time did she leave? Where did she go? What was the plan?"

With a heavy sigh, I tell her everything I know. Rahn jumps in with a few details and ten minutes later, everyone's up to speed.

"What's going on out here?" Mrs. Barlow appears behind her daughters, smiling at Rahn and then giving me a quizzical look. "And who are you?"

Max catches my eye and kind of winces before looking to Maddie.

The older twin stares at me for a moment, then turns to her mother and tells the truth. "Mom, this is Vincent, Chloe's boyfriend."

Mrs. Barlow's blonde eyebrows disappear beneath her bangs. "Excuse me?"

I try for a smile, but it's kind of impossible to muster one right now.

We don't exactly have time for pleasantries, so I cut to the chase and destroy the woman's morning.

"Mrs. Barlow, if your husband's not home, you need to call him right now." I pull in a breath. "I was supposed to meet Chloe last night and I couldn't make it. And now she's missing."

"Missing?" Mrs. Barlow's face flickers with a disbelieving frown. "She was staying the night with you, Rahn." The woman points at Chloe's friend, realization creeping in as Rahn sucks in a watery breath and then starts bawling.

"I don't know where she is!" she wails between sobs.

I rest my hand on her back and silently ask if I can usher her inside. Max reads my expression and moves aside.

Soon we're piled into the living room. Rahn is slumped on the couch, still crying, while Max awkwardly tries to comfort her. Maddie is pacing from the wall to the archway, her glare landing on me every time she freaking turns around.

"I don't know!" Mrs. Barlow's voice pitches. "Just get home, Reece. Get home right now!"

Something slams onto the dining room table. I assume it's the phone.

Maddie rushes out of the living room to talk to her mom while I dig my hands into my pockets and lean against the wall.

I need to think.

I need to process what the hell is going on so that

when Chief Barlow walks through the door set on murdering me, I'll have some kind of way to defend myself. He can kill me later, *after* we've found Chloe.

It takes less than ten minutes for my executioner to arrive. The door bursts open and he storms into the house, Holden frickin' Carter in his wake.

Maddie called him to let the guy know they couldn't make the game and what do you know, Prince Charming ditched his teammates to come and support his girlfriend.

"Are you okay?" He pulls her into a hug the second she's within range, cupping the back of her head and glaring at me over her shoulder.

I roll my eyes and look away from him, only to be confronted by Chief Barlow. He's standing in the archway, his arms crossed and a murderous look distorting his features.

"Where's my daughter?" His voice is stretched thin, trembling slightly with what I can only assume is the desperate kind of rage I'm feeling.

I swallow and force my gaze to his. "I don't know, that's why I'm here."

He points a quivering finger at me. "You better

start talking, and I want every single detail. Nothing is unimportant, do you understand me?"

"Yes." I nod and pull in a breath. "Where do you want me to start?"

"Explain why my daughter was sneaking out to see you." His eyes dart to Rahn, who cringes and curls in on herself.

I clear my throat to catch his attention. Honesty is the only card I have to play so I go for it. "We've been secretly dating for a while and uh, we don't get much time to see each other, so Chloe told you that she was staying with Rahn as a cover. I'd arranged to pick her up from the bus stop at the end of Rahn's street. I was going to take her to a quiet spot in Cullington...near that pond, just so we could talk. She said she had so much to tell me and I needed to catch her up on..." I glance to the floor. "On some stuff."

Chief Barlow starts breathing like a bull ready to charge. Storming the space between us, he towers over me. I shuffle back just an inch but he grabs my collar and hauls me back.

"Why didn't you meet her?"

I resist the urge to fight him off me, although it's pretty damn hard. My brain's kicking into survival mode and I'm going to throw a punch soon if he doesn't let me go.

"I couldn't make it because my uncle was being

an asshole," I rush out. "I tried to get away, but they…" I'm loath to say it, so I settle for "They locked me in my room."

He lets me go and points at my face. "Is that how you got those bruises?"

I start to nod, but then shake my head.

"I got them this morning fighting with my cousin. He tried to threaten Chloe last night and I was scared he wasn't kidding. So I went after him and I wasn't going to let up until he told me the truth."

He lets me go, his expression telling me that he's struggling to figure me out. I'm challenging all his preconceived ideas about me and all he can do is rasp, "And? What did he say?"

My jaw is shaking so I slam my teeth together and grit out, "He hasn't seen her."

Chief Barlow scrubs a hand down his face and mumbles a soft curse. Yanking out his phone, he makes a quick call.

"Yeah, Mike. Chloe's missing … Since last night." He looks to Rahn.

She jumps under his gaze and squeaks, "She left my house just before eight."

"Eight o'clock … I don't know, but she was last seen walking to the bus stop on the corner of Stanton and Emery. Can you and Hayley start canvassing the area for me? … Yeah, I know, forty-eight hours, but hopefully we can find her before we have to call them

… Yeah … Yeah … Just keep me posted, okay?" The officer must say one more thing because Chief Barlow nods, then hangs up.

Glancing down at his wife, he gives her a weak smile and rubs her shoulder. "It's okay, Krisi, we're going to find her."

The woman's face bunches as she fights her tears. "What are the police doing?"

"They're going to go door-to-door and ask if anyone's seen Chloe."

"Do they need a photo? Text them a photo." Mrs. Barlow covers her mouth with shaky fingers as her husband quickly sends a photo from his phone to his officers.

"Is there anything else I should know?" He looks up from his phone and hits me with a molten glare.

Shit, he wants to kill me with his bare hands.

I rake my fingers through my hair.

"He asked you a question!" Holden snaps, his gaze telling me the same thing.

I glare at the guy, used to the look of disdain he's throwing me. I'm not afraid of that arrogant punk.

He stands a little straighter and I start picturing how I'll take him down before I have to ready my fists for Chloe's dad.

Curling my fingers, I breathe through my nose, but am distracted by Max's soft voice behind me.

"If you guys are thinking about fighting, don't be

dickheads. Chloe needs us to focus right now, so Vincent, if there's anything else you want to tell us, rest assured you can say it without getting your ass kicked. Right, Dad?"

I spin to see her silent plea. She's looking at her father, her blue eyes bright with her appeal.

"Of course," Chief Barlow croaks. "Chloe's all that matters right now. It's time to speak up, son."

I whip around to face him, licking the edge of my mouth before admitting, "We've been looking into my brother's conviction. Chloe's dead set on proving him innocent and I'm really scared that maybe she's followed some kind of lead. I told her to leave it alone, I swear, but she's so passionate about injustice!"

Maddie's lips twitch, her eyes glassing over. "She really is, and she's stubborn too. Especially when she believes in something."

My insides fold.

Shit.

She believed in me...and I let her down.

I bend forward, resting my hands on my knees as the thought tries to annihilate me.

"Maddie, get me Chloe's computer." Chief Barlow snaps his fingers.

"What?" She frowns.

"Do it, Madelyn!"

"Reece, talk to me." Mrs. Barlow grabs his wrist

and squeezes.

"The other night Chloe was trying to convince me to reopen Nick Mancini's case again. She was researching on her computer."

Maddie runs back into the room with Chloe's laptop and we all follow Chief Barlow into the dining room.

Crowding around him, we strain to see over his shoulders as he opens the laptop and checks the history.

I read as fast as I can, noting the pages on my brother, then gasping when I spot an article about the new club in Brazenwood.

"There!" I point at it. "That's that new club in Brazenwood."

Chief Barlow's skin turns this sick ashen color. "But I paid him. We were set. We... He said he'd leave my family alone."

Chloe's father turns dark with rage, but he's distracted by the phone in his pocket. "Yeah, Mike, talk to me ... Reliable? ... And you showed her Chloe's picture? ... Okay, okay, great. Get in touch with the bus company, see if you can track down the driver and find out where Chloe got off ... Yeah. Thanks ... Call me back."

"What'd he say?" Mrs. Barlow grips her husband's arm while everyone stares at him expectantly.

"A lady saw Chloe getting on the bus at 9:05 last

night."

Shit, she waited over an hour for me.

"It was bound for Cullington."

"Cullington?" Maddie frowns. "Why would she go there?"

"She may not have. Mike's going to find out where she got off the bus and we'll go from there."

"So we just have to wait?" Mrs. Barlow paces away from the table, pissed off and desperate. I know how she feels.

I can't just stand here doing nothing while someone else chases down that bus lead.

"Well, at least she didn't jump on a bus to Brazenwood," Max mutters.

Brazenwood.

Grabbing Chloe's laptop, I turn it to face me and bend down to get a better look at the images. Three people are standing outside the club, two men and a short woman.

She catches my eye for some reason. She's short, Latina...really beautiful.

"Shit," I whisper. "Is that her?"

"What?" Holden glares down at me.

"The woman." I point at the photo. "Chloe went and saw Todd McCrae's girlfriend, and the lady said a female detective came and took Todd's photos and notes. She said it was evidence for the case. But Armitage has never had a short Latina female detective, right? And—"

"You let her interview some woman without me?" Chief Barlow's anger snaps back to attention.

"No." I shake my head. "I didn't even know she was going there. She told me about it afterward."

"When?" He's back in my space again, no doubt ready to grab my shirt and slam me against the wall.

I force myself not to cower away. "She went on the last day of Spring Break, okay? She told me about it the next day and I told her to stop, but she wouldn't let it go."

"So this is Chloe's fault? You're blaming my daughter?"

"No! I—"

"That's Luisa Garcia," Max interrupts us. "Cairo knows her. Her husband and brother own the club we auditioned in."

Chief Barlow spins to face her. "But Chloe didn't head to Brazenwood."

"I'm calling Cairo." Max slips out of the room, the phone already to her ear.

Her dad scowls at her back before training his dark gaze on me.

"Did Chloe find out anything else about this woman?"

"I'm not sure, but if she's researching this woman then maybe Chloe thinks it's the lady who took the stuff from McCrae's house, which means she's not a detective at all. She pretended to be so she could get whatever information Todd McCrae had. I'm telling you, something is off with that guy's murder. My brother's lawyer convinced him not to appeal, the cop who conducted the investigation was scared into hiding and now this chick shows up stealing evidence...covering up the truth. I don't know what the hell Todd McCrae was into, but they killed him and then they set my brother up."

My voice rings with conviction as I clump all the pieces together.

"The investigating cop was scared into silence?" Chief Barlow frowns at me.

I close my eyes and squeeze the back of my neck, readying myself for another attack.

"We found him and went to see him over Spring Break. He told us to stay away from it. That it was too big."

"What was his name?"

"Scott Tannon."

"The former police chief?" Chief Barlow's face flickers with confusion. "He left because he was sick with cancer."

"No. He left because they threatened his family. He now lives in the middle of nowhere with two scary-ass dogs and a 12-gauge shotgun."

"Oh my God." Mrs. Barlow flops into a dining chair, her blue eyes glassy with horror.

"You took my daughter where?" Chief Barlow bellows.

Nausea sweeps through me while guilt has another go at my heart.

"I should have tried harder!" My voice splinters. "I even broke up with her, hoping she'd leave it alone, but she just wouldn't...and I couldn't..." I shake my head, emotion clogging my throat.

Chloe's dad goes still, his eyebrows flickering as he takes in what I'm saying.

"I love your daughter. I know you probably hate that I do. And you have every right to blame me. I come from a shitty family and Chloe deserves better than me. I'm sorry I didn't have the strength to stay away from her."

Shit, am I crying?

Swiping at my eyes, I back away from the table and turn around so no one can see me.

An awkward silence descends. I don't understand why they're not yelling and throwing punches right now. They can. I won't even fight back.

I deserve to get pummeled. I let Chloe down last night. I should have been there.

I'm so cut up and broken right now.

But I can't keep failing her.

I have to find her.

Sniffing at my stupid-ass tears, I smash my teeth together and bite down so hard it hurts.

"Her husband owns a club in Cullington too." Max's voice makes me spin. "Club Matrix." She's talking to her dad. "Maddie, Holden, and I have been there with Cairo. Velocity plays there sometimes."

Her dad bulges his eyes, then drops his head like if he has to hear one more exposed secret he's going to combust. Scratching the back of his neck, he lets out a heavy sigh and turns to his wife.

"I'm gonna go check it out. I'll call the Cullington PD on my way there, see if they can't help me track her down."

"Okay." She crosses her arms, tears brimming on her lashes.

Chief Barlow cups her cheek. "It's going to be all right. I won't stop looking until I find her."

"I know."

He kisses her forehead. "I need you to stay here, in case she comes back."

The doorbell rings.

Max bolts away to answer it and I soon hear Cairo's voice, asking if she's okay. Her reply is muffled and I assume he's hugging her the way I want to hug Chloe.

Chief Barlow tenses, letting out a soft huff as he leaves to grab his stuff. Cairo and Max walk into the room holding hands. Cairo gives me a pained smile. Max must have given him a quick update on the phone. I look to the floor, lightly kicking the table leg until I hear Chloe's dad thumping down the hall.

I move into his line of sight. "I'm coming with you."

"No, you're all staying here." He ignores my shaking head and points at Rahn. "Except you. I want you to head home in case she returns to your place. Is your phone charged?"

"Yes, sir." She bobs on her toes.

"Then get going." He tips his head at the door before looking at the rest of us. "Keep me posted."

"Yeah right, Dad. Like we're going to sit here and wait," Maddie argues.

"Madelyn, this is my job now."

"And she is *my* sister and I'm *not* going to sit here and wait for news. Let us at least walk the streets asking if people have seen her. I have to do something!"

Chief Barlow's jaw clenches. He's obviously straining for calm. "The cops in Cullington will help me."

"As will we." Maddie doesn't give him another chance to argue, storming for the door with Holden in tow.

"Madelyn!" Chief Barlow dashes after her while his wife plunks back into her chair again.

"Come on, Vincent, we'll give you a ride." Max tips her head at the door while Cairo cringes at her mother and then gives me an awkward look before heading out the door.

"Maxine!" Her mother's call is in vain and she knows it. She doesn't even rise from her chair.

As I walk out the door, Cairo pats my shoulder. "I'm sorry, man. We're going to find her, okay? It's going to be all right."

I wish I could believe him.

I trail Max down the path and slip into the back of the yellow Camry. I'm determined to hope for the best, to fight with every ounce of strength I have to bring Chloe home, but I can't ignore the torturous questions in the back of my mind.

What if we don't find her?

What if we do, but we're too late?

#41

CHLOE

Silenced

I've been struggling with these ties for an eternity.

The skin on my wrist feels raw and I won't be surprised if I'm bleeding.

My cheeks are damp with tears. I've fluctuated from moments of stubborn determination to heart-wrenching sobs. I've been desperate, enraged, and exhausted.

Everything aches and quivers, but my effort has led me nowhere.

I'm still on this damn leather couch, tied up and gagged.

I don't know where Luisa and the mayor have gone. They're off somewhere setting up my boyfriend and I don't know how to make them stop.

Vincent won't kill me. Whether I'm masked or not, he's not the type to pull a trigger. Even if he puts on that front, he won't do it.

Right?

I mean, he'd never get mad enough to actually kill someone, would he?

I have to believe in him.

They'll just have to come up with another plan to save their asses.

But what if they kill Vincent too?

I squeeze my eyes shut, my body convulsing with the thought.

Shit!

I *have* to get out of here.

Shaking my woozy head, I attempt to stand again. My last few tries have failed, but maybe if—

The door punches open and Mayor Carter rushes in. Yanking my arm, he throws me over his shoulder and hustles toward the closet.

Luisa appears in the doorway, smoothing her hair back.

"We should just pretend we're not here," Mayor Carter whisper barks.

"No, I'll go smooth things over. Throw them off our scent so they don't come back later. Just keep her hidden and quiet!" she snaps before dabbing a little more gloss on her lips and putting on a demure smile.

"No!" My scream is muffled by the gag, but I fight like an angry toddler, flailing my body to get away.

Someone's here. I have no idea who it might be, but they're here. And I have to let them know where I am.

"In here!" I scream, kicking and bucking as Mayor Carter struggles to walk me to the closet.

"Shut up," he barks, roughly dropping me onto the floor.

Pain fires through my body as I smack onto the wood.

He puffs and glares at me, panic flickering over the edges of his expression. Opening the closet, he drags me inside.

"No!" I kick my bound legs, catching him in the thigh.

"Arghh!" He slaps me across the face, then points at me. "Shut up!" His voice breaks with desperation.

A stinging pain radiates across my cheek and tears blur my vision before I can stop them.

"Keep your mouth closed. You hear me?" Spittle

coats his lips as he shoves me into the closet and slams the door shut.

I'm instantly shrouded in darkness, but I'm not about to let that stop me.

Bringing my heels down on the wood, I squirm and pound the inside of the closet until the door's whipped open again.

Light pours in, creating an ominous glow behind Mayor Carter. He crouches down, grabbing my face and giving me a shake. "Don't make me hurt you."

I narrow my eyes, pouring every ounce of anger and disgust into my glare.

"Stop looking at me like that," he spits.

He pushes my face away, but I just turn right back and keep glaring at him.

His jaw juts out and he sniffs, reaching behind his back and hesitating over something. "Shit!" he barks and then powers his fist at my face.

He clips me on the side of the cheek and my head smacks against the back of the closet. Darkness creeps into the edges of my vision as the band of pain around my skull tightens.

My throbbing heart is now pounding in my brain, tugging at my conscience and trying to drown out the world around me.

I have to fight it.

I can't black out now.

The words keep screaming through my head as

my eyelids slide shut and I'm once again shrouded in darkness.

#42

VINCENT

The Only Name to Yell

Being mid-morning, the club is locked up tight, but Chief Barlow's not going to let up banging on that door.

I look over my shoulder. Maddie and Holden have gone to ask around the local shops for any glimpses of Chloe.

Cairo wanted to stay and talk to Luisa since he

knows her, but he lost the argument pretty quickly and Max dragged him away before her father could find another excuse not to like him.

From what Cairo said in the car, he's doubtful Luisa would be capable of murder or kidnapping, but he did concede that he doesn't know her that well. She turned a blind eye when Max was in trouble at *Escapar*, so maybe she's not as nice as she appears.

When we arrived on the scene, Chief Barlow was on the phone to the Cullington PD. "I don't care about a warrant!" he barked. "I just want to talk to the owners … Okay, fine, I'll wear that, but if I sense something's off, I'm calling you guys in for backup." He growls in his throat and finishes the call with a terse "Just send a squad car down here!"

I don't know if they will. All I can hope is that we don't need them.

Bile swirls in my stomach as I try to ward off images of what Chloe might be going through right now.

I close my eyes and force air through my nose as Chief Barlow pounds his fist on Club Matrix's big black doors.

"Police, open up!"

Stepping back with a sigh, I can see him eyeing up the doorframe and then hesitating. He so wants to kick it in, but he's got no warrant and no proof in order to get one.

Maybe if he showed Luisa's picture to Todd McCrae's girlfriend and she gave him a positive ID…but we're working on a clock here.

"Do you want me to kick it in?" I murmur. "You can arrest me later for destruction of property."

He gives me a sidelong glare and is about to reply when the locks on the door start turning.

Luisa Garcia appears. She eyes us up and down before pasting on a pleasant smile. "Good morning, gentlemen. We're actually closed until five. Is there something I can help you with?"

I step forward with a snarky answer prepared, but Chief Barlow shuts me up with a tight squeeze to my shoulder. He's still pissed off that I'm standing here. He tried to send me away with his kids, but I refused. If Chloe's in here, I want to be able to reach her quickly.

Pulling out his badge, Chief Barlow quickly flashes it at her before stating, "Are you Luisa Garcia?"

"I am." She smiles. "How can I help you, Officer?"

"We're looking for a missing girl and have reason to believe she's in this area. We were wondering if you could tell us anything." He shows the picture on his phone to Luisa and watches her face carefully while she glances at the image.

"Wow, beautiful girl," she murmurs before giving us a pained smile. "I'm very sorry, but I haven't seen her."

"Okay." Chief Barlow nods. "Were you at the club last night?"

"Yes, I was. Do you think she was here?"

"Maybe." He nods, gazing past her shoulder to get a look inside. "I don't suppose you'd mind if we check the bathrooms. Maybe she got a little tipsy and fell asleep in a corner somewhere."

Luisa's smile tightens. "Officer, we have very strict rules here. No underage drinking."

"I didn't say she was underage."

"She looks young in the photo. I just assumed." Her smooth reply riles me. "As I was saying, we have very strict rules and this club is always empty before we lock up. Every corner is checked."

"Are you sure?" Chief Barlow crosses his arm, looking taller and wider than usual as he bores the petite woman with a look that would make most quake in their boots.

Her red, glossy lips pull into a patient smile. "I really don't want to waste your time. I would never do anything to impede an investigation, particularly concerning a missing young woman, but I cannot help you."

"Then you won't mind us looking around," I growl, pushing past her before Chief Barlow can stop me.

"Hey!" she shouts, trying to grab my jacket.

I flick her off me and stalk into the empty club.

"Chloe! You in here?"

My voice bounces back to me as it pings around the cavernous space.

"Boy, get out of my club!"

"He's just having a look, Miss Garcia." Chief Barlow's voice is gruff as he trails after me.

"You have no authority being in here. I will happily file a lawsuit against the police department unless you can show me a warrant!"

"Chloe!" I ignore the woman's threats and shout my girlfriend's name, heading for the bathrooms.

She's still spouting off when I emerge empty-handed.

Chief Barlow's trying to calm her down and I can tell by the look on his face that he's going to call me out of here soon.

Before he can say anything, I duck through an archway leading backstage.

"Get out of there!" Luisa yells. "Are you just going to let him walk through my club? He's not even a police officer."

"I guess I don't have to worry about you suing my department, then," Chief Barlow clips.

"He is trespassing!" she screeches. "Now you get him and drag him out of my place or you will most definitely regret it. I highly doubt your supervisor will let you keep your job if you're planning on behaving so unprofessionally. And I don't think your city council will appreciate having a lawsuit on their hands."

Her voice fades as I delve farther into the back passageways.

"Chloe!"

My gut pinches as I'm met with nothing but silence.

Rubbing a hand over my mouth, I head past one more door and notice a stairwell on my left.

Do I take it? Or am I wasting my time?

That lady out front is going ballistic. If the Cullington PD show up, whose side will they take?

Shit, I'll probably get arrested.

Scraping my fingers through my hair, I look up those stairs and murmur, "Who fucking cares."

Thumping up the steps, I risk arrest and shout the only name I care about. "Chloe!"

#43

CHLOE

A Whole New Level of Terrifying

"Chloe!"

The name is a distant shout but it pulls me into consciousness.

My eyes pop open. I'm still in the closet, shrouded

in darkness. I'm still tied and gagged, and my head is killing me.

But I heard my name.

I swear it wasn't a dream.

"Help!" I scream against the gag, kicking the wood beneath me and trying to create as much noise as I can. "Help me!"

It's so hard to be heard when my voice is muffled by the gag, but I keep screaming until the closet door is flung open.

"Shut up." Mayor Carter grits out the words, pulling me out of the closet.

My feet drag along the ground as he painfully wrenches me under the arm.

I scream and buck, trying to squirm free, but he just tightens his hold on me.

"Shut up!" His voice rises with desperation. Crouching down, he wraps his arm around my waist and hauls me to my feet.

"Chloe!"

My name's closer this time, and I think I recognize the voice.

Vincent?

"Chloe, can you hear me?"

Vincent!

He's here!

He's come for me.

"Vincent!" I scream.

"Stop it!" Mayor Carter warns, clamping his hand over my mouth and finally producing the one thing that can shut me up for good.

I can't see it, but when that cold metal presses against my temple, I know exactly what it is.

A breath catches in my chest, stuck there while my heart beats wildly with fear.

There's a creaking on the stairs outside the door.

It's Vincent.

He's coming for me.

He's walking straight into a trap.

"Chloe?" His call is softer now, like he's not sure whether he just imagined my muffled cry a moment ago.

He didn't rush up the stairs when I shouted, so maybe he didn't hear me anyway.

I finally take in a breath, my chest heaving when his silhouette appears in the glass doorway.

A tear slips from my eye as he walks straight past it. There must be another room on this floor. The one where I heard these killers discussing how they were going to set Vincent up.

Shit, is this all part of their plan?

How'd he find me anyway?

Or did they lure him here?

The questions jump through my mind, only stirring up more tears as the gun pokes into my cheek, telling me my time is nearly up.

Vincent's heavy footsteps lead him back to the door and I shake my head as he goes to open it.

I whimper behind the gag and Mayor Carter squeezes me so hard it hurts.

The second the door swings open, he tightens his grip even more and calls across the room, "Take one more step and she's dead!"

#44

VINCENT

All That Matters

I jerk to a stop in the doorway.

My heart jumps into my throat the second I see that asshole holding my girl.

Tears are trailing down Chloe's gagged and bruised face. And his talon grip around her body is obviously causing her pain.

Anger flares bright and it takes everything in me

not to run across the room and rip his face off.

His…

Holy shit, that's Mayor Carter.

I blink, kind of astonished, before my brain tells me to focus on the main problem.

He has a gun pointed at Chloe.

I raise my hands in a symbol of surrender and slowly inch toward them. I hope my eyes don't give away how much I want to kill this guy.

I don't give a shit that he's the mayor. He could be the president of the whole fucking world and I wouldn't care. He's hurting my girl and he's going down.

But first I need to get Chloe to safety.

"Just let her go," I say, as calmly as I can.

"Stop walking!" He digs the gun into her cheek and she whimpers.

The sound breaks my heart, stirs the protective rage flaring inside of me. Forcing myself to stand still, I lift my hands a little higher and try again. "Let her go."

"She's seen too much," the mayor's voice quakes. "Now you shut that door. You—"

"Hey, Vincent, you up here?"

Chloe's eyes pop wide while Mayor Carter flinches at the sound of Chief Barlow's voice. I can tell they both know it's him. Chloe's eyes are so bright blue right now and Mayor Carter looks like he's ready to throw up.

Panic sets in at the first creak on the stairwell.

Mayor Carter points the gun at me, then at the door, his voice fast and panicky. "Get rid of him. Turn around and tell him you saw nothing."

I shake my head, but freeze when he cocks the gun and presses it back against Chloe's cheek.

"You want to save her life, you walk away."

"I can't do that," I whisper.

"I will blow her brains across this floor, do you understand me?"

"Don't do it." My voice catches. "Please, just put the gun down."

"Tell him to go. If he reaches the top of these stairs, she's dead."

Okay, he's seriously starting to freak out. I can tell by the wild look in his eyes that he's losing it. I can't have him kill Chloe, but I won't turn my back on her either.

Shit! What do I do?

"Vincent! Where are you?"

Chief Barlow's nearly at the top of the stairs. I inch back, hoping the move will calm the mayor enough to relax his finger on that trigger.

"Keep moving," the mayor mutters.

Chloe's chin starts to tremble, fresh tears lining her lashes as I back away from her.

I don't know what to do or how to save her.

"Vincent!" Chief Barlow's at the top of the stairs now, and he's sounding pretty pissed that I'm not answering him. "Vincent!" he snaps and turns my direction.

I can feel his eyes on me now. He's spotted the back of my head through the door.

If he appears behind me, will Carter pull the trigger?

I step back, desperate to stop this, but Chief Barlow's only two steps away. His feet jerk on the floor behind me.

Shit, I'm too late!

"Chloe?" He chokes out her name, and I hear the sound of a weapon being drawn.

I quickly glance over my shoulder.

"No, stop!" I shout before whipping back to face Chloe.

The mayor's upper lip curls, panic distorting his features as he aims the gun straight and fires.

I lurch to the side, jumping in Chief Barlow's way just before the bullet hits me.

Chloe screams as I jerk and drop to the floor.

One more shot goes off—another muffled scream—a cry of pain.

What just happened?

I scramble to see through the blur.

Is Chloe okay?

Did he shoot her?

A body thumps to the floor and my insides scream in despair until I see Milo Carter writhing in agony, shouting curses to the air as he holds his arm and curls into a ball on the floor.

Chief Barlow rushes past me, kicking the gun away from the mayor before spinning him over.

"You have the right to remain silent..." He keeps reading the agonized mayor his Miranda rights while snapping the cuffs on. Leaving him cursing on his stomach, Chief Barlow spins to check his daughter. She's on her knees, sobs punching out of her. Her bright blue eyes are staring at me across the room and it's only then that I can inhale a full breath.

She's alive.

Thank you, God, she's alive.

I close my eyes, my head flopping back onto the wood as relief floods through me.

Something is burning my shoulder. The pain blooms from my wound and spreads down my arm. I don't know how bad it is, but I'm just going to lie here for a second and breathe.

Because Chloe's okay. She's safe now, and that's all that matters.

#45

CHLOE

Hospitals and Soft Confessions

I can't take my eyes off Vincent as Dad gently removes my gag and cradles my face.

"You okay?" He winces as he looks at the wounds on my forehead and cheek.

His eyes are glistening. His fingers on my face tremble while he gazes at me.

"I'm fine," I murmur and lick the edge of my aching mouth. "Vincent," I whimper.

Dad gasps, racing back to my boyfriend and shouting his name. "Vincent!"

He quickly inspects his shoulder before whipping off his jacket and then pulling his shirt off. Balling it up, he applies pressure to the wound, then forces Vincent into a sitting position. He groans and my heart constricts.

As soon as he's resting against the wall, Vincent opens his eyes and whispers, "Untie Chloe. I'm fine."

"Keep pressure on that wound." He makes sure Vincent's hand is steady and holding before leaping back to me. Pulling a knife from his pocket, he frees my wrists and legs.

I can't help a small cry as I move my arms. My muscles are screaming in agony.

"Just stay put until the paramedics get here." Dad tries to stop me while yanking out his phone and making a call.

"No," I whimper, shaking his hand off my arm and scrambling to my feet.

I try to walk to Vincent's side, but the world turns sideways on me again. I drop to my knees and end up crawling across to him.

As soon as I'm within reach, he lets go of Dad's

shirt and holds his good arm out for me. I scramble into his embrace, quickly picking up the shirt and reapplying pressure to the wound. He's been shot in the shoulder. I have no idea how bad it is or if he'll need surgery.

The thought makes me blubber, tears streaming down my face as I rest my head against his good shoulder. His arm curls around my back and his lips brush my forehead. I close my eyes and let the tears flow. I'm completely exhausted and now that it's over, I want to shatter like glass hitting ceramic tiles.

"Yeah, I need an ambulance at Club Matrix," Dad's voice is low and hollow. He looks over his shoulder and stares at Mayor Carter. The man's gone quiet, his cheek lying on the wooden floor as he stares across the room. He's not seeing anything. His expression is one of complete desolation.

He's probably just as shocked and horrified as the rest of us.

He's been caught. There's no way out now. No cover.

I can't believe this is happening.

Holden's father.

My body convulses as the aftermath hits me. The repercussions are huge, and a lot of people are going to be hurting over this one.

Will they try to pull strings and cover it up again?

Will someone get threatened?

Or will justice finally be served?

Feet thump on the stairwell. I don't know who's coming, but two bodies jerk to a stop in the doorway.

I glance up to find Holden and Maddie gaping into the room as they quickly figure out what happened. Holden's face puckers with surprise. "Dad?"

Mayor Carter flinches, his eyes shooting up to his son before he frowns and turns his head the other way.

The dawning realization is brutal.

Maddie's blue eyes fill with tears as Holden rushes across the room.

"Dad!" He lands on his knees, forcing his father onto his back and gripping his collar. "No! What did you do?"

My dad walks over, calmly placing his hands on Holden's shoulders. "It's okay, son. Let him go."

"You shit!" Holden sobs, shaking his father as anger distorts his handsome face.

"Let the law deal with him." Dad's voice is soft and calm. "He won't get away with anything else. We'll make sure of it."

Holden's upper lip curls with disdain as he lets his father go. Mayor Carter thumps back to the floor. I flinch and Vincent holds me a little tighter.

Maddie kneels down beside us, covering her hand with her mouth as she looks at the blood oozing between my fingers. Dad's shirt is now saturated with blood.

I push it against Vincent's wound.

He lets out a feeble grunt but I don't let up. He's losing too much blood.

"Where's Max?" Dad asks while guiding Holden back to us.

"She and Cairo are downstairs with the police," Maddie murmurs. "Luisa tried to flee the scene, but we kind of stopped her before she could. We were going for a citizen's arrest, but then a squad car pulled up and they took over. They're taking statements and I told them I thought you were in the building. As soon as backup arrives, they're going to sweep this whole place." Maddie frowns. "Dad, I don't know if they're going to arrest her. If she's anything like her brother, she might have the wrong people in her back pocket."

"I'll go down and give them an update, make sure she gets taken to the station. Don't worry, they won't get away with it this time." Dad's voice is somber as he points down at Vincent. "Keep pressure on his wound. I'll send the paramedics up as soon as they arrive."

He walks through the door, his footsteps loud on the stairs.

Holden crouches down beside us, scrubbing a hand over his face before muttering to Vincent, "He shot you?"

"Rather me than Chloe," Vincent rasps.

A fresh set of tears fills my eyes, my chin bunching as I try to hold in my sob.

Holden nods, quickly assessing the situation and taking charge of Vincent's care.

"It's okay. I've got it." He gently removes my hand from Dad's shirt and continues to plug Vincent's wound.

Maddie comes around to me, assessing my forehead. "That looks nasty."

"I'm okay."

"Are you dizzy? Blurry vision?"

I want to say no, but I can't lie anymore. "Yeah, a little."

"I'm going down to wait for the paramedics. I'll lead them up here." Maddie squeezes her boyfriend's arm and they share an agonized look before she jumps up and disappears.

Gently gripping Vincent's side, I nestle my head into his shoulder, aware that his hold on my back is going slack.

Sitting up, I gaze down at his pale face and panic starts to rise to the surface.

"Vincent?"

He responds with a groggy groan and struggles to open his eyes.

"He's losing a lot of blood," Holden whispers, his

eyes brimming with sympathy.

"No!" I whisper. "He's going to be fine. It's just a shoulder wound. Vincent!" I grip his shirt, begging him to open his eyes. "Come on, stay with me! Vincent!"

He's still not opening his eyes and the panic is now in full bloom. My erratic heart is threatening to explode if he doesn't answer me.

"Vincent!"

Footsteps arrive on the stairwell, rushing up to meet us.

I let out a strangled cry as two paramedics burst through the door. Holden moves aside, telling them what he can while I crumple on the floor and turn into a useless quivering mess.

They get busy administering to Vincent and Holden's soon crouched beside me, his arm wrapped securely around my shoulders.

He doesn't say anything. All he can do is hold me tight and stare across the room at his shame-faced father. A paramedic is checking out his wound as two officers enter and stand guard beside the fallen mayor.

"Step back, please." A paramedic orders us aside and before I know it, Vincent is being rushed out to an ambulance.

Holden supports me down the stairs. My legs act like cooked spaghetti and he basically has to pick me up and carry me.

Two steps onto the empty dance floor and I'm soon surrounded, being fussed over by loving family as they cart me out to the second ambulance.

The first one is pulling away, its sirens blaring as they transport Vincent to the nearest hospital. It kills me not to be with him.

Tears trail down my cheeks as I watch it drive away without me and I start to pray that Vincent will be okay.

Although, right now, I can't see how anything will ever be okay again.

I sit in the treatment room, my legs swinging back and forth as I wait for the nurse to find me a room for the night. They're making me stay for observation thanks to the concussion I scored last night. And there's a chance I may have a CT scan in the morning, just to double-check that everything in my brain is okay.

My superficial wounds have all been treated. I have bandages around my wrists and balm on my ankles.

Mom's been in here fretting up a storm, but I finally managed to persuade her to go and check on my sisters. I need a second to breathe.

Holden's in shock. Maddie's with him while they wait for his mother to arrive.

Max and Cairo have been freaking amazing, wiping up a constant stream of tears and being the quiet oak trees everyone needs to lean on. Cairo's parents arrived at the hospital before we did. They must have driven like a tornado was chasing them. It's a good fifty minutes from Armitage to Cullington. They must have done it in forty. I'm glad Mr. Hale floored it, because he and his wife have been on hand to help with any requests. I know my mom spent a few minutes crying in Mrs. Hale's arms while a nurse cleaned up my wounds.

I can't stop asking for updates on Vincent. He's in surgery now and I'm sick with worry.

I don't even know what the operation entails, but he better make it out alive.

Yet more tears sting my eyes as I relive a few harrowing moments of my ordeal.

I can't believe Milo Carter covered up Todd McCrae's murder and framed Nick Mancini. I can't believe he threatened to kill me. I can't believe he shot my boyfriend!

Shit, if Vincent hadn't jumped in the way, that bullet would have gone straight into my father.

I pull in a ragged breath and grip the edge of the examination table.

Dad's apparently at the station, making sure the arrests go through without a hitch. He'll have a battle on his hands. Luisa Garcia is connected to some powerful men. They'll be hard to take on, but Dad's got it in him. He'll be worried about our safety, but he can't be bought and he won't be scared off.

I, for one, will not be running to the hills or hiding myself away.

Luisa Garcia and Milo Carter will be tried and convicted for their crimes. I don't care how good their lawyers are. They're not getting away with it this time.

I'll happily testify against them.

The door eases open, and I flinch at the sound.

"It's only me," Dad murmurs, slipping into the room.

My lips curl into a sad smile as he slowly approaches the bed.

"How you feelin'?"

I shrug.

"They'll be transferring you to a room soon. Mom's fought to get you some privacy, so you won't be sharing."

I snicker and look down at Dad's black shoes.

"I'm sorry," I whisper. "I'm sorry for this whole mess. I never should have gotten on that bus, and broken your rules. I was just so desperate to find you some proof."

"It's not your fault, sweetie." Dad's voice is thick with emotion.

I glance up and notice the glistening in his eyes.

"You tried to tell me to reopen the case. I should have listened to you."

My throat is thick and gummy, making it impossible to respond.

"You girls are…" He lets out a broken kind of snicker. "I've made liars out of you. I've been so hard and judgmental. I pushed so much that Max couldn't tell me she was over baseball and you couldn't tell me that you were dating Vincent Mancini. My own daughters are too scared to talk to me about what's going on in their lives." He shakes his head and squeezes his eyes shut. "I'm a police officer and you couldn't even tell me what you were trying to do for Vincent and his brother. You nearly died today!" His jaw works to the side. It's trembling as he sucks in a shaky breath. "I should have listened. I should have heard you, read between the lines."

"I probably could have been clearer." My shoulder hitches. "But I figured you wouldn't understand. That you'd stop me somehow. People never give Vincent a chance because they hear his family name and take one look at his face and then make all the worst assumptions. They don't want to hear that his brother's innocent because they want to look up to people like Milo Carter." I scoff and press my quivering lips together. "But Vincent saved your life today. He's the hero."

"I know," Dad rasps, his shoulders slumping forward like he's run out of fight for a minute.

Easing off the bed, I shuffle across to him and wrap my arms around his thick torso. "I love you, Dad."

His arms come around me in an instant, cradling me against him while we quietly sniff and cry in each other's arms.

#46

VINCENT

The Heart Expansion Project

Someone has injected concrete into my brain, I swear.

With a soft groan, I ease my eyes open, squinting against the light.

A body shifts in a chair near the window. I turn to my left, only to be met by the towering chief of police as he stands and walks to my bedside. He's in uniform, his expression ominous.

"Am I being arrested?" I croak.

With a soft snicker, he shakes his head. "For saving my life? No. For dating my daughter behind my back? Tempting, but..." He raises his eyebrows, his mouth tugging up at the corners. "What you did was very brave."

I close my eyes and lick my lips, suddenly aware that my shoulder is killing me.

With a wince, I reach up to investigate.

"The bullet went straight through your shoulder and chipped the bone. You lost a lot of blood, but the surgeon cleaned you up and you're going to recover just fine."

"It hurts," I rasp.

Chief Barlow reaches for my head. I lean away from him with a wary frown and don't relax until I hear the beep of the call buzzer behind me.

"I'm not going to hurt you, son. You saved my life. You saved Chloe."

"I'd never do anything to hurt her," I whisper. "Is she okay?"

"She's still a little traumatized, but she'll get there."

My face crumples as the urge to find Chloe and

see for myself swamps me. I just want to hold her. I struggle to sit up, but a gentle hand on my chest forces me back down.

"Hey, she's all right. She's going to be fine. We all will be."

I swallow, the sound audible in the silence between us.

"Are you going to let me see her?"

"I'm pretty sure she'll kill me if I don't." His wink is so subtle I nearly miss it. "But she's sleeping right now and I'm not going to let you wake her."

"Sleeping," I whisper, relaxing my head onto the pillow and picturing her curled up in bed. I hope she's not having nightmares.

I know what it's like to relive a beating. It took me weeks to sleep through the night after the first time Enzo got to me.

Shit, Enzo.

I grimace and glance up at the police chief. "Is my family...?"

"They're still in Armitage. I suggested that it'd be better if they stayed put. I'll look after you. Your uncle wasn't too keen but I've managed to talk him around, for now." His voice takes on a hard, unimpressed edge.

Dread simmers through me as I imagine going back there, having to deal with their shit while I recover. I don't know if I can do it.

"You know, the Hales have offered to let you stay with them until you're better."

"What?" I frown.

"Mr. Hale, the music teacher from school."

"I know who he is," I murmur. "But why would he do that?"

The policeman gazes down at me. I can't read his expression. It's maybe a mix of sympathy and understanding, I'm not sure.

"Not everyone in this world wants to hurt you, Vincent. Some are dead set on taking care of you."

I snicker. "Chloe's proof of that."

"She's not the only one who cares, and when I spoke to your brother earlier, he specifically requested that I find somewhere safe for you to go until he gets out. I can't exactly have you moving in with my family, but—"

"He's getting out?" I hold my breath, hope daring to surface.

Chief Barlow bobs his head. "Milo Carter signed his confession while you were in surgery, which seems to have started a chain reaction. Luisa Garcia is reluctantly telling her side of the story now that her brother Tomas has completely denied all knowledge of it." He lets out a derisive snort. "Guess family bonds aren't as tight as she thought they were, but it works in your favor, kid." He taps the end of my bed. "It'll take some time, but your brother should be fully exonerated."

"You mean he's free?"

"He will be."

Thick emotion kills my ability to speak.

"How are we doing in here?" A nurse bustles in with a sweet smile. She has a short black ponytail and big brown eyes. Her olive face is round and friendly.

Chloe's dad steps back so she can stand beside the bed and look at me. "Nice to see you awake."

I lick my dry lips again and let her check my vitals.

"Any pain?"

"My shoulder."

"Okay." She bobs her head while checking my chart. "Looks like I can give you some more meds in about ten minutes. You sit tight, I'll go and get things organized for ya."

"Thank you," Chief Barlow answers on my behalf.

She nods and smiles at him, looking like a dwarf next to the towering man.

He steps forward as soon as she's left. "So, you think you could live with the Hale family for a while?"

"I guess." I shrug, then wince, my shoulder reminding me not to move around. "Not sure Enzo will be too happy about it though."

"Hey, you leave Enzo to me."

"You can't watch him every second of the day. He's not just going to let me walk away."

"If he lays one finger on you, I'm taking him

down."

I glance at the man, surprised by the strength of his statement.

"Don't be afraid to trust me on that one, kid. Chloe tried to tell me what an excellent guy you are, and you showed me how right she was."

There's this warm thing happening in my chest right now. I'm not sure what it is, but no adult has ever made me a promise I could believe in. But I trust this guy. I trust the look on his face, the confidence in his tone and posture.

He's not going to let me down.

A smile creeps across my lips before I can stop it. "So, am I allowed to date your daughter, then? You know, in front of your back?"

My joke falls a little flat and I cringe, looking down at the white blanket covering my legs. It was a lame joke anyway.

"Of course you can date me." The soft voice at the door makes my heart sing.

I strain to see her, ignoring the pain searing my shoulder.

Gritting my teeth, I hold back my hiss and smile at the vision shuffling into view.

"Hey," I whisper, drinking her in. My beautiful Chloe.

"Hi." Her smile is pure sunlight and I reach for her face, but can't get my arm high enough to touch her.

"It's okay." She perches on the edge of the bed, leaning close so I can cup her cheek.

"You all right?"

"Yeah, I am now." Her blue eyes sparkle, but don't hide the trauma of what she went through. I wish I could wipe it from her mind. I wish I had a magic touch to heal the wound on her head and the bruise on her cheek.

Anger flares briefly as I picture Milo Carter punching her, but she takes the emotion away with her delicate fingers.

"How bad are you hurting?" She traces the contours of my face. It kind of tickles, but I'm not moving for anything.

"My shoulder's not great, but I'm going to be fine."

"I know you will be. You're the toughest guy I know."

I grin and pull her in for a kiss, but a little throat clearing makes me pause.

Chloe rolls her eyes, but doesn't turn to acknowledge her father.

She keeps gazing at me like I'm the most important thing in the world.

No one's ever looked at me like that before and it's hard to know what to do with it. My chest feels like it's going to burst; the emotion bubbling inside of me is indescribable.

JORDAN FORD

"Okay, fine. I'll let you have a moment," her dad finally mutters. "Not too long though. You both need your rest."

Chloe grins as her father steps out of the room. As soon as the door clicks shut, she leans down to kiss me. It hurts my split lip but I don't care. Running my fingers into her blonde locks, I cradle the back of her head and skim my tongue against hers.

It's warm and comforting, enveloping my senses and taking all the pain away.

She smiles against me, running her thumb across my cheekbone and murmuring, "I love you."

The words only add to my heart expansion. I swear I'll be floating soon. It's like there's this balloon inside of me that she keeps inflating and I don't want it to ever pop.

For a second, I glimpse my future. Instead of dread and resignation, I spot something bright and brilliant. Chloe's holding my hand, smiling her sunshine smile and letting me lead her out the door to prom.

I've never let myself imagine something so *High School Musical* before, but there it is. And I can't help hoping the vision will come true.

It'd be so normal, so unlike anything I've experienced before.

#47

CHLOE

Red, White and Blue

"Would you stop fussing!" Max smacks Maddie's hand away. "I look fine."

"It's prom! You're supposed to look more than fine!"

Rahn giggles behind me, winking in the mirror as she finishes twisting my hair into some elaborate design she saw on Pinterest.

Max groans. "I'll be playing for most of it. I need to be comfortable."

"Okay, fine, no heels, but do you seriously have to wear those red Converse?"

"Yes." Max nods, her expression emphatic.

Maddie rolls her eyes. "Well at least let me put a little makeup on you. Please! Rock stars wear makeup."

Max sits down with a huff. "Fine, but make it quick. I don't want to be late for the sound check."

"Is Cairo picking you up?" I wince as Rahn tugs my hair a little too hard.

"Sorry," she squeaks.

I wrinkle my nose in forgiveness.

"No, I told him it'd be easier if we just met there."

"Wow, you guys are so romantic." Maddie bites back a grin when Max slaps her on the knee. "Sit still. Unless you want eyeliner on your cheek."

Max goes still while I giggle in my chair. I'm so excited I could burst.

The last five weeks have been insane.

Between studying, baseball...and recovering from the aftermath of what happened, life has been overwhelming.

Dad made us all see a counselor and we've been going to weekly sessions to talk through what happened. I haven't been allowed to sit in on any of Vincent's, but something in him is changing. I don't know if it's living with the Hales or what, but he's lighter somehow. He actually smiles without thinking about it. Even people at school are noticing.

You should have seen their faces when we finally returned to school, walking hand-in-hand down the corridor. I swear, the gossip train is still going strong on that one. It'll probably be going until we graduate. Our senior year together. It's going to be amazing. I'm determined to make it the best year ever.

There's really mixed emotions as we scream toward Maddie and Max's graduation. Maddie decided to go to USC and Holden's heading there too. Cairo's off to Berkeley, which is killing Max as she's made the decision to stay put, work her ass off, and learn everything she can from Mr. Hale.

She's going to miss Cairo big-time, but she'll survive. That's what Dad says whenever he hears her complaining about it.

I swear that man has forgotten what young love feels like.

"There you go. What do you think?" Rahn turns my head so I can see my profile.

"It's beautiful!" I finger the layered French braids and smile at my reflection. "I hope Vincent likes it."

"Oh please, you could be wearing a sack and have twigs in your hair and the guy would still drool at your feet." Max looks to the ceiling while Maddie applies mascara to her lower lashes.

"He seriously has the worst case of goo-goo eyes I've ever seen." Maddie laughs.

"That's because you can't see a mirror when you're looking at Holden," I retort.

Rahn laughs. "All three of you are ridiculous. Seriously, Barlow girls, you're all stuck in that super-in-love, gushy phase." Squeezing my shoulders, she bends down and kisses my cheek. "I hope it lasts forever."

I smile at her reflection and squeeze her hand.

Zane's taking her to prom tonight. They're just going as friends, but who knows what might come from it? Rahn doesn't seem too bothered. She's convinced she's too young to fall in love and is quite happy to wait for some college man to sweep her off her feet.

Standing tall, I check out my dress. It's a simple red number with a fitted, beaded bodice and a skirt that spins out when I twirl. I'm not sure how much twirling I'll be doing tonight, but I love the fact that it can. When I tried it on in the store, I made myself dizzy spinning in front of the mirror, but I just couldn't help it.

Rahn and I found these wicked red pumps with ribbon that winds around my ankles. Okay, they're a touch uncomfortable, but so worth it.

I shuffle back so I can get a full view.

"You look gorgeous, Chlo-Chlo." Max stands and holds up her foot. "Oh look, we're both wearing red shoes!"

Maddie groans while I giggle at my sister's teasing. She loves to rile Mads when she's stressed. And of course Maddie is stressed because she wants to look perfect for Holden, who we all know will be smoking hot in a tux.

What she fails to realize is that she is just as gorgeous as he is. The slinky, blue, off-the-shoulder number we found for her floats around her toned legs. The split goes all the way up to the top of her thigh, but it's elegant, not slutty. Mom had to say that a few times before Dad actually believed her.

But seriously, Maddie is dominating that dress right now. She looks like a supermodel. With half her hair up in this cool twist and the rest in loose curls around her shoulders, she looks incredible. Holden's going to be speechless. I'm certain of it.

"Right, I gotta go." Max puffs up her loose curls at the back before smacking her red lips together and tearing out the door.

She's in this short, backless dress. It's black and looks amazing on her slim figure. She was worried that it might slip off her shoulders when she's rocking out, but Mom produced some kind of tape and Max is basically stuck into that dress for the night.

Dad laughed when Mom told him, telling us it was

a good safety precaution and maybe we should all be taped into our dresses so we couldn't get up to any mischief.

"Honestly, Dad, like I'm going to lose it on prom night. That's way too cliché."

Maddie swanned out of the room with a teasing wink while Dad's smile disintegrated. I giggled behind my hand and trailed after my sister.

It was pretty hilarious.

Poor guy. Three daughters, all in love. That's got to be rough.

"Are we ready?" I swing my arm around Rahn's shoulders. She snuggles in beside me while Maddie takes the other side and we all admire our dresses. Red, white and blue. How patriotic. Rahn's in this funky two-piece with an embroidered bodice. It's totally unique and so her. I love that she doesn't even want to be like anybody else.

"We're ready." Maddie nods, then grins at me. "Let's go knock these guys off their feet."

#48

VINCENT

The Simple Things

The limo is kind of stuffy and quiet as we make our way to the Barlow house. Holden and I are the first two in it. He picked me up from the Hales' place. Avia made us stand and pose for some photos before Cairo had to split with his dad. She's dying to see what the girls look like and made us promise to send as many selfies as we can.

"You've got your phones, right?"

We both nodded.

Yeah, I have a phone now. I never want Chloe not to be able to reach me again, so I swallowed my pride and asked Mr. Hale if he could loan me the money for a simple cell phone. He agreed and ended up buying me something really nice.

"Only pay back what you can. The rest is a gift from us." He winked at me, once again sending my head into a spiral. I'm not used to adults being so damn nice.

I've found myself an after-school job at Armitage High. I help the janitor with cleaning and classroom lockup. I was surprised he said yes when Principal Sheehan asked him, but everyone has been putting in good words for me around the place and things are finally going right.

It sometimes makes me feel like a bit of a charity case, but Chloe told me off for saying that.

"Don't buy into that crap," she warned me. "People like to bless others. It makes them feel good. If you reject their generosity, you're hurting more than just yourself. Don't be proud. Be grateful."

And I am. I'm really grateful.

I shuffle in my seat, feeling awkward and uncomfortable in these fancy clothes.

"You look good," Holden murmurs, catching my eye and trying to smile.

He's been having a really hard time accepting everything that's gone down. His life has been turned on its head and not in the good way mine has.

He's gone from golden boy to the son of a criminal.

It's impossible not to feel sorry for him.

I open my mouth to talk, but then don't know what to say.

We've hung out a little because of the girls, but Holden's going to need more than five weeks to accept what's happened.

"You doing all right, man?" I can't believe the words just popped out of me like that.

My eyes bulge and I look out the window, hoping he doesn't mind my question.

He pauses for a second, then lets out a dry snicker. "Yeah, I'm... It is what it is, you know?"

I bob my head.

"When does Nick get out?" he asks.

"Should be next week. Courts are just finalizing the paperwork."

"Sorry it's taken so long."

"It's all good." I shrug. "He's been moved to minimum security while he waits, so it's been pretty cushy for him."

"Nice." Holden tries to smile again.

I wince and scramble to change the subject. What the hell can I talk about that's happy?

The girls. They make everything better.

I'm about to open my mouth and say something, but he starts talking before I can.

"Shit, man, I'm really sorry for how everything went down."

"It's not your fault," I reassure him. "And you don't have to keep apologizing."

"I know." He sighs and shakes his head. "I just hate what he did."

"How's your mom taking it?"

"She's in rehab at the moment. Took me a while to get her there, but my older brother flew back from New York to give me a hand. He's staying with me until the summer starts, and then my other brother is gonna move in and help me prep for college. I told them I'd be all right on my own, but they wouldn't believe me."

I grin at him.

"It's weird. I didn't even think they cared anymore."

"Yeah, well, a crisis can sometimes bring out the best in people."

"You're living proof, man."

Holden's compliment stuns me and all I can do is blink at him. A half smile tugs at his lips. He rubs a hand over his mouth, obviously embarrassed by how candid he's being.

I want to croak out a thanks or something, but I

can't quite manage it.

"Here we are, guys." The driver pulls up against the curb.

Holden and I flash each other a nervous look before getting out of the limo.

I've never been to a dance before. I hope I don't make a complete fool of myself.

Buttoning Mr. Hale's jacket, I smooth a hand over my hair and follow Holden to the front door. No matter how many times I walk up this path, I always feel nervous.

Chief Barlow's kept his promise and so far, Enzo and Diego haven't even tried to get near me. It's like they've forgotten we're related or something. I mean, I haven't ventured into that part of town again, but still...I honestly thought they'd come after me.

Chief Barlow has turned out to be much cooler than I thought. He's even helped me get Selena out. It took a little convincing, but he managed to persuade her to flee the house when Enzo and Diego weren't there. She's now living in San Diego, cleaning houses, and happier than she's ever been.

I thought Enzo would kill me for sure after he lost her, but whether stuff's gone on without me knowing or not, I haven't seen him once.

Holden rings the bell and then glances over his shoulder.

"Smile, man." He winks and grins as the door

flicks back and Mrs. Barlow greets us with an excited smile.

"Oh, you two look so great!" She stands back to admire us as we step into the house.

Her eyes kind of glisten as she moves into my space. "Vincent, you scrub up real nice." She smooths the collar of my jacket and gives me a motherly smile, just the way Avia does.

Shit, I feel like their pet project sometimes, but I'll do my best not to complain. They're good people.

"Is Zane here yet?" she asks.

"He was running late, so we'll collect him on the way to the school." Holden gives her a closed-mouth smile.

"Oh, poor Rahn, she—"

"I'm good, Mrs. B. Don't you worry." She skips into the room, her brown eyes dancing with excitement as she eyes us up and then turns to look down the hallway.

I glimpse Maddie walking toward me. She looks freaking hot in that blue dress, but the second I catch a flash of red, I'm owned by the one and only Chloe Barlow.

She looks amazing. That dress is so her—sweet and gorgeous, like a red rose that brightens up someone's day.

I glide my arm around my flower's waist and lift her into a hug. She giggles against my cheek before taking a step back to check me out.

"You're looking pretty hot there, Mr. Mancini."

"Watch it," her father clips, leaning against the living room archway and checking us all out with a narrowed glare.

"Oh, Reece, stop it. They all look hot." Mrs. Barlow giggles and holds up her phone, snapping photos while Holden and Maddie share a blushing moment and Chloe wraps her arm around my waist. "Can you pose for a couple of these?"

She lines us up, snapping an insane amount of pictures before finally letting us leave.

"We'll see you guys there." Mr. Barlow stands at the door with his wife tucked under his arm.

"So you *are* coming, then?" Holden threads his fingers through Maddie's.

"If Max wants to study music at college, then I need to see how good she is."

Chloe gasps. "Oh my gosh, Max will be blown away."

"Don't tell her I'm coming. I don't want to make her nervous."

Chloe lets go of my hand and races back to the door, wrapping her arms around her father's neck. "Just make sure she sees you before you leave."

"I will."

"So proud of you, Dad."

He hugs her tight, blinking rapidly before

suddenly pulling out of the embrace. "You better get going. Don't want to be late."

She kisses his cheek and then bounces down the steps, back into my arms. I rest my hand on her lower back and guide her to the limo.

"Take care of my girls!" Chief Barlow calls to us.

I help Chloe into the limo, then raise my hand in farewell. Mrs. Barlow rests her head against her husband's shoulder, her smile wide and proud.

As soon as the door is closed, the limo pulls away from the curb, heading for Zane's house. This is still so weird. I'm sitting in the back of some fancy car with people I never even thought I'd speak to.

But they're becoming my friends.

Chloe leans against my arm, curling her fingers around mine as we smile at Rahn's enthusiasm and her story about Maddie and Max arguing over a pair of red sneakers.

I laugh with Chloe, loving the sound of her giggle, the shape her face makes, the way her eyes dance.

She's captured me and drawn me into a life I never thought I could have.

Every day I wake up and find something new to love about her and her family.

Every day I wake up with these feelings I never thought I'd experience.

Hope and peace.

It's a trip, and I don't know if I'll ever get used to

it.

But maybe I don't want to.

Because I never want to take those simple things for granted.

#49

CHLOE

A Knight in Shining Armor

This prom is amazing.

I think it's mostly got to do with the guy beside me, but even so...I've never had so much fun.

I'm in his arms, swaying to "Carry You Home"

which my sister is singing. She's beautiful on stage—electrifying. Watching her and Cairo rock out together, and seeing that sheer joy on her face...even Dad can't deny that dropping the whole baseball thing was the right move for his daughter.

I've never seen Max so happy.

"Has she seen him yet?" Vincent glances over his shoulder, checking out the stage, then tracking back to where my parents are leaning against the wall of the gym.

They snuck in about five minutes ago and Dad hasn't been able to take his eyes off Max since. There's this awed kind of smile on his lips and I swear, he's crying on the inside.

Max started off the song we're dancing to right now, her clear voice piercing the air as she sung, "When it all comes caving in..."

I love this song.

Playing with the ends of Vincent's hair, I gaze up at him with a dreamy smile and start mouthing the words.

He smiles, his eyes sparkling as he swoops in for a quick kiss.

I giggle against his mouth, deepening the kiss as the music envelops us.

His fingers lightly dig into my back when he pulls me against him, suctioning our bodies together. Gently lifting me off my feet, he leans back so I can gaze down at him.

"You saved my life. You know that, right?" His voice is husky and sweet. "I didn't know what the word 'home' meant until I met you."

"Well, I guess we're even, then." I thread my fingers into his hair as he gently swings me around.

The song comes to an end and he places me back onto my feet.

There's a pregnant pause as a hush settles over the gym. I frown and glance at the stage. Max is standing by the mic, her glassy eyes fixed on Dad. She's obviously supposed to start the next song, but she can't move.

Because Mom and Dad are standing there.

And they're looking pretty damn proud.

Cairo glances down and sees what she's gazing at. His smile is instant. Tipping his chin, he acknowledges our parents before strumming the opening to "Great Escape."

Roman comes in with the drums, snapping Max out of her surprise. With a stunning smile, she leans into the mic and raises her fist in the air.

"Woohoo!" she cries before kicking into the first verse with Cairo.

The crowd mimics her move and soon we're all jumping and singing along with Velocity. The entire gym is vibrating with their magical energy, and I swear I have never been this happy before.

Vincent's arm snakes around my waist. I lean back against my unexpected warrior, smiling at the turns life can take you on.

When we left our life in Columbus I wondered how we'd survive this transition, but sometimes the best things in life come from the hardest moments. If I hadn't been attacked that night, I never would have seen Vincent for who he truly was. I never would have gotten his notes and fallen in love with him.

My terror in the darkness allowed Vincent to show me his light, and unveiling it to the world has been nothing but an honor and a privilege.

There's still more in there too. I can feel it.

And I'm going to cherish every beam of sunshine that comes out of my guy.

Spinning in his arms, I lock my fingers behind his neck and grin up at him.

"What?" He brushes his knuckle down my cheek, a tender smile lighting his expression.

I shake my head, too overcome to find my voice. Instead, I rise on my tiptoes and press our smiles together. The dancing crowd fades into the background as the world becomes just two people— me and my knight in shining armor.

THE END...

or maybe not...

Extended epilogues are always popular with my readers.
Keep reading to find out how the Barlow Sisters are getting on one year later...

Epilogue #1

Maddie

"Madelyn, come on! You're killing me, baby."

I frown at Holden's hassled tone and pop my head out from the behind the closet door. "Did you just call me by my full name?"

"I got your attention, didn't I?" He smirks, spinning the keys around his index finger. He's leaning against the doorframe of my dorm room looking all kinds of delicious...until he taps his watch. "Hurry up. We're going to be late."

I huff and rush to finish getting dressed.

I don't know what his problem is today. Geez!

Pulling on my sundress, I wriggle my hips and tug the sides until it's sitting right. This bodice hugs me like a glove. It's hard to get on, but so worth the effort.

I smile at my reflection, then glance at my watch. "We're not going to be late. We've done this trip a hundred times. It takes two hours twenty-five minutes." I slip my shoes on. "And that's allowing for traffic."

Grabbing my overstuffed bag, I hoist it onto the bed and then scan my closet one last time to make sure I'm not forgetting anything. I've been packing all week, ready to head back to Armitage for a chunk of the summer. We'll pop back here a couple of times to check on Holden's mom, of course. He lives with her, about a ten-minute drive from campus. She's doing so much better since she came out of rehab, but she's still kind of fragile and Holden likes to keep an eye on her.

My boyfriend tips his head, his eyes running over me with an appreciative smile. I love the way my skin tingles when he looks at me like that.

He inches into my room, clicking the door shut behind him.

My roommate, Joanne, has already left for the summer so we had the place to ourselves last night. He stayed pretty late and I concluded that sleep would be impossible the way my body was feeling. I had a really long shower and read until I fell asleep around three.

My lips curl at the corners in spite of my tiredness. Holden Carter is my happy place and I swear I've fallen more in love with him this year. Being at college together is all kinds of amazing. I love the studying, the social life, the freedom of being treated like an adult. I've never been so happy and content before, and this guy in front of me is a huge reason why.

"You're not allowing for make-out time." His eyes glimmer.

"Make-out time?"

"Yeah, you know the 'Oh look, we're ready five minutes early, let's make out while we're waiting.'"

I laugh. "You are unbelievable. How is it that we've been going to college together and practically living in each other's pockets for a year now, and I've never heard of you allowing for make-out time?"

"It's just something new I came up with." He rounds the bed and steps into my space.

Crossing my arms, I try to suppress my giggle. "I thought you would have had enough of me last night."

"Baby, there is no such thing as having enough of you." Placing his hands on my hips, he pulls me close and murmurs against my mouth. "You're looking so freaking hot today."

Unable to resist, I thread my arms around his neck and melt against him. Who cares if we're a little late, right?

Holden

With one hand on the wheel and my other resting on Maddie's thigh, I'm the luckiest guy in the world right now. Her blonde hair dances in the wind. She catches a few stray hairs and tucks them behind her ear. They'll fly free again soon, but it's too nice a day not to have the top down.

The sky is blue, the sun is hot.

We made it. Our first year in college is done and now we can look forward to some time in Armitage and a camping trip that Vincent wants to surprise Chloe with. The six of us are going to head to Utah after the Fourth of July weekend. Apparently Chloe's been wanting to hike around some of the national parks, and Vincent wants to make it happen for her before college begins.

"I can't believe my little sister's graduating tomorrow," Maddie murmurs, resting her elbow on the window ledge and smiling up at the sky.

"You look like a proud mama."

"I kind of am. I mean, I've been such a huge part of her life, and living away from her and Max has been so weird."

"Good weird?"

"A mix weird. Like sometimes I love that I don't have to be responsible for anyone other than myself." Her nose wrinkles. "But other times I miss them. They've been living without me and I can't help feeling left out sometimes."

"After this summer, all three of you will be spread."

"Not really. With Vincent and Chloe both getting into San Jose, they'll be super close to Cairo and Max."

"And not too far from us." I wink, trying to make her feel better.

She grins and bobs her head. "You're right, and at least she'll have Vincent to look out for her."

"I'm pretty sure they'll look out for each other. And not to sound overly female, but they are seriously a cute couple. I'm so glad Vincent got that scholarship in the end."

"Yeah, I didn't think it'd come through. Man, I would've loved to have seen his face when he got that letter."

"I'm pretty sure Chloe screaming excitedly into the phone captured it."

Maddie giggles. "I swear my ear was ringing for the rest of the day."

"I was on the other side of the room and I heard her." I snicker and put my blinker on, cruising into the other lane so I can overtake the pickup truck.

Thanks to a little make-out time, we are running late now, and I want to check in on Grandpa before we head to the Barlow house.

Chloe and Mrs. Hale have been helping me out, being my points of contact with anything Grandpa related. It makes me wish I hadn't kept him a secret for so long because those two have been awesome. Even Vincent's gone along to help out with Bingo nights occasionally, although I think he finds it kind of awkward.

He'd do anything for Chloe though.

I glance to my right, knowing exactly how he feels.

Being in love with Maddie Barlow has changed me. And I really like the change. I cringe to think about who I could have become if she hadn't stepped up and challenged me.

Thoughts of Dad flash through my mind. I still haven't visited him and I know this is something I will have to face eventually, but I'm trying to get to a point of forgiveness first. I want to be able to look him in the face and tell him that I'm over it. But I'm still fluctuating between "he'll always be my father and I'll definitely forgive him" to "that two-faced asshole can rot in jail, and I hope he never gets out on parole."

My knuckles turn white as I grip the wheel.

At this stage, I'm pretty ashamed that the guy's

my father.

Mom tells me the sooner I forgive him, the better I'll feel. I know she's right. But it's really hard. How do you forgive a murdering cheater who framed an innocent guy...and then nearly shot Chloe?

The family counselor Mom and I have been seeing tells me these things take time to process. It's been over a year and she's now got me practicing saying the words "Dad, I forgive you."

Maddie said she'll come with me if I find the courage to say it to his face this summer. Man, I don't know if I can. A big part of me wants to dig my heels in, but there's a small voice inside warning me that if I don't forgive the guy soon, my anger will fester and rot until it owns me. The best way to free myself is to just do it.

I swallow, shoving the thought from my mind and focusing on the road ahead. A road that leads to people I love.

Maddie

Visiting Grandpa John is always so much fun. Even though he doesn't remember us, he's still a sweet man, and watching Holden with him makes my insides all warm and fuzzy.

I love the way he holds his hand and rubs his thumb over delicate knuckles. John's skin is like tissue paper now, wrinkled and spotted brown. We're not sure how much longer he has, which is why we make him our first visit every time we arrive in Armitage.

Glancing at my watch, I can't help a rush of jitters. I'm about to catch up with my family. It's been close to two months since I've seen my sisters and I can't wait for hugs and catch-up time.

Chloe's pretty good at staying in touch, but Max is useless. It's not that she doesn't care, she just gets so busy living life that she forgets about how much a text, email, or phone call can mean. At least she's always pleased to hear from me when I initiate.

Man, I wonder if I'll see her at all when she moves to Berkeley.

She got in on a partial scholarship, and between selling a bulk of her baseball card collection and Mom and Dad's penny-pinching, they've managed to put together enough money for tuition fees.

Chloe won a scholarship too, which has really helped. The fact that she's attending the same school as her boyfriend is like the icing on the cake for her.

Vincent's older brother, Nick, has found work as a mechanic in San Jose, and Vincent will be moving in with him. It's great that he doesn't have to scrounge up money for an apartment or move in with people he doesn't know.

Tapping my watch, I catch Holden's eye and he nods.

"Okay, John, we better get going."

"Nice to see you, my boy." He pats Holden's hand, obviously in a good mood today. It's such a relief when he is.

I rise from the bed, then lean down to kiss him.

He chuckles. "You take care, pretty lady."

"We'll come back and see you again for Bingo night." I crouch beside his chair with a grin.

"Bingo night?" His eyebrows pop high. "They do that here, do they?"

"Oh yeah, and I'll be here to make sure you get the perfect card with no tens."

He shakes his head. "I don't like the number ten."

"I know." I wink and give him another quick kiss on the cheek before taking Holden's hand.

"See you again soon, John."

"Bye-bye now." He waves at us but is already looking at the painting on the wall, his scrambled brain no doubt trying to figure out who we are.

Holden drapes his arm over my shoulders with a sigh.

"That went well." I wrap my arm around his waist. "He was happy."

"Yeah," Holden murmurs.

"Hey." I squeeze his side until he's looking at me. "Leaving him here was the right thing to do. He needs the routine and familiarity of this place. Moving him to LA would have been too disruptive. He's happy. That's what matters."

Holden's smile is sweet as he leans down to kiss me. I meet him halfway, pouring as much love into the moment as I can. I just want to bathe him in it. The poor guy's had a rough time with his dad and everything. I want to be a pillar he can lean on, just like he is when I'm stressed about studying or missing my sisters.

I can't believe how good we are together.

Considering how we first met and started, it's almost comical.

That feels like an eternity ago sometimes. I can't imagine him not being a part of my life.

Resting my head back in the car seat, I slide on my shades and grin the whole way home. By the time we pull up outside our house, my insides are bubbling with excitement. The yellow Camry is in the driveway, which means at least one of my sisters is home.

"I can't believe Vince still owns that blue piece of crap," Holden mutters as we park behind it.

"I can't believe it still works." I laugh, jumping out of the car and rushing up the path.

If Vincent's car is here, Chloe must definitely be home.

Holden chases me and I'm about to open the door when it pulls back before I can.

"Hey." I smile at Max as she jolts to a stop in front of us.

Her face lights with a grin as she grabs me into a quick hug. "Hey! So good to see you, sis." She pulls back and kisses my cheek. "I gotta go."

"What? Where?"

"Cairo just got back," Chloe answers from the hallway while Max rushes out the door, waving us a haphazard goodbye.

"See you soon!" she yells before tearing out of the driveway.

Her tires squeal as she takes off down the road.

"Don't speed!" Mom yells from the kitchen window, then gives up with a sigh.

Holden and I glance at each other and crack up laughing as we step into the house and are soon enveloped by my family.

Epilogue #2

Max

This stupid car won't go fast enough!

I tear down the street, Cairo's message burning a hole through my phone.

He's back! He's back for the summer!

I've missed him so much this year it's insane. It's not like I haven't seen him at all. He's been back every holiday, and I've even gone to Berkeley for a couple of weekends, but it's not the same as day-to-day contact.

Oh man, this next school year is going to be amazing.

I've been working so hard with Mr. Hale, plus Mom got me a job at the store. It's sucked, but I've tried to focus on the fact that it's getting me money for college. Thanks to my practice plus hard work, I got accepted into Berkeley with a partial scholarship.

Mom and Dad said they'd cover the rest of my fees, plus pay for my housing, so all I have to shell out for is books and resources. So yay! I'm going to study music at Berkeley. And I'll only be a year behind Cairo.

I put my blinker on and whip around the corner.

When Cairo first left after last summer, I had my doubts.

Could we make it?

Or would he find some gorgeous college musician to replace me?

But nope, the guy has stayed one hundred percent loyal. We talk or text every day, and he's even let me help him with a few assignments, asking for my feedback. With Maddie gone, I've got my own room and we've stayed up on FaceTime until the early hours, talking music and working on his assignments.

I've loved every second of it.

But nothing beats being in his arms.

Screeching to a stop in his driveway, a laugh punches out of me as I see him racing down the porch steps.

He stops on the path, grinning while I sprint around the car and straight into his arms. My legs wind around his waist and he holds me tight.

We don't bother with words; our kisses say it all. I wrap my legs tighter around his waist as we walk and kiss our way to the front door.

"I've missed you," he murmurs against my mouth.

I lean back with a smile. "That all ends today."

"Yes it does." He leans in for another kiss and I happily oblige.

Our tongues start a familiar tango that we've been practicing for months. It's already the perfect dance, but we don't mind spending the hours trying to make it even better.

"Oh, all right, you two!" Mr. Hale barks from the porch. "I get that you're in love and all that, but you don't need to eat each other's faces off. Get into the house!"

I laugh at his teasing, then grin when he winks at me and waves his hand to usher us inside.

Cairo reluctantly drops me to my feet, but keeps a secure arm around my waist as we walk into his house.

"Hey, Max," Mrs. Hale calls from the kitchen.

"Hi, Avia! Ooo, smells good in here." That woman has transformed my palette, I swear. I never would have touched curry before dating Cairo, but she's taught me to love Indian food.

She's even given me a few cooking lessons, something my mother doesn't have the patience for.

But Cairo's mom is just so relaxed and cool. I've spent so much time here in the last year. This is where Mr. Hale tutors me, and his wife always feeds me while he's doing it.

"Right, sit down." Cairo's dad pulls out my usual stool and taps it with his fingers. "Lover boy here was just telling us how his last week of school went."

I chuckle and grab an almond from the bowl as Cairo sits down beside me and regales us with the final week of his freshman year. It sounds like really hard work, but I'm so ready for it.

This past year has been good for me. I've spent hours doing things I both love and hate, but it's given me the discipline I need to cope with college life.

Dad's been going on about how focused I'll have to be. Now that I've dropped baseball, he's throwing his energy into making me the world's best musician. Groan! The guy just doesn't know how to do anything but push me. Chloe assures me it's because he knows I could conquer the world if I wanted to and he wants the best for me.

"He loves you, Max. If you don't remember anything else, remember that. It might drive you crazy, but if he didn't care about you at all, he'd leave you alone."

What's the bet I'll end up missing him once I'm away.

I roll my eyes, but then purse my lips as I imagine

how much he's going to miss me.

Poor guy's losing all three of us after the summer.

I hope he copes okay.

"So, you're staying for dinner, I assume?" Avia captures my attention.

"Actually we've got a family dinner tonight. Maddie and Holden just got back."

"Oh, how lovely. It's so nice that you can all be here for Chloe and Vincent's graduation."

"We wouldn't miss it for the world."

"I'm so proud of those two." Her warm brown eyes light with a smile I have to reciprocate.

"And I'm proud of you." Mr. Hale grabs me in a sideways hug, kissing the top of my head and reminding me why he's my favorite adult.

I giggle against his chest while Cairo complains, "Dad, stop suffocating my girlfriend."

"I've got to get my hugs in before she leaves and your poor mum and I will be left all alone."

"Yeah, like that's going to hurt." Cairo rolls his eyes. "You can't wait for an empty nest."

"That is true." Mr. Hale tips his head, then clicks his fingers and points at his wife. "Sex in every room, love!"

Avia wiggles her eyebrows, putting on a sexy little smirk.

"Aw, gross. You guys!" Cairo drops the piece of naan bread he was nibbling on and I crack up laughing.

I love this family so damn much.

Because Cairo complained, his dad's taken it the next level, wrapping his wife in a hug and kissing her passionately in the middle of the kitchen.

"Don't eat each other's faces off," Cairo warns as he jumps off his stool and grabs my hand. "Come on, gorgeous, let's hang at yours for a while." I thread my fingers through his. "We'll be back after dinner for a jam with the guys!" Cairo calls from the door.

His parents fail to respond, which means they're obviously still making out.

"I wonder if they'll do it on the kitchen floor," I tease him.

He gives me a deadpan glare and shakes his head at me. "Don't ruin my life, please. I'll never be able to step into that kitchen again."

I giggle and rest my head against his shoulder. "One day you'll get to torture your own children in exactly the same way."

He stops in the path, turning me to face him while wrapping his arm around my lower back. "I'm going to enjoy that." His brown eyes sparkle. "Do you think our kids will be musical?"

The air in my lungs dries up for a second. It's such a casual little question but it says so much.

He's picturing a life with me. He's imagining making out in our kitchen while our children tell us we're gross.

I can't answer him with words. All I can do is smile and tell him I love him with a searing kiss.

Cairo

I strum the strings and grin as Max steps up to the mic and starts singing, "Ocean Avenue." I lean in and add a harmony on the word *ni-ght*. Damn, we sound good together.

Roman goes for it on the drums, pumping up the song until the walls of the garage vibrate. The beat thrums through me, my spirit soaring as we take on the song and own it.

Considering it's just the three of us, we sound awesome.

Max is actually on bass. Dad's been teaching her both electric and bass. It's cool that she's so versatile, especially since we lost Latifa.

Yeah, much to Roman's heartache, our girl fell in love with someone new at college. And to make it even worse, she followed the guy to Nashville. They left a couple of weeks ago and according to Max, Latifa was so excited, she didn't even pick up on Roman's despair.

Poor Rome.

He's been slogging it out at the community college in Cullington and been pretty damn miserable about the whole thing.

I spin around and watch him go for it on the drums. That's his salvation right there. I grin and strum the last riff of the song. He hits the final beat and I hold my note, dragging the song to a finish.

Max whoops into the mic, tossing her hair back and giving us a goofy smile.

She's so cute when she plays.

"What time is Austin getting here?" Roman flicks his stick in the air.

Max pulls out her phone to check the time. "He's probably still stuck at his family dinner. Kingston got back this afternoon, I think, plus his grandparents have come for the graduation too."

"Yikes." Roman cringes.

"I know." Max nods. "They're going to hassle him about his bleached hair and ask him why he's not being a good Chinese boy and studying something boring."

"I bet they flipped when they found out he's going to CCM," I murmur.

CCM is the California College of Music, and that place is freaking amazing. They know how to rock out, but it's not exactly the formal education his family wants for him. I think it's awesome that he's following his heart on this one.

Max bulges her eyes at me and then winces. "Poor guy. He came and hid out at my place for the whole weekend after he got his acceptance letter. My dad loved it."

I snicker at Max's sarcasm.

Her dad is definitely softening up, but it's going to take a really long time to accept that any of his daughters have fallen in love. I think I'm the hardest pill to swallow. Holden is golden and he can relate to the guy easily. Vincent saved his life and there's this protective fatherly thing going on. But me...I'm just the punk that dragged his daughter into a nightclub where she nearly got killed.

I'm the jerk pulling her away to study music at Berkeley.

I'm the idiot who drove all the way back to Fresno so we could try out for the Summer Rock Festival again. We missed out last year, and when the chance came up to audition again, I pulled an all-nighter to make it.

This year, we were successful and we're playing on one of the smaller stages for the Fourth of July weekend. We're even playing the song Max and I wrote together—"Spell Caster." We're all pumped and have been working damn hard to pull it together without Latifa. But we have Max on bass now and it's gonna be great.

Both our families are coming to watch and then

we're going camping, apparently. Some surprise that Vincent's been cooking up for Chloe.

The internal door clicks and we all spin to watch Austin lope down the stairs.

"Hey, Cai! Good to see ya, man."

"Hey, graduate." I grin and hold up my hand. "You made it."

He laughs and I pull him in for a quick hug and back pat.

"How was dinner?" Max lightly thumbs the bass strings.

Austin groans as he sets up his keyboard. "Painful, as expected."

"Sorry, dude. Old people just don't get it sometimes, right?"

"Yep." Austin flicks the bleached hair out of his eyes.

"The main thing is you're following your heart. And that's what counts."

I glance over my shoulder to smile at Max's words. I love that we're so often thinking the same thing. I love that she found the strength to follow her heart as well.

Shuffling back, I close the gap between us and lean in for a kiss.

"Ewww, seriously!" Austin starts making gagging noises behind us so I deepen the kiss to rile him.

Okay, maybe I deepen it because I've spent the

last year pining for my girl and now she's right beside me. And this time, I don't have to say goodbye, because she's coming to Berkeley too.

I'm so excited for this new chapter I can hardly stand it. Max is going to love it there, I just know she is.

And we'll be together.

An image of the first time I saw her flashes through my mind. Those big blue eyes staring at my guitar, her flustered words as she tried to get away from me.

I grin against her mouth, my body sizzling with pleasure as I think about how far we've come, and how much further we'll journey together.

My beautiful spell caster. She owns my heart, just like I own hers.

Epilogue #3

Vincent

I clear my throat and cringe as Nick adjusts my tie. I'm pretty sure he's going for some kind of chokehold knot.

"Stop whining, you big man-baby," he mutters.

"I didn't say anything!" I snap back.

"Your face is saying it all, man."

"It's just graduation," I grumble. "Why the hell do I have to wear a tie anyway?"

He slaps my shoulders and looks me in the eye. "Because it's graduation, and you're the first Mancini to ever get there."

My brother's eyes sparkle with pride and I pull him into a quick hug.

We never used to hug before, but since he got out of jail, everything's changed. I have my brother back, and I never want to take that for granted again.

Thanks to Chloe's dad, Nick's transition back into society has been as smooth as it can be. Not perfect, of course. The guy's qualifications weren't exactly stellar, so finding a job was tough. But thanks to one of the officers at Armitage PD, he managed to get an apprenticeship at the local garage. He's worked like a dog and learned everything he possibly can. And now he's got a job in San Jose working as a mechanic.

I told him he didn't have to come with me, but I think he's just as keen to leave Armitage behind as I am.

I didn't find this out until after it happened, but Nick ended up giving Chief Barlow a few key nuggets of information that helped the Armitage PD bust Enzo's drug operation wide open. My abusive uncle and cousin are now behind bars for at least eight years. I don't know what the rest of the Mancinis are up to and I really don't give a shit. Chief Barlow's been keeping a close eye on them and making sure they leave me and my brother alone.

Nick's moving to San Jose in a few days. He can't wait to be free of this place. He's going to find us an apartment and start his new job over the summer so that by the time I arrive, everything will be set up.

He's really doing everything he can to look after me, and I've never been happier.

My senior year at Armitage High was the best year of my life. I have the world's prettiest, sweetest girlfriend, I'm living in a house I'm not afraid to go home to each night, and for the first time ever I've been able to focus one hundred percent on my studies.

It meant I excelled in my course work and scored a scholarship. The guidance counselor worked overtime on my behalf. It's been so bizarre. Everyone has gone out of their way to make my life a success. I had no idea people actually cared or could be so awesome.

I smooth down my tie and look in the mirror, my lips curling at the corners as I picture Chloe and wonder what she'll have on under her gown. Probably some pale pink summer dress that will fit her perfectly.

"Here you go." Nick holds up my gown for me and I slip my arms into it, adjusting my shoulders until it sits right.

He stands behind me, his eyes glassing over. "Mom would be real proud."

I swallow, the sound thick and audible in our little apartment.

With a wonky smile, he lightly smacks my arm with the back of his hand. "Come on, you little jerk, let's do this."

I grab my cap off the table behind the couch and play with it the whole way to school. Threading the fine red tassel through my fingers, I gaze out the window as we head down these streets that are so familiar, yet I'm not going to miss them.

Armitage will never be home for me.

I don't know where home is. Not geographically anyway.

I hope I'll find it one day, a place that I can settle in, but right now, my home is in people. Or at least one very important person.

As we pull into the parking lot, I spot her on the grass. She's standing with Rahn, Max and oh hey, there's Cairo and Roman. They're all laughing together, Rahn and Chloe looking jittery as they fidget with their caps.

A smile spreads my cheeks wide as I watch Chloe's blonde hair dance in the breeze. She giggles and turns my direction just as Nick's parking the car. The second she sees me, her face lights like a Christmas tree. She ditches the others without a backward glance and walks across to me.

I jump out of the car as Nick cuts the engine and meet her halfway. My arms are spread and waiting so she can walk right into them.

"Good afternoon." I kiss the top of her head and feel myself relax as she rests against me.

"Happy graduation day," she murmurs into my chest.

I lean back and smile down at her. "We did it."

"I knew we could."

Her blue eyes tell me they love me and I lean down to kiss home. My place of refuge, comfort, joy and inspiration.

She always goes on about how I saved her life that night, but she has no idea. It doesn't matter how many times I try to argue that she was the one who saved me, she just doesn't seem to get it. She'll always underestimate the power of her love, but I'm quite happy to spend the rest of my life convincing her that I might be a warrior, but she is my superhero.

Chloe

Vincent looks so handsome in his graduation robe and cap. My insides are bursting with pride as Principal Sheehan calls his name.

My poor boyfriend is so nervous. I can tell by the way he's refusing to look down at the crowd. His hand is making and releasing a fist as he walks across the stage and accepts his diploma.

As he moves his tassel across his hat, I let out a loud whoop and pump my fist in the air.

It makes him glance my way, and I give him the biggest and best smile I can.

The audience behind me is making a lot of noise and I know it's the Hales, Nick, and my family that are cheering the loudest.

Vincent did it.

He's worked his ass off this year and he's getting out of Armitage to start his life anew...with me.

Senior year has just been one miracle after another. Vincent's brother got out of jail, Dad helped him score a job, and then found them a little apartment only ten minutes from school. My parents have been completely won over by my boyfriend and just quietly, I think Vincent's become Dad's favorite. It's a huge triumph and yet another reason why I'm so proud of my man.

He's shown the world who he is this year and they're finally starting to see what I see.

His smile and wink make my heart somersault as he saunters down the steps and finds his seat. As soon as this ceremony is over, I'm stealing him away and showing him just how I feel with a kiss that will curl his toes.

And that's exactly what I do.

"Come on." I walk past him, capturing his wrist and pulling him around the side of the gym while my family is busy chatting with the Hales.

Rahn is locked in a flirt-a-thon with Roman

Sanchez. It's kind of adorable. I didn't even know they liked each other, or maybe today is just the start of something new. She can't stop giggling around him, and his shy smile is the sweetest thing.

I glance over my shoulder, watching Rahn cover her mouth as she laughs at something Roman said. Austin glances at Cairo and rolls his eyes while Max and her boyfriend start laughing.

"You okay?" Vincent places his hands on my hips the second we stop walking.

I push him back against the building and grin at him. "I'm more than okay."

Lacing my arms around his neck, I rise on my tiptoes and press my mouth against his. Our kiss is slow and languid, filling me up from my toes to the top of my head.

He softly moans against me, curling his fingers into my robe and tugging me as close as he can.

I grin against him, gently sucking his bottom lip before pulling away and whispering, "I'm so incredibly proud of you."

He loves it when I say that to him. I can tell by the way his eyes sparkle. "I couldn't have done it without you."

"Yes, you could—"

"No." He shakes his head. "You believed in me, and I don't think I could have done it without that. I love you."

My heart turns to putty every time those words leave his mouth. I lean into another kiss and he cups the back of my head, deepening our moment to something hot and searing. A promise of things to come.

We still haven't slept together. Vincent has flat-out refused, not because he doesn't want to, but because he won't disrespect my dad.

"The guy has done way too much to help my family. I'm not sleeping with you yet, Chloe. It'll gut him if he finds out."

"It's not his decision," I argued.

"I know, but please, you know he thinks you're too young to lose it, and seriously, what's the rush? We're going to be together forever, right?"

Those words matched with that grin always win me over and so I remain a virgin...for now.

Vincent

I ease out of the kiss, brushing my lips across Chloe's nose before smiling at her. "We should probably get back before they notice we're gone."

"We probably should." She wrinkles her nose.

"Hey." Resting my fingers on her cheek, I whisper with a smile, "We've got the whole summer ahead of us, baby."

Aw man, I can't wait to tell her about the camping trip I've got planned. We're heading to Utah straight after the Summer Rock Festival. Thanks to Holden's help, the six of us are going for ten days of camping and hiking around these national parks that Chloe's always wanted to see.

She's going to love it.

I still haven't decided when I'm going to tell her. I was thinking I might take her out one night this week. We'll go for a romantic drive somewhere, maybe have a picnic, and then I'll gently mention it to her while we make out under the stars.

My insides stir with desire.

Chloe's eyes narrow as she studies my face. "What?"

"What?" I blink, going for innocent.

"What are you thinking right now?"

That I'm totally busted.

I can't help a grin. "Nothing."

"Liar." She gently pokes me in the stomach.

I capture her hand and start to laugh. "Don't make me tell you here. It's a surprise."

"What are you up to, Vincent Mancini?"

I clear my throat, still cringing when she uses my last name. I'd seriously love to change it but Chloe told me that's dumb. It's just a name, and it's up to me to change what people think about that name.

"Don't let those assholes make you feel ashamed. Just live the kind of life that makes people revere the Mancini name."

And I swear, I'm really trying to do that.

"Hey!" Chief Barlow appears around the corner. "We've been looking for you two. Now, stop kissing my daughter and come pose for some photos."

He points at me, then flicks his hand to beckon us out of hiding.

I rest my hand on Chloe's lower back, gently pushing her forward.

"So, when are you going to tell me?" She bobs on her toes and grins up at me.

"How about I take you out for a date this week, and I'll tell you then."

She tips her head back with a groan. "Don't make me wait!"

I laugh and shake my head. She's seriously too cute.

Rounding the corner, we're met with a mixture of cheers and wolf whistles. I can't help blushing as I'm teased for pulling my girl away to make out.

But she pulled me away, something I will always love about her. I never have to doubt her feelings for me.

"All right, let's get some photos!" Mrs. Barlow claps her hands and starts organizing us. She hired a professional photographer to snap some pics of our big day.

I actually hate having my photo taken, but I do as I'm told and huddle up with my family that's grown from just Nick and me into this beast that now includes a little Mancini, Carter and Hale, mixed with a whole heap of Barlow.

It's the perfect combination, if you ask me, and I'll happily stay connected with these people for the rest of my life.

"Okay, just a few more!" The photographer raises his hand to grab our attention.

Threading my arm around Chloe's waist, I pull her back against my stomach and softly whisper in her ear, "Cairo, Holden and I are taking the Barlow sisters camping in Utah after the Summer Rock Festival."

At first there's a gasp, followed by a pause, and then Chloe lets out an excited squeal. "I love you, Vincent Mancini!"

Everyone glances our way, then starts laughing.

I hope the photographer's finger is planted for this moment, because I'm pretty sure there will be some golden images captured on screen. I want to frame them and hang them on my wall so I never, ever forget how blessed I am, and how much my life has changed.

Thank you so much for reading Foul Play. I really hope you enjoyed it. If you'd like to support my work, please leave a review on Goodreads or Amazon. This validates the book and helps me reach new readers. Thanks for your support.

Author's Note

There's something very special about Chloe and Vincent's story. From book one, my readers wanted to see them together. And that was always the plan. Chloe's a sweet flower. Vincent's a dark knight.

But they work so well together.

They balance each other, and watching them fall in love was so special and precious.

I flew through this book. My fingers were desperate to write this story, to finally unfold the big mystery. I love the combination of danger and sweetness in this book. The brutality Vincent faced at home was tempered by the tenderness he found in Chloe's arms.

In the prom scene, Chloe talks about how sometimes the best things can come from the worst. I've experienced this firsthand in my own life. Sometimes we have to go through the lowest points we'll ever face before discovering something amazing. I don't know why life works that way; maybe it's so we'll appreciate the good stuff when it comes along.

Thank you for reading this trilogy. I appreciate you and I'm so very grateful for your support. Writing is a huge privilege that I will never take for granted. It's my dream come true, and I wouldn't be able to do it without you. So thanks :)

And I'd like to thank a few more people too...

Cassie, Rae, Lenore, Beth, Kristin and my eagle-eye proofreaders. You make these books publishable! I also need to give Kristin an extra special mention for all the baseball help and guidance she gave me when I was mapping out this trilogy.

My assistant Rachael—what would I do without you? Thank you so much for being amazing!

My husband—thank you for being my perfect match.

The Holy Spirit—you fill my heart to overflowing. With you, I am never alone.

xx

Jordan

Jordan's Books

BIG PLAY NOVELS
The Playmaker
The Red Zone
The Handoff
Shoot The Gap

THE BROTHERHOOD TRILOGY
See No Evil
Speak No Evil
Hear No Evil

FAIRYTALE TWISTS NOVELS
Paper Cranes

THE BARLOW SISTERS TRILOGY
Curveball
Strike Out
Foul Play

Jordan hasn't announced her next project yet, but something is brewing for 2018.
Keep an eye on her website for more information:
www.jordanfordbooks.com

About the Author

Jordan Ford is a New Zealand author who has spent her life traveling with her family, attending international schools, and growing up in a variety of cultures. Although it was sometimes hard shifting between schools and lifestyles, she doesn't regret it for a moment. Her experiences have enriched her life and given her amazing insights into the human race.

She believes that everyone has a back story...and that story is fundamental in how people cope and react to life around them. Telling stories that are filled with heart-felt emotion and realistic characters is an absolute passion of Jordan's. Since her earliest memories, she has been making up tales to entertain herself. It wasn't until she reached her teen years that she first considered writing one. A computer failure and lost files put a major glitch in her journey, and it took until she graduated university with a teaching degree before she took up the dream once more. Since then, she hasn't been able to stop.

"Writing high school romances brings me the greatest joy. My heart bubbles, my insides zing, and I am at my happiest when immersed in a great scene with characters who have become real to me."

Connect Online

Jordan Ford loves to hear from her readers. Please feel free to contact her through any of the following means:

WEBSITE:
www.jordanfordbooks.com

FACEBOOK:
www.facebook.com/jordanfordbooks/

INSTAGRAM:
www.instagram.com/jordanfordbooks/

NEWSLETTER:
This is the best way to stay in touch with Jordan's work and have access to special giveaways and sales.
www.subscribepage.com/jordanfordfreebies

CPSIA information can be obtained
at www.ICGtesting.com
Printed in the USA
FSHW022110030420
68807FS